RED TIGER

A RYAN LOCK NOVEL

SEAN BLACK

ABOUT THE BOOK

The winner of the 2018 International Thriller Writers Award returns with his latest explosive thriller featuring ex-military bodyguard Ryan Lock and his business partner, retired US Marine, Ty Johnson.

When the daughter of a Chinese billionaire is kidnapped from her mansion in Arcadia, California, Ryan and Ty find themselves caught in the middle of a vicious standoff.

Emily Yan is a Chinese 'parachute kid', one of thousands of children sent to study in America by their ultra-wealthy parents. Living in a multi-million dollar mansion in Arcadia, California with her hard-partying cousin Charlie, it's not long before their ostentatious displays of wealth attract the wrong sort of attention in the form of some MS-13 gang members.

But someone else has been looking for Emily, a shadowy figure from back home known only as The Red Tiger.

Two very different worlds collide in this explosive new thriller from Sean Black as Ryan Lock and his business partner, wise-cracking US Marine Ty Johnson, set out to save Emily from a violent tug of war between two deadly forces; the brutal members of America's most dangerous gang, and an equally determined Chinese enforcer called the Red Tiger.

PRAISE FOR SEAN BLACK

"This series is ace. It stars bodyguard Ryan Lock, here hired to protect a glamorous movie star with a headless corpse in her car. There are deservedly strong Lee Child comparisons as the author is a Brit (Scottish), his novels US-based, his character appealing, and his publisher the same. " – Sarah Broadhurst, *The Bookseller*, reviewing Gridlock

"An impressive debut thriller from Sean Black that introduces a new full-on action hero. Clearly influenced by Lee Child and Joseph Finder, Black drives his hero into the tightest spots with a force and energy that jump off the page. He still has a little to learn when it comes to depth of character and pacing, but that won't take long. Lock is clearly going to be around for a long time. With a spine-tingling finale that reminded me of Die Hard, this is a writer, and a hero, to watch." – Geoffrey Wansell. *The Daily Mail*, reviewing Lockdown

"Sean Black writes with the pace of Lee Child, and the heart of Harlan Coben. Lockdown is a sure-fire winner" – Joseph Finder, New York Times Bestselling Author of *Buried Secrets*

"In Lockdown, Sean Black's hero, Ryan Lock, causes New York to be sealed against a terrorist threat. The synergy between name and title matters because it highlights the artifice underlying an excellent first novel. Like Lee Child's Jack Reacher, Lock is an ex-military policeman. Unlike Reacher, he has a job (as an elite bodyguard), a home, friends and a sense of humour. Lock's likeability contrasts with Reacher's pomposity and Black's style is supremely slick." – Jeremy Jehu, *The Daily Telegraph*, reviewing Lockdown

Sean's books that were nominated for, or have won, the International Thriller Writers Award (previous winners include Stephen King, Jon Gilstrap Megan Abbott & Joseph Finder) presented annually in New York City.

Post (nominated in 2015)
The Edge of Alone (nominated in 2017)
Second Chance (winner in 2018)

AUTHOR'S NOTE

In China and Chinese culture, names are written, and expressed, with the family or surname, coming first. For ease of reading in English I have reversed the order to the more conventional (for English language readers) Western order. So, for example, Yan Emily is written as Emily Yan.

PART I

1

The Red Tiger stared down at the man's bloodied face. There were several deep cuts above his right eye. His cheekbone was shattered, and his scalp was crisscrossed with hundreds of small incisions. The man's hands were secured behind the seat back. His legs were tied together at the ankles. His mouth wasn't covered but that hardly mattered. Even if someone from the nearby village heard his screams, they wouldn't come to investigate. Nor would they tell the authorities.

They were simple country folk, who avoided trouble at all costs. Not that avoiding trouble was the reason they would keep their own counsel. People in this area loved the Red Tiger. He was a bringer of justice. A righter of wrongs.

There was fear too. How could there not be? He had done terrible things. He had killed without mercy. But, mostly, love and admiration ensured their silence.

To the people of the village, and hundreds like it across the vast expanse of mainland China, the Red Tiger offered something that no policeman could. In their time of deepest need he offered hope.

"You know who I am?" said the Red Tiger.

The man began to cry. His head bobbed up and down.

"Then you must also know why I'm here."

The furious nodding stopped. "I can't."

The Red Tiger reached down, opened the bag of salt and scooped out a palmful. "Where?" said the Red Tiger.

"They'll kill me."

"That happens either way. But I can make it go fast."

The palmful of salt hovered over the man's scalp. He swallowed hard. "They'll kill my family too," he said.

"And I won't?"

"You never have. You don't touch the innocent. Everyone knows that."

The Red Tiger seemed caught off guard. The salt spilled through his parted fingers and landed harmlessly on the floor. Some caught on the shoulder of the man's jacket.

"This is different."

"How? How can it be different?" said the man in the chair. It was a genuine question. What faced him was grotesque and violent. He accepted that. In some ways, he deserved it. But it wasn't any different from any other time.

Men, sometimes women, taken somewhere quiet. Tortured until they died or gave up their secrets. Then dumped, after night had fallen, by the side of the road. Sometimes a poster was left with them, a child's face staring back at whoever found them.

Justice delivered. Swift, macabre, a warning to others.

The Red Tiger produced a piece of paper. He unfolded it and held it up for the man to examine.

It meant nothing to him. "I don't remember anything about this one. There have been so many."

"Look at the name."

The man peered at the bottom of the poster. He read the name out loud. Before his mouth had stopped moving he knew what he had just been told. He swallowed again. It hurt his throat. He started to cry again. Not for himself. For those he loved.

"Your family," said the Red Tiger. "A wife. Two sons. You're a lucky man to have had two sons when you did."

Until a few years ago the Communist Party had decreed that each family could have only one child. Unless, of course, there was special dispensation, or you had a good reason for another, such as adopting a relative's child.

"My brother in the country. He died. His wife couldn't cope," said the man.

It was a lie so well rehearsed that he had finished repeating it before he realized how absurd it sounded in the present company. The Red Tiger must have heard it, with some slight variation, dozens, maybe hundreds of times.

"You recognize the name?"

The man nodded.

"You still think I wouldn't kill your family?" asked the Red Tiger.

"No. I believe you. You would."

The Red Tiger leaned down.

The man felt hot breath next to his ear. "Your wife is already dead, Xi. Your sons, they are alive, but gone. You'll never see them again. If I have to, I can arrange that they die."

Xi felt a deep ache of grief flood through him. His wife. It had all been for her. That was how it had begun many years ago when he had come home from the factory to find her staring at the wall. She'd seen the doctor. The news had been bad. Xi had done what he had to. Once he had started, and realized the demand, he had been sucked into the life. Now it was time to pay the price.

Xi Yow Chang blinked the blood from his eye. The Red Tiger's face came into focus. Nothing special to look at. Nothing to suggest that this was someone dangerous.

The Red Tiger's features softened. "Tell me what you know."

Xi began to talk. He stumbled and strained over some details. It had been a long time ago. Almost two decades. His memory was hazy. But he confessed enough to satisfy the Red Tiger.

When he was done, the Red Tiger gave him a cigarette. When he was halfway through and had just drawn a fresh puff of smoke deep into his lungs, the Red Tiger walked behind him, and shot him twice in the back of the head.

2

Li Yeng grabbed his cell phone from the seat of his car. He tapped the answer icon. His hands were trembling slightly. The boss called every week, on the same day and at the same time, to get an update on his daughter, Emily. The other kid, Charlie, Emily's cousin, was mentioned in as much as he impacted on Emily, which was more frequently. Charlie was trouble. Not a bad kid, but reckless and thoroughly spoiled by the boss's sister.

This was not the usual time or day of the week. That alone unsettled Li Yeng. His boss was a man with an iron routine. You didn't gather the wealth and power he had without such self-discipline. To make a fortune in America was one matter. To do it in China, where everything could be taken from you on the whim of a government official, was something else. Americans didn't know how lucky they were.

Li greeted his boss. He was always formal with him. Always.

"It's happened," said Chow Yan.

It took a moment for Li to realize what "it" was. The clue was in how his boss said the word. He sounded fearful. That narrowed the possibilities down to one.

"How?" asked Li.

"That's not important."

"What should I do?" asked Li. He had a thousand other questions, but this was the only one that felt appropriate. Whatever the boss asked of him, he would do. Regardless.

"There's nothing to do. Be thankful you're there and not here. I just wanted you to know."

The boss hung up without a goodbye or any further instruction. Li Yeng sat there for a moment. A car horn sounded behind him. He watched in his rearview as the driver leaned out of his window. "Wake up, asshole," the man shouted.

Li lowered his window and hit the button. The machine spat out a parking ticket. He snatched it. The barrier lifted. Li drove through, went up a level and found a space.

He visited this building in downtown Los Angeles once a month. Just to make sure that everything was as it should be. An American agency managed the day-to-day running, but it was always good to make sure they were doing their job. His boss had purchased it back in 2008 after the financial crash, along with two others in a six-block radius.

As Li exited his car, the irate driver who'd shouted at him sped past. Li raised his hand in apology, the way people did here. It was important to blend in. Not to upset the Americans. What was the expression people here used? To fly under the radar.

If they could all do that then perhaps nothing would come of the news he had just received from home.

3

O*ne week later*
 Arcadia, California

"WOULD you *please* turn down that music?"

It was two in the morning, her cousin Charlie was driving like a complete a-hole, and Emily Yan needed to be at her first class of the day in six hours. She hadn't even wanted to go out tonight. Who went to clubs on a Tuesday? But she knew that if she didn't go with him Charlie would only get into even more trouble than he usually did. Only last week he had almost gotten arrested. He would have been if Li Yeng hadn't paid off the kid Charlie had punched.

"What? You don't like Kanye?" Charlie shot her the easy smile that girls who weren't his cousin fell for.

"No, he's an idiot. Which maybe explains why you like him."

"You're funny."

Charlie laughed and pressed down even harder on the Lamborghini's gas pedal. The fresh burst of acceleration pushed Emily back into her seat. Charlie had no business driving a car like this. He only did it to keep up with his idiot friends. She'd wanted to take the Audi, but Charlie had insisted they take the "Lambo". He said it like that, Lambo, and sounded like a complete tool.

Emily really wished her aunt would send for her cousin, but there was no chance of that happening. The family was all about them getting their education here in America. America was safe. The schools were good. They had the money, so why not?

She and Charlie were *parachute kids*. Chinese kids sent to America to get an education while their parents stayed in China. There were thousands of them up and down both American coasts. San Francisco, Los Angeles, Vancouver, Toronto, New York.

Emily and Charlie lived in a seven-thousand-square-foot house her father had bought for them in Arcadia, thirteen miles north-east of Los Angeles. It was pretty much little China, but for rich Chinese families rather than poor immigrants from places like Taiwan. Over half the population was Chinese, with many parachute kids, like Emily and Charlie. There were also lots of *ernai*, the beautiful young mistresses of wealthy Chinese businessmen and government officials.

The street where Emily and Charlie lived was known as an *ernaicun*, a mistress village. It drove Emily crazy. She didn't want anyone to think she was an *ernai*. On the other hand, Charlie loved it. He was always hitting on the cute little *ernai* across the street. Emily had warned him what would happen if her "sponsor" found out but, as with everything else, Charlie didn't care. As far as he was concerned, he was untouchable.

The Lamborghini was almost flat out. The speed made Emily nervous. She checked WeChat on her iPhone X as Kanye blasted from the speakers and the wind whipped her hair across her face.

The supercar slowed abruptly.

Charlie angrily thumped his hands against the wheel. The engine was making a metallic whining noise.

"What is it?" Emily asked.

"How do I know?"

He pulled the Lamborghini into the breakdown lane, opened his door and got out. He walked to the front and tried to yank up the hood so he could look at the engine. This would be good. Emily still had to show him how to put gas in it. He couldn't even lift the hood so the idea of him fixing the problem was pretty hilarious.

"I told you we should have taken the Audi. How many times has this thing broken down?"

"Can you just be quiet?"

"Fine." She went back to scrolling through her WeChat messages.

Charlie grabbed the hood and tried again to pull it up. "Can you see a catch in there to open it?"

"No."

"Can you at least look?" he said.

PONY LEANED over in the passenger seat and tapped Joker's elbow. "Check it out, *ese*."

Joker looked across to what had caught Pony's attention. On the opposite side of the freeway a white Lamborghini was pulled over. Some young Chinese dude was stood next to it, his piece sitting in front.

Joker slowed the beat-up Dodge pickup they were driving.

"Nice whip," said Joker.

"Maybe they need some help," said Pony.

Joker knew what he meant. He just wasn't sure it was a good idea. They could take the car, that wasn't an issue—it would be like taking candy from a baby—but would they be able to get it back home to East Los Angeles without being stopped?

The pickup they were in, with the lawnmower and gardening tools thrown in back, had been their secret weapon since they'd started working Arcadia. Any time they were stopped they just pulled the *no habla English, Officer* routine and made out they were driving home from a day doing yard work. So far it had worked like a charm.

Why mess up a good thing? thought Joker, the older of the two by three years.

"What's the matter?" said Pony. "It's right there. I don't see no cops."

"You not forgetting something?" said Joker.

"What's that?"

"The dude's broken down, dummy. How are we going to get it moving?"

"We could tow it."

"You serious?"

"Not all the way back. Take it somewhere off the road. Throw an old tarp over it. Come back later and get it," said Pony.

That was why Joker liked working with Pony. He was crazy, like you had to be in Mara Salvatrucha, but he was crazy smart too.

Joker slowed and spun the wheel. The Dodge turned, bumping over the median, crossed two lanes and headed for the broken-down Lamborghini.

～

EMILY YAN SHIELDED her eyes from the glare of the truck's headlights as it drove the wrong way down the breakdown lane, and stopped in front of them. Charlie was so dumb. He couldn't even call a proper tow truck. He was lucky he was born rich. If he'd been born poor, he would have starved to death.

Charlie sprang back at the truck's approach. He popped the door and climbed in. He was in a panic, but Emily didn't pick up on it.

"These are the guys you called?" Emily said to him, as two young-looking Hispanic guys got out of the truck's cab. They looked more like gangbangers than mechanics. Not that she'd seen many of either group, apart from on TV.

"I didn't call them. I haven't called anyone yet," said Charlie, leaning over her and flipping open the glove box.

Emily's heart rate jumped. The two guys were strolling toward them. They looked relaxed but the way they walked carried menace. "Then who are they?"

The two young men were almost level with them. One had

stepped to Charlie's side of the Lamborghini, and the other was closing in on Emily. They should have at least put the top up, but it was too late for that.

"Nice whip," said one, running a finger down the bodywork. "Real smooth."

"This your *chica*?" said the other, his eyes all over Emily.

That was when she saw Charlie pull the gun from the glove box. It was big and black and frightening. She'd had no idea it was even there, and he'd never mentioned having a gun.

Now he had it in his hand, and was pointing it up and out at the guy closest to him. The guy seemed more than amused than anything. He smiled and put his hands up, like he was in a low-budget gangster movie. "Easy there. We just wanted to see if you needed some help."

"We don't need your help, thanks," said Charlie.

He didn't seem nervous any more. Emily put it down to the gun. Charlie wasn't much of a fighter, and he definitely wasn't a tough guy, like her father or his friends. Charlie was rich and soft and had always had the family's money to get him out of trouble. Which made the gun all the more surprising.

"Okay, homie," the guy was saying. He made a gesture to the guy who was on Emily's side of the car.

They both started to back up.

Charlie started to get out. Emily reached over to grab him and pull him back in but he shrugged her off. "They're leaving," she said.

"Yeah, we're leaving," the guy said to Charlie.

"So hurry up and get the fuck out of here, beaners," said Charlie.

The guy's smile fell away. His brow furrowed, his face tightened and he turned side on. The headlights caught his face. That was when Emily noticed the tattoos that ran all the way up his neck to his forehead. She couldn't make out much. At least one was in Spanish. She picked out the number 13.

"What you say?" the guy said.

Even with the gun in his hand, Charlie seemed to sense he'd overstepped some invisible line. It was like a line he'd heard and spat out without thinking.

The guy took a step towards Charlie. His chest was puffed out, his shoulders back. He didn't blink.

The guy on Emily's side said, "*Chota.*"

That one word seemed to break the spell. The two guys walked back to their truck, got in, and turned around before taking off.

Seconds later, a wash of red lights explained their sudden departure as a California Highway Patrol police car pulled in behind them. Emily snapped the glove box open. Charlie jammed the weapon inside. Emily closed it again.

The truck was gone. The patrol car pulled around them and parked in front of the Lamborghini.

"I'll speak to them," Emily hissed at her cousin.

"Whatever. You see those Mexicans shit their pants?"

She rolled her eyes. The two guys had taken off because of the cops, not because of her cousin, but try telling him that. "Shut up, Charlie," she told him. "Let me do the talking."

REMOVING HER MAKE-UP, Emily stared at herself in the mirror. She would have to speak with Li Yeng about Charlie. Li Yeng was her father's . . . She wasn't sure what his official job title would be. She guessed the English word 'fixer' would be close. Officially, he looked after her father's investments, but he also kept an eye on her and Charlie.

Emily had never really gotten a read on Li Yeng. He was detached and business-like. He looked like the kind of man who got out of bed already wearing a blue Brooks Brothers pinstripe suit. She knew he was from Beijing and had studied for his MBA at Harvard. She also knew that he came from a poor family in Henan province.

What had never been explained was how he had made the transition from being the son of a poor farmer to his present position. For all the talk of Communism being about equal opportunities, China was like most countries. If you weren't born into a family with money and connections, it was hard to make anything of yourself. Not impossible, but the odds were stacked against you.

She did know that Li Yeng had relied upon her father's patronage. He had paid for him to study in America. But, like everything her father did, it had been an investment that Li Yeng was expected to pay back, with interest. That was why he had been charged with keeping an eye on them as well as all the real estate.

She finished removing her make-up and applying moisturizer. She glanced down at her iPhone. Messages were stacked up. Dumbass Charlie had been all over his social media about how he had scared some gangbangers. Sent them home to the barrio with their tails between their legs.

He had been going on in group chat about Chinese power, and other kinds of stupidity. Those two guys hadn't been scared of Charlie. Not even when he had a gun pointed at them.

That was what had unsettled Emily the most. Someone pointing a loaded gun seemed like just another day at the office for them. They probably knew it wasn't the gun so much as who had their finger on the trigger.

At least she was home now. She would get some rest, maybe skip her first class, and start tomorrow fresh. Next time she would insist they take the Audi rather than that penis on wheels.

4

The BMW rolled slowly down the street. They had ditched the pickup and made a call. Two of their homeboys had delivered this new whip. It had been stolen the day before from long-term parking at LAX so the cops wouldn't be looking for it just yet.

In two days' time it would be in an auto shop being broken up. But for now it would help them prowl Arcadia without drawing the kind of attention a pickup would at this hour. Even the most eager gardening services weren't out blowing leaves at three in the morning.

"Slow down," said Pony. "I can't see."

They were scoping each driveway for the car. After the cops had arrived, Joker and Pony had watched from a safe distance as the tow-truck guy had gotten the Lamborghini started.

Usually they would have let it go. But not after the Chinese kid had pulled a strap on them. Now this whole thing was a matter of honor. Of pride. MS-13 pride.

Mata, roba, viola, controla.

Kill, steal, rape, control.

That was the Mara Salvatrucha motto.

Not run like a couple of punkass bitches because some rich kid pulled a gat.

He should have let them have his car. Instead he had played it like he was some kind of gangster.

"What's with all the lions?" said Joker.

It was true. Lion statues stood guard outside many of the houses.

"They're supposed to ward off bad spirits," said Pony.

"Good luck with that," said Joker, and they laughed.

They came to the end of the block.

"Down there," said Pony.

Joker made the turn. Pony had a weird sense about things like this. He always had. Ever since they'd been little. It was like he had some sixth sense about stuff. It was freaky. Give him a haystack and Pony would know where the needle was.

The BMW crawled down the block. Pony hit the button to lower his window. He leaned out. "Stop," he told Joker. He popped the door and got out. He walked up to a gate, a lion at either side, bigger than any of the neighbors had. Joker promised himself that next time they were out here with the truck, he would take a pair of these lions and put them outside his mom's house. Maybe start a new trend in the barrio. Why not? They looked pretty cool.

Pony waved at him. He flashed their sign.

"You found it?"

"Yeah," said Pony.

Joker threw the BMW into park, left the engine running and got out to see for himself.

There it was. Right out front of the house on the driveway. The white Lamborghini.

What an asshole, thought Joker. Not putting a car like that in the garage when you had one. It was like you were begging to get jacked.

"Mark it up," said Joker.

Pony took a few steps back, and looked up at the house. All the lights were out, save one that burned upstairs. "We're here now."

Joker shook his head. That wasn't what had been agreed. They were already pushing their luck coming back. This wasn't like jacking up a car. A car just went where you pointed it. People weren't like that. They had their own ideas.

If they were going to do this, they needed to do it properly. That meant they had to know exactly what they were walking into.

Plus they needed a green light from up above. You couldn't be MS-13 and just go do stuff like this. It had to be run past a shotcaller first.

"Mark it," said Joker.

Pony pulled the chalk from his pocket, and scrawled the sign down low so no one would notice it. He kept looking up at the house. He was still staring at it as they got back into the car and pulled away.

5

———————

*I*nternational Arrivals Hall
    Los Angeles International Airport

THE RED TIGER stood behind the line and waited to be called. Finally, it was his turn.

He walked forward. He handed the Customs and Border Protection officer his passport with his documents tucked inside. The officer took them without a word and began to look through his passport.

"What's the purpose of your visit to the United States?" asked the officer.

"I'm attending a business conference."

Before he had left, he had searched the internet for conferences in the Los Angeles area. He had found one for businesses that manufactured store displays and signs. Less than three hours later, he had a website online for such a business with his name and picture as CEO.

He had booked a hotel close to the venue in downtown Los Angeles, as well as a place at the conference. His story would check out.

"How long will you be in the United States?"

"One week."

That was what his return ticket said. The truth was he would stay as long as it took, but a week was about as long a stay as was credible for a sign maker attending a business conference.

The officer stared at the screen in front of her. She tapped a few times at her keyboard.

The Red Tiger stood in silence.

"Okay, sir, if you could place the four fingers of your left hand on the scanner."

The Red Tiger did as instructed.

"And now the four fingers of your right."

Again, the Red Tiger complied.

"If you could look at this camera."

He looked at the lens, his eyes unblinking, his expression perfectly neutral. His picture was taken.

More tapping at the keyboard. More checking of his documents. Finally, his passport was handed back to him.

"Thank you, sir."

He nodded, walked to the escalator that would take him down to the baggage-claim area. As he stepped onto the escalator he slowly exhaled. The hard part was done. He was here.

6

Li Yeng ran his hand along the side of the Lamborghini. There was no question that it was a beautiful piece of machinery, so stunning in its form that it qualified as a work of art.

But it was not a car for a twenty-one-year-old Chinese boy with impulse-control issues and a history of making bad decisions. He would mention it to the boss. Discreetly, of course. Perhaps the boss would suggest to Charlie's mother that something more modest would be appropriate. Not that modesty was a trait of this generation.

The house in front of him was one of a dozen he had presented to the family for purchase. It was the largest, the most expensive, and the gaudiest of the twelve. It was absurd that two young people barely out of diapers would require a seven-thousand-square-foot home with a swimming pool, spa area, and wine cellar.

Li Yeng lived in a one-bed apartment in downtown Los Angeles. It was a nice building, but it was no more and no less than he required. He was kept so busy that he was rarely there so he didn't need frills or luxuries beyond somewhere to sleep, bathe and, on rare occasions, cook and eat.

The front door opened and Emily stepped out. She startled at the sight of him.

"I was about to knock," he said.

"You scared me. Why do you have to creep around?"

He ignored her. One of his hard and fast rules was not to upset Emily. In a country that normally venerated sons, his boss worshipped the ground that Emily walked on. Li Yeng suspected it was because he recognized something of himself in his daughter. She was what the Americans called a tough cookie.

Yes, she liked the trappings of wealth, but she was also serious and hard-working. Her grades were excellent and she always applied herself. When the boss retired it would likely be Emily who took over the family business and interests. He could only hope that she would keep him on as the family's trusted first lieutenant.

"How was the party last night?" he said, changing the subject.

She rolled her eyes. "So boring. You know, the same people we see back home."

That much was true. It seemed like half the children of China's wealthiest families were within twenty miles of Los Angeles. They hung out together. They went to the same clubs. They dated each other. The only difference was the location.

"So nothing interesting happened?"

Emily stared at him. He always did this. Asked questions like he knew more than he did. She studied her nails. She badly needed a manicure. "Not really. Why do you ask?"

"No reason. Is Charlie awake?"

"Why don't you go see for yourself?" she said, clicking the button to open the garage.

The door whirred open. She walked past him. He could smell her perfume, French and expensive. She was wearing heels. She was always dressed like a runway model.

Li Yeng had watched her turn from a precocious brat into this self-assured, self-contained young woman. He had found himself thinking about her when he was alone. As soon as he did, he pushed the thought away. He could never allow himself to see her in that way.

He was so blinded by all of this that he had almost forgotten why he was there. "Before you go."

"Yes?" she said.

"I'm to remind you both to set the alarm, even when you're inside at night."

Suddenly he had her attention. "Why?"

"What do you mean? It's just important. That's all."

She stopped and walked back to him. "Yes, but why mention it now? Has something happened?"

This was bad. The boss had warned him not to alarm her unduly but to make sure she was vigilant. He didn't know how you did one without the other. Vigilance required some level of heightened awareness.

He had to think of something quickly. "There have been some robberies. That's all. Nothing to worry about, but if the alarm isn't set our insurance would be invalid."

"Our?"

"Your," he said, correcting himself.

"Maybe you should speak to Charlie. He's the one who has trouble with the rules."

"I will."

With that, she disappeared in a cloud of Chanel and the clip-clop of red-soled shoes. He stood back and watched as she drove past him, and roared out into the street, the Audi bottoming out at the end of the steep driveway.

He should have said more while he'd had the chance, made his warning more specific. He should have told her she needed to be careful. To tell him if anyone approached her.

How could he, though? Even something as simple as suggesting the alarm was set had raised her suspicions.

This was an impossible job. Secrets always were. No good ever came of them.

PART II

7

Ty Johnson stood in the middle of the arrivals area at Terminal 2 of the Los Angeles International Airport, plain old LAX to the locals. This was one upside to being six feet four inches tall. People he was collecting from the airport couldn't exactly miss him.

Just look out for the huge black dude with the bad attitude and shades.

Not that he'd needed to give a description on this occasion.

He checked the time on his phone, then the screen above his head. Lock's plane out of JFK had landed fifteen minutes ago, which meant he should appear any moment now.

Ryan Lock was Ty's business partner and best friend. He'd been in New York for the past few days conducting a counter-security review for a Russian oligarch. It would have involved finding the holes in the man's existing security arrangements, showing how a hostile party could exploit them, and telling him how they could patch them up. Lock saw this as an elaborate game, one that sharpened his own, already razor-edged, close-protection skills. Ty liked the fact that these gigs paid the kind of money it had taken him a year to earn when he'd worked for Uncle Sam.

Ty had stayed in California because of some minor legal difficulties involving his part in ending an armed hostage situation at a hospital in Long Beach. A man he'd served with in the Corps had flipped out when the staff had refused to treat an injured animal he'd brought in. Ty was facing a number of charges that would likely be dropped but for now it was easier for him to stay in California.

Lock appeared, carrying an overnight bag and a laptop case. He threaded his way confidently through the throng.

As Ty headed over to intercept him, Lock suddenly changed direction, picking up his pace and veering left, heading toward the exit that would take him outside to the nearest parking structure.

Weird, thought Ty, as he briefly lost sight of his friend.

Maybe he should have texted to let him know he was picking him up. No matter. He edged his way through the throng to intercept him.

Ty stopped in his tracks as he saw Lock pick up his girlfriend, Carmen Lazaro, and spin her round before planting a kiss on her lips. She ran her hands through his hair and pulled him in for an even more passionate smooch.

"Goddam," Ty muttered.

He wasn't big on PDAs (public displays of affection), and until right now he'd thought Lock wasn't either. Ty started to back up, away from the happy couple. He turned and began to head in the opposite direction.

"Ty!" Lock called.

Ty pretended not to hear and kept walking.

"Ty, wait up!"

There was nothing else for it. Ty turned around, doing his best to pretend that he hadn't already seen him.

Lock was walking toward him, hand in hand with Carmen. "You here to pick me up?" he asked.

"Yeah," said Ty, shuffling his feet. "I didn't realize Carmen was meeting you."

Carmen smiled at him. "I had a free day. Well, technically, I'm working at home."

Lock squeezed her hand. "Was that what we were going to call it? Working from home?"

She playfully punched Lock's arm. "Behave."

"Absolutely not," said Lock.

Lock had it bad. He never lacked for female attention, but this was the first serious relationship he'd been in since his fiancée had died right here in Los Angeles. With the job that they did, relationships were hard to establish and even tougher to maintain. Ty was pleased for his friend, but he didn't want a courtside seat for all the mushy stuff.

"You kids go do whatever it was you planned," said Ty.

"Hang on a sec," said Lock. "Did I miss anything while I was up there? The WiFi was down so I haven't checked email or messages."

"Yeah, but it can wait."

"Sure it can," said Carmen, pulling at Lock's hand.

"What was it?"

"Some Chinese guy's been calling. Li Yeng. Name ring any bells?"

"Can't say it does. What did he want?"

"To speak with you. Wouldn't say why. But he's called like four times in the past three hours."

"Sorry," Lock said to Carmen, and turned to Ty. "You have a number for him?"

"Sure," said Ty, handing Lock his cell. "It's the last call right there."

"I'll be two minutes and then we can split," Lock said to Carmen.

"It's fine."

Lock moved away from them to make the call, leaving Ty alone with Carmen.

"Kind of awkward," said Carmen. "We should probably coordinate airport pickup."

"I thought you'd be at work," said Ty.

"Ty, can I ask you something?"

"Sure."

"Don't take this the wrong way, but are you jealous?"

"Jealous? What do you mean?" he said, feigning ignorance. Ty knew exactly what she was driving at.

"Well, you and Ryan are tight. Best buds. Joined at the hip almost.

Then I come along, and all of a sudden you don't get to collect him from the airport anymore."

"You're fucking with me, right?"

She grinned. "Maybe just a little."

Lock walked over to them. He handed Ty his phone.

"What's the deal?" said Ty.

Carmen had already read the change in Lock's demeanor. "Something tells me our plans for the day just took a hit."

"I'll make it up to you."

"Serious?" said Ty.

Lock nodded. "Double abduction in Arcadia."

"Abduction or kidnapping?" said Ty.

"Too early to say. No ransom demand's been made, but that's not unusual at this stage."

"You want me to call the office, see what I can find out?" Carmen asked.

"No point. The cops haven't been told, and that's the way the family wants it to stay. For now anyway."

8

They cleared the worst of the traffic surrounding LAX and took the ramp onto the 105. They would switch to the 110 before getting on to the 10 freeway that would take them all the way out to Arcadia.

Ty was driving but they had elected to take Lock's car. A pearl grey Audi RS7 was a better match for a job that demanded a low profile than Ty's tricked-out purple 1966 Lincoln Continental, with its leopard-spot suede interior and the sound system that Lock was convinced Ty had bought from a dance club. Ty had many great qualities, but keeping a low profile was not one of them.

As Ty wove through traffic, Lock did his best to gather what intel he could on the man who wanted their help. The information available online did not suggest a man who'd find himself in the middle of a double abduction.

The unwillingness to involve law enforcement worried Lock. The first hours after a kidnap or abduction were the most crucial. Whether they were local, state or federal, law enforcement possessed expertise and resources that no one else could come close to offering.

It suggested that more was going on. Maybe something illegal or straight-up criminal. That was the usual reason for people who didn't wish to involve the cops when a crime was committed.

Of course, there was another factor. One that Lock couldn't ignore. Immigrants and immigrant communities often had a built-in reluctance to involve law enforcement, especially when they came from a country where institutions were either corrupt or incompetent.

Lock wasn't sure how much either of those charges would apply in China. It was such a vast nation that he imagined there were places where the cops were on the ball and fairly straight up, and others where they weren't. He'd have to explain to their new potential client that the cops here could be trusted, and did a good, often exceptional, job.

"So what you got on this guy?" Ty asked, piloting the Audi across two lanes to make the transition to the 10.

"Not a whole lot," said Lock, scrolling down his phone.

"Twenty-nine years old. Chinese national. Moved to the States to study for his MBA. Was already working for a heavy business hitter back home who paid his fees. Now he manages the guy's property and business interests out here on the west coast, and his kids by the look of it."

"Man, I hope he's doing a better job with the real estate."

"We don't know what's happened to them yet. Maybe they're out partying and he's jumped to the wrong conclusion. There's no ransom note and no contact from any kidnapper."

"False alarm?" said Ty.

"It's a possibility."

"That might explain why he wanted us to check it out first, rather than call the cops and get them all up in his business."

"It might," agreed Lock. "Or he's panicked and thinks he can deal with it himself without his boss back home finding out."

"We have any steer on who's missing?" asked Ty.

"One male, one female. Both family members of his boss, but he didn't say how they're related. They're both over eighteen, but he was asked to keep an eye on them while they're studying over here."

Ty made a low whistling noise. "Boss's family. Best not be asking for a raise anytime soon. He told him yet?"

"No idea."

"So, we have a couple of kids who may or may not be missing," said Ty, summarizing. "May or may not have been kidnapped. No motive if they have been or idea who took them. No one wants to call the cops, and no one knows if their family's been told. Sounds like a complete mess."

"In other words, just our kind of gig," said Lock.

Lock's phone beeped. He had texted Li Yeng and asked for the names of the two missing individuals. There was no point waiting until they got there for the information. He opened the reply.

"What he say?"

"Will discuss when you get here," said Lock, reading the text to Ty.

"Maybe this isn't a good idea," said Ty.

"I was just thinking the same thing. Hard to work with someone who won't give up any information."

Lock's cell rang. It was Li Yeng.

"Ryan Lock."

"Mr. Lock, I apologize. I didn't mean to be rude. It's just that this information is very sensitive, and I never fully trust electronic communication."

That made some kind of sense to Lock. It was easy to forget that paranoia wasn't really paranoia when you grew up in a country where people disappeared if they said something that someone in power deemed out of turn. He was prepared to cut the guy some slack. "Okay, well, listen, we're about twenty minutes out. You can bring us up to speed when we meet."

"I appreciate your understanding. I'll see you at the house."

The call completed, Lock turned to Ty.

"I heard," said Ty.

"There's something else that's bothering me about this," said Lock.

"Listen, about the airport, if I'd known Carmen was collecting you . . ."

"Not that. You guys will just have to fight it out for my affections. No, what I'm wondering is, why us? If this is a missing persons or a kidnap for ransom there's a bunch of people he could have called. LA County is crawling with ex cops doing PI work."

"Maybe it's that cop thing again," offered Ty. "If the guy won't even share names over the phone, why would he involve someone who might just go straight to law enforcement?"

"And he thinks we won't?" said Lock.

"Given our recent record . . ." said Ty. He didn't need to finish. A few weeks ago both of them had been in cuffs, and one of the charges Ty was facing involved locking a member of the Long Beach Police Department in the trunk of his own patrol car.

"I hear you," said Lock.

9

Arcadia reminded Lock of its near neighbour, Pasadena. Clean, tidy, upmarket. The kind of place you'd want to raise children if you had a million to drop on a small family home.

Cruising through downtown, Lock took in all the businesses with some kind of Chinese association. Even the realtors' signs sported Chinese names alongside the major brands such as Century 21 and Re/Max.

The town may have had a large Chinese population but this wasn't Chinatown, an area carved out by poor immigrants. It was a town populated by people who had already made their money by the time they got here.

They headed for a neighborhood known as Upper Rancho. Here a couple of million dollars might get you the house, but it would be small and likely wouldn't have a yard. They turned off Rancho Road onto Hacienda Drive, passing a large corner lot where the existing house had been scraped to make way for a brand new bigger home. It blew Lock's mind that people would spend millions on a perfectly fine house so that they could reduce it to rubble and build something else, only larger and in a different style. Lock made good money, but he struggled to come to terms with the wastefulness of the wealthy.

"It's just down here on the left," he said to Ty.

He was glad they'd used his Audi rather than Ty's pimp-mobile. The Audi, even with its eye-watering price tag, blended in here. Ty's car would have had people calling the cops before they'd reached the end of the block.

Ty pulled up to the curb. "This it?"

Lock checked the address. "Yup."

Ty gave a low whistle.

"Nice house, huh?" said Lock.

Ty raised his sunglasses. "The lady across the street is what I'm talking about." He was busy checking out a young Asian woman who had just gotten out of a Mercedes Benz in short shorts and a halter top with a bag of groceries. "We should speak with her. See if she saw anything."

Lock passed his hand in front of Ty's face. "Ty, can you focus?"

"I'm focused like a motherfucker."

"On this," said Lock, with a nod towards the house. A man in a Brooks Brothers suit, presumably Li Yeng, was walking down the driveway toward them.

Lock got out of the car and Ty followed.

"Mr. Lock," said Li Yeng. "Mr. Johnson. Thank you for coming so quickly."

He made it sound like they were there to install cable or spray for termites rather than assess the site of a possible abduction. There was cool and business-like, but this was a different level.

Lock and Ty shook his hand. There was nothing clammy about it. It was as cool as his demeanor.

Lock decided to start with the basics. The kind of stuff a normal person would have given the dispatcher when they called 911. "So, who are we missing?"

"Right," said Li. "Emily and Charlie Yan. Emily's my boss's daughter and Charlie is her cousin. They both moved here about a year ago to study."

"You mind if we head up to the house?" Lock asked.

"Of course not. Go right ahead," said Li, waving them forward. They walked through the gates. Lock couldn't see a camera at the entrance. There was a cavity for a keypad and intercom system in one of the pillars, right at car-window height, but it hadn't been fitted.

"This is new construction?" Lock said, as they cleared the gates and hiked up toward the house.

"Yeah. I think it was finished right before Mr. Yan purchased it for his daughter."

"You didn't get round to fitting a security system?" said Ty, trying and failing to keep a hint of incredulity out of his voice. Like Lock, it always took him aback that people who would drop six or seven million on a house wouldn't drop fifty thousand on a security system to protect themselves and their investment.

"We have an alarm system that covers the house."

"Cameras?" Lock asked.

"Yes. Four outside, and one in the front hallway."

"Everything was switched on?"

Li hesitated. "I'd reminded the kids about setting the alarm but I don't know if it was on."

"What about the cameras?" said Lock.

"I haven't looked yet. I guess."

That was a lie, thought Lock. It had to be. You didn't have two people go missing from a house with cameras and not check the footage.

"How old are Emily and Charlie?"

"Emily's nineteen and Charlie just turned twenty-one."

"And why do you think something's happened to them? Kids that age can lose track of time. Go out partying with their friends, forget to check in."

"Charlie, yes, that wouldn't surprise me, but not Emily. Both their cars are missing, and it looks like something happened inside the house. You can see for yourself."

They were almost at the front door. It was wide open but Lock couldn't see any damage or sign that it had been forced.

"It was like this when you got here?" Ty asked Li.

"Yes."

"With the door open?" said Lock.

"Yes, that's why I knew something was wrong. Even Charlie wouldn't leave the door open with no one home. He can be reckless at times, but not like that."

Lock made a mental note to ask what Li meant by that. Reckless could cover a wide range of behavior. But, for now, one huge question loomed over all of this.

Crossing his arms, and standing just outside the front door, Lock asked the man in front of him, "Why didn't you call the cops? Why spend hours trying to get hold of someone like me when you potentially have two young people who are missing? You realize that this is America, right?"

None of the questions seemed to faze him. "I know. It looks bad. But I spoke to the family and they didn't want me to contact the authorities until we knew for sure that it was a kidnapping."

"Why?" said Ty, his expression as serious as a heart attack.

The implication was unspoken but clear. People didn't call the cops when they had something to hide.

"It's not what you may think." said Li. "People like Emily's father, they don't involve the authorities unless they absolutely have to. It's cultural."

Cultural, my ass, thought Lock. That was everyone's get-out, these days. He took a breath. "I get why that might be the case back home, but the cops here are on the up and up. It's not like they're going to ask you for money before they open an investigation. A town like Arcadia, they'd be all over this like a rash."

"And if it's a kidnapping that could be very bad for Emily and Charlie," said Li.

That was the first thing out of this man's mouth that actually made any sense, or explained his reluctance to inform local law enforcement of his suspicions. "Okay, let's take a look inside. Maybe they left a note saying they were going somewhere and you missed it," he said. He doubted it. You didn't make a call to people like him and Ty if you thought someone had gone walkabout or was out party-ing. "I take it you've tried all the usual ways of contacting them?" he asked Li.

Li nodded. "First thing I did."

"Calls go to voicemail, ring out? What?" said Ty.

"Both their cell phones are switched off. No voicemail. Nothing."

"What about social media?" said Ty.

"Nothing posted since they disappeared. Not publicly anyway. I'm not in some of their friends' groups for obvious reasons."

"Okay, we can dig a little deeper on that if we need to. They may still be in touch with someone," said Lock.

"Not if their phones are switched off they ain't," said Ty.

Ty was right. Both phones switched off wasn't good. The first thing any even semi-intelligent kidnapper would do was get rid of them: they were essentially portable surveillance devices. You didn't even need to have the cops triangulate cell masts. All you needed was the location services button to be toggled to the on position, which it was on most devices. If you ever used Google Maps or its equivalent on your cell phone, you were being tracked.

Li bent down to take off his shoes. Lock and Ty followed suit. Together, the three men stepped through the front door and into the cavernous front hall with its standard McMansion double-swoop staircase and polished floors.

A mountain bike lay propped against one of the walls. Ty had pulled out his cell phone and was shooting video for review later.

Lock walked back to the front door and took a closer look. He bent down, closing one eye to get a closer look at the keyhole from the outside.

"What is it?" asked Li.

Lock straightened up, walked across the hallway and into the first room he saw, the kitchen. It was large, and well equipped enough for an outside caterer to use. He walked over to the refrigerator, and opened it. They obviously ate out a lot or ordered in because, apart from water, diet sodas and a couple of beers, it was fairly bare.

"Give Ty the details of the two cars, their license numbers, and whether they have any Lo-Jack or other tracking devices fitted," said Lock, closing the fridge door and looking around for any sign of a note.

"I know the Lamborghini had some kind of Lo-Jack deal. I'm not sure about the Audi."

Lock stopped and looked at him. He'd been around enough kids of the ultra-wealthy not to be surprised but somehow he still was. "They have a Lamborghini?"

"Sweet ride," said Ty, unhelpfully.

"It belongs to Charlie. His mother bought it for his twenty-first."

"I got a birthday card and a six-pack of Coors," said Lock.

"I got a ride to Iraq," said Ty.

"You win," said Lock.

"What can I tell you? He's *fuerdai*. They're spoiled," said Li.

"*Fuerdai*?" said Lock.

"It's what they call rich kids in China. You know, the ones who've had everything handed to them," said Li.

"Like a Lamborghini Aventador?" offered Ty.

"Yeah, like that," said Li. "They're actually not bad kids, especially Emily."

"You have pictures of them both? Recent ones."

"Sure. I can pull some from their social media for you."

Li followed Lock and Ty out of the kitchen. They trailed around the rest of the ground floor. There was nothing to indicate a struggle had taken place, or that someone had been dragged out of the house against their will.

Li walked into the living room, still behind Lock and Ty. "You have to understand that when it comes to the *fuerdai*, and even their parents, we're talking about wealth that even Americans struggle to understand. China is so vast, and the economy was so underdeveloped for so long, that the small number of people who made money made a lot of it, and they made it fast. We're talking billions of dollars."

Lock picked up a biology textbook from a couch. It was well

thumbed and marked with Post-it notes. "All the more reason to have good security."

"Believe you me, once you locate Emily and Charlie I'll be putting everything in place that you recommend. No expense spared," said Li.

"Good, but unfortunately throwing money at things isn't always the answer," said Lock. "Sometimes you have to do the opposite. The Russians learned that the hard way. Now they keep their wealth a lot more on the down-low. Like not giving their kids three-hundred-thousand-dollar supercars."

"People like Charlie's mother have never seen money like they have. Never been around it. They want to give their kids everything."

"And what about you?" Ty asked Li.

"I've had to work for what I have."

"But this gravy train will come grinding to a halt if anything bad's happened to your boss's daughter?"

"I expect it would. I also expect I would find something else," said Li.

It didn't come off as boastful, more as a simple statement of fact.

"Let's look upstairs," said Lock.

Li started to follow him and Ty up one side of the double staircase. "Go get us the info on the cars and those pictures," said Lock. He needed a moment alone with Ty without the gofer in tow.

THE TWO BODYGUARDS stepped into Emily's bedroom and closed the door behind them. Besides some puddles of discarded clothes, and an unmade bed, the room was neat and tidy. A large desk was piled with textbooks. They sat next to a Mac computer. Study plans were tacked up on the wall.

Other than the room itself, which was big enough to qualify as an apartment, there was a bathroom and a walk-in closet.

"What you think?" said Ty.

"He's full of shit," said Lock.

"That's the vibe I was getting."

"The question is, what's really going on?"

"Maybe he's involved," said Ty.

The same thought had crossed Lock's mind. Here was a guy who'd had to work his ass off for what he had and was babysitting two rich kids not that much younger than himself who had everything in life gift-wrapped for them.

"If he is, then why call us?"

"Easier to control someone you're paying than the cops?" offered Ty.

"We're not easy to control."

"He's not to know that."

Lock wandered into the walk-in closet. He didn't know much about fashion but he had been around enough women who did to be aware that the clothes and shoes in it would have likely cost hundreds of thousands of dollars.

Ty picked a skimpy black dress off the rack. It still had the store tag on. He showed it to Lock. It had cost a little under four thousand dollars.

"Wasn't a robbery," said Lock.

"I wouldn't be so sure," said Ty. "You steal, you have to fence. Some broke-ass neighborhood where the hos are wandering about in Chanel and red-soled Louboutins rather than sweatpants and clear heels. That's going to lead back to you real quick."

Lock wasn't convinced, but he took the point. It was always worth bearing in mind what the score was. Two living, breathing family members of a billionaire were worth a lot more than stolen goods that had to be sold off at a ninety per cent discount. Cars were a little different, but stolen was stolen. It was why kidnap for ransom was one of the fastest-growing crimes worldwide.

"We need to ask Li if someone can take a look at their bank accounts and credit cards," said Lock, walking back out into the bedroom.

"So what's the plan?" Ty asked. "Think we should call the cops?"

"Absolutely, but what are they going to say?"

"Same as we just did. Missing less than twenty-four hours. No sign of a struggle. Or robbery. Cars are gone, but why wouldn't they be if both occupants have left the house?"

"Phones could be switched off because, hey, kids who're out partying don't want to speak to Mom or Dad," added Lock.

"And no ransom demand."

"It's a big pile of nothing at all," said Lock. "Let's check the other rooms, then go see if Li's located the security-camera footage."

10

E mily's pupils widened as big as dinner plates as the girl walked the length of the room toward her. Maybe fifteen or sixteen, she was chewing gum, which smacked against the side of her mouth. She was dressed in black shorts, black sneakers with no socks, and an oversized LA Kings shirt that revealed white bra straps. Her neck, arms and legs were heavily tattooed and she wore cheap gold chains. Two black and silver skull rings adorned her right hand, the index and middle finger.

"How you doing?" she said, the 'you' sounding like 'choo'.

When she spoke, her lips peeled back to reveal gold-capped teeth that made her look even more sinister. The boys called her Princess. Emily could tell it served as both nickname and in-joke. Princess Nightmare would have been a better name.

"I'm okay," said Emily. She had to say something. She also knew that whatever she did say would be wrong somehow.

"You're a princess too, huh?" said the girl, her closed fist coming up, the skull rings pressing hard into Emily's cheekbone. "*Niña consentida.* You know what that means?"

"No," said Emily, her mouth so dry with fear that she was barely able to speak.

"It means spoiled little bitch," said Princess, drawing her fist and faking a punch that stopped just short of Emily's nose.

Emily flinched. She couldn't stop herself. It was reflex. She didn't remember ever having been hit, apart from maybe once by a boy in school who'd made a tearful apology after the teacher had intervened. Charlie had heard about it and beaten the living shit out of him when the boy started high school. The school had threatened to expel Charlie. Her father had intervened. Suddenly it had a new swimming pool and Charlie stayed.

Emily doubted that these people would be so easily bought off. She'd already had to listen to Charlie being beaten shortly after they'd got here, hurried into this house in the dead of night. He had pleaded for them to stop. That had only seemed to make them more excited.

If possible, Emily was not going to plead. She was going to get through this. Somehow.

Princess had her face right in Emily's. Her perfume was vile. The smell made Emily want to be sick. Emily closed her eyes as Princess's tongue touched her cheek, and ran all the way across her face and to the nape of her neck. The girl's long black hair swept across her face. Emily had to clamp her lips together to keep it out of her mouth.

"You like that?" Princess whispered in her ear.

Emily tried to catch her breath. "No."

Princess stood back. Emily opened her eyes.

"Don't worry. You'll get to like it."

"No, I won't."

"We'll see."

Princess stood back and cocked her hand to her hip. "You know, Joker likes you. I see how he looks at you."

Joker was one of the gang members who had taken her and Charlie at gunpoint and brought them here. Emily was sure she had heard that name. "Why are you telling me this?" she said to Princess.

"Maybe I can persuade him to leave you alone."

Emily knew what that meant. "Leave alone" meant "not raped".

"Why would you do that?" she said, although she had an idea already.

Princess shrugged. "I like you. We may as well enjoy ourselves."

Emily needed to change the subject. "My family has money. If you let us go, they'd pay you."

Princess started laughing. "Oh, don't worry. We know that." She bent down and went to kiss Emily. Emily turned her head.

"That's okay," said Princess, running a finger down Emily's cheek to her neck. "I like a *chica* who fights first."

11

The Red Tiger drove his rental car from LAX to Kingman in Arizona. His business was back in California, but Arizona was where he had to collect what he would need.

On the way to Kingman he made two stops. First he went into a Walmart to purchase a burner phone and a pre-paid SIM card. Second, he pulled into a gas station to refuel and use the restroom. He also bought some caffeinated energy drink and two packs of cigarettes. Energy drinks and cigarettes were the staples of his diet, his two main food groups. Out of habit, he paid with cash for all of his purchases.

When he was a half-hour away from Kingman, he texted the number of his contact. In under sixty seconds there was a reply, giving an address of a parking lot on the outskirts of town.

Twenty minutes later, the Red Tiger pulled in. There was a supermarket, a drug store, and two fast-food restaurants, one serving hamburgers, the other Mexican food. He parked near the exit, ready to get out of there and back on the freeway if the sale went bad. Transactions such as this could easily go bad.

He had cash, the seller had guns. It was the perfect recipe for robbery.

Sitting in his car, he smoked another cigarette. He was starting to feel tired. The last week or so had been frenetic. He'd averaged four hours of sleep a night, if that. Nervous energy had kept him going. That, and knowing that his long journey was near an end.

Not knowing had always been the worst part of this. Where was she? Was she alive? Was she happy? Did she remember anything about her old life? What had they told her? Did she remember him?

Some of these questions were answered. The rest would be soon enough.

People would stand in his way. That was why he needed a gun.

A dark red sedan circled the parking lot. It pulled up next to his rental car. A white man with a beard and a baseball cap leaned out of the driver's door. He was in his late fifties, or maybe his early sixties. The Red Tiger couldn't see anyone else in the car. Unless someone was lying down on the backseat, the man had come alone.

The man pulled into a parking spot in the next row, and got out. He walked over to the Red Tiger's car. The Red Tiger got out.

"You found the place okay?" said the man.

The Red Tiger nodded. He planned on speaking as little as possible. He knew he had an accent when he spoke English. He also knew that Americans like this man didn't trust foreigners. It didn't upset him. The Chinese distrusted foreigners too. It was the way of the world.

"Come on over. I'll show you what I got."

The Red Tiger followed the man back to the dark red sedan. The man popped the trunk to reveal a half-dozen gun carry cases.

"You got the money?" said the man.

Another nod. The Red Tiger looked around. He couldn't believe how relaxed the man was about conducting business right out in the open.

The man seemed to sense his unease. "Relax, you're not in California anymore. This is Arizona," he said. He opened one of the smaller cases to reveal a handgun. He took it from the protective foam insert. "Okay, lemme see here. I think I got everything you asked for. This here's the Glock 43. Single stack. Nine mill with a mag extender." He took it out of the case. "Let me just clear and safe this bad boy."

He handed the gun to the Red Tiger. He weighed it in his hand. It was a nice gun. "I'll take it," he said.

"Damn, you're my kind of customer."

"Shotgun?" said the Red Tiger.

The man put the Glock back in its case and closed it. He reached deeper into the trunk and pulled out a pump-action shotgun.

"Here you go. Mossberg 590 Shockwave, Twelve-gauge, fourteen-inch barrel. Army buddy of mine calls this the head eraser." The man chuckled at his own joke, and handed it over.

The Red Tiger took it into his hands. It was beautiful.

"Good car gun. Great for home defense. Have a couple of them myself," said the man. "Just don't get caught with it in California, okay?"

"I understand," said the Red Tiger. "How much?"

"For both?" asked the man.

"Yes. And ammunition."

"How much ammo you need?"

The Red Tiger gave him the number.

The man stepped back and muttered his calculations under his breath. "I ain't asking any questions. What you do with them once you leave here is your business."

"Yes, of course."

"Why don't we call it two even?"

"Two thousand dollars," the Red Tiger repeated.

"Like I said, no questions, and I'll throw in some extra rounds."

"Deal," said the Red Tiger. "You take cash?"

The man smiled. "Don't take anything but. Nice doing business with you. Mr. . . . .?"

The Red Tiger pulled out his money clip and began to count off the money in fifties. He didn't give the man his name. There was no need.

∾

BACK IN HIS RENTAL CAR, the Red Tiger watched the man drive away with the two thousand dollars. He left the Glock 43 in its case. He took the Mossberg, racked a round into the chamber, and laid it on the passenger seat next to him, the barrel facing the door.

He switched on the engine and drove out of the parking lot. A few minutes later he picked up the freeway and headed back west.

He lit a fresh cigarette and lowered the window, enjoying the breeze. He glanced back at the gun on the passenger seat next to him. He doubted he would need it. But it was always best to be prepared, especially when you were a stranger in a strange land.

Lock, Ty and Li had gathered in the living room to watch the last thirty-six hours of security footage on a sixty-inch display mounted on the living-room wall. The screen was divided into sections. Each showed the output from a single camera.

Lock was still struggling with Li's assertion that he hadn't seen any of this before he'd called them. If he was lying, and the recording showed them what had happened to Emily and Charlie, Lock was certain Li's reaction, or lack of one, would give him away.

Ty held the Creston remote control. He was busy fast -forwarding through the early part of the footage. They had reached the time-stamp for the previous evening. An internal camera had caught Emily and Charlie together in the kitchen. Then they had walked up the stairs, presumably to go to bed.

That had been a little after midnight. So far there was nothing out of the ordinary.

The footage rolled on at sixteen times normal speed. Lock leaned forward in the armchair, elbows on his knees.

"Okay, what's that?" he said.

Ty hit the pause button and pulled the footage back.

"Where?" asked Li.

"Top right," said Lock.

He had noticed a sudden change in brightness in the footage from the outside camera that covered the garage area. Now, even as Ty rewound, Lock could see movement. He side-eyed Li, who was sitting a few feet away on the couch.

"Who are they?" said Li.

It was always hard to tell if someone you had only just met was genuine or faking, but Li's surprise seemed to Lock like the real deal.

Ty tapped the remote display. The view from the garage camera filled one half of the screen. The other displayed the recording of the other cameras.

Lock's eyes narrowed. He'd assumed the sudden brightness had been a motion-activated security light switching on. Depending upon the sensitivity level it had been set to, the light could be triggered by something as small and innocuous as a domestic cat walking past. Coyotes, possums and raccoons were favorite culprits.

The light hadn't come from the bulb mounted above the garage door.

On screen, car headlights splashed out from inside the garage. It looked like someone was taking one of the vehicles for a late-night drive. They had watched both Emily and Charlie heading upstairs, which didn't mean that one or both of them hadn't snuck back down.

Before Lock could prompt him, Ty pulled back the footage, and checked the inside of the house. There was a door that led from a pantry next to the kitchen directly into the garage. But to reach the kitchen you would have to come down the stairs and walk across the hallway.

Lock kept one eye on the screen, and the other on Li as the hallway area stayed the same. There was no sign of either Emily, Charlie, or anyone else.

"Okay," said Lock. "Keep it rolling."

They watched as the front of the Lamborghini inched forward out of the garage, the high, fixed angle of the security camera making it impossible to see who was at the wheel.

"We have sound on any of these?" asked Lock.

"Nope," said Ty. "Just a visual."

The Lamborghini inched a little further out of the garage. The hesitant, stop-start way it pulled out suggested to Lock that whoever was behind the wheel was unfamiliar with the vehicle. Had Emily ever driven it? Could she have found a way into the garage that avoided the hallway camera? It seemed unlikely. If she had decided to take it for a spin she wouldn't have worried about a camera catching her.

Now lots of things happened all at once. Outside the garage, two figures appeared from the edge of the frame and rushed towards the Lamborghini as its high-mounted brake lights lit up.

Ty paused the footage again. Lock got up from the armchair and walked toward the screen, studying the figures. They wore sneakers, baggy jeans and equally baggy shirts. Bandanas covered the lower part of their faces. Baseball caps took care of the rest, leaving only the area around their eyes visible.

Li had also stood up and was standing next to Lock. Again, his reaction seemed one of complete and genuine shock. "What the hell?" he said to Lock.

He could be acting, Lock reminded himself, but something told him that he wasn't.

It was a fine process of calibration, but it was also one that Lock was adept at. He could usually spot a liar at six hundred paces: even if their words were consistent, their body language betrayed them. The only exception Lock had found were individuals with socio- or psychopathic personalities and ice water for blood.

That was a possibility that he could not dismiss. So far Li had been extremely focused and business-like. This reaction could simply be a mirroring of what he knew to be a normal human being's reaction.

"Who are they? How did they get into the garage?" said Li.

"I can tell you what they are," said Lock. "It's a little early for the who and the how."

"They're gang members," said Ty. "Come to jack that sweet ride of your boy's."

"I tried to tell them that car was a bad idea," said Li, coming off like he was making a final plea to a jury. It was a little too strident for Lock's liking.

In his head Lock circled back to Li having waited until now to find out what had happened when it was playing out in front of them. "Half speed," he instructed Ty.

Ty hit play, then slowed it down to one half of real-time replay. He tapped between screens, blowing up the ones with signs of activity and shrinking the others.

Presumably alerted by the roar of the Lamborghini, Charlie came tearing down the stairs. Outside the garage, a third gang member had appeared on the forecourt. There had to be one driving inside the car, and possibly a second riding shotgun.

"Okay, pause," said Lock. "Go back to Charlie. What's he holding there?"

The frame froze. Charlie was mid-step, three steps from the bottom. He had something in his right hand. A pistol. It was either a Glock, or a SIG, almost certainly the former from the finer details and shape.

"You know he had a gun?" Lock asked Li.

"No idea."

He was lying. Lock was certain of it. He let it go. For now.

"Does Charlie have any kind of training?"

Li shook his head.

Lock's stomach sank a little. A gun for home defense wasn't the worst idea but only if you knew what you were doing with it. If you didn't, it could quickly become a liability. Time at the gun range with an instructor did two things. It taught you how to hit a target. But, more importantly, it helped make trigger-pull a habit that wasn't overridden by uncertainty.

There was no point in having a gun in your hand, and aiming the end of the barrel at a bad guy, if you didn't have what it took to squeeze off a shot.

Ty hit play but kept it on half speed. Charlie disappeared frame left. He was headed towards the kitchen and in the direction of the garage.

A few seconds later, the gang members standing outside seemed to react. Two of them ran down the side of the Lamborghini and towards the open garage.

Back in the hallway, Emily was coming down the stairs, still in her pajamas. She appeared hesitant. At one point, she seemed to turn back. Even though he knew she wasn't here, part of Lock was willing her to run back up the stairs, lock herself into a bathroom and call the cops. That would have been the smart thing to do.

He made a mental note to discuss panic-room installation with the family, if they resolved this mess. It was nuts that someone could drop this kind of cash on a trophy home and a trophy car without even a basic panic room to hole up in while they waited for the cavalry to crest the hill.

On the street, in your car or in your home, if the bad guy couldn't get to you, you were safe. That was rule number one. It was hard for anything bad to happen to someone who was sitting behind a blast-proof door.

At the bottom of the stairs, they all watched helplessly as Emily headed in the same direction Charlie had moments before. Her mouth opened and shut. She appeared to be shouting. Then she, too, exited the frame.

Back outside, two of the gang members had disappeared into the garage. One stayed next to the Lamborghini. Its brake lights still flared.

Lock sensed what he would see next before it unfolded on the screen. Not even sensed. He knew. What was missing and what was present from the house told him.

Ty let the next brief section play in real time before slowing the footage again as the two gang members reappeared, dragging Charlie between them. He was no longer holding the handgun. But one of the gang members was holding what looked awfully like a Glock. He held it by the barrel and smashed the butt into Charlie's face. Over and over. At least four heavy blows to his face and then the back of his head as he crumpled.

The third gang member skipped over to join the beating. Lock motioned for Ty to pause the footage.

"What is it?" Ty asked him.

Lock walked up close to the screen, and jabbed a finger at the third gang member. A mass of long black curly hair spilled down their back.

"That's a girl?" said Li.

"It's not exactly unheard of," said Lock.

"Or it's a guy with long hair," offered Ty.

Lock shook his head, and tapped the screen. "Not unless he's had breast implants too."

"Fair point," said Ty.

The footage resumed. Charlie was thrown to the ground. The girl swung a kick, full force, at his head. Even Lock winced. Li's hand covered his mouth.

"You don't have to watch the rest of this if you don't want to," Lock offered.

The question was loaded.

If you didn't know what happened next, no matter how shaken you were, you'd want to see it. If you did know, you might try to over-think how a regular person would react.

"No, I'm good," said Li.

Now the gang members were dancing about in front of Charlie. One leaned in and spoke to whoever was at the wheel of the Lamborghini. They seemed uncertain of their next move, like this hadn't been in the plan.

No doubt they had figured that if anyone interrupted them it would be the cops, not a fresh-off-the-boat rich kid, who'd spent his life having his ass wiped for him. As assumptions went, it was reason-able. Make entry to the garage, steal a quarter-million dollars' worth of supercar, and get the hell out of Dodge. Not a bad evening's work for a bunch of street rats. Lock was certain that had been the plan. Especially as they looked down at Charlie writhing in agony on the ground in front of them, like they had no clue as to what should happen next.

The smart money would have been on a hasty escape. Lock knew that hadn't been the call.

Two seconds later, his heart sank further as Emily stepped to the back of the car. She was agitated, hopping from one foot to the other. She had something in her right hand. When he saw what it was, Lock's agitation came close to matching hers.

13

On screen, Emily stood in front of the three bandana-masked gang members, waving a kitchen knife. It was the kind used to chop vegetables. A big black handle. A six-inch blade.

In Lock's mind, pulling a knife on someone, especially when you didn't know how to use it, was almost as dumb as pulling a gun. A gun, you could pull the trigger and get lucky. A gun gave you a better shot at fending someone off. Pull a knife and you'd better have the physical power and fighting skills to deploy it.

Stabbing someone took a colder heart than shooting them. It was more intimate, more physical. It required a deeper level of rage.

The girl gang member was the first to react. Reaching back, she magicked up her own pistol from where it had been tucked into the waistband under her shirt. She aimed it squarely at Emily, who was shifting her weight from side to side. The girl was perfectly calm. She took a step towards Emily, who retreated.

Lock glanced back at Li. He seemed utterly transfixed by the nightmare unfolding on the screen directly in front of them. The moment had a surreal quality to it. Here they were, standing less than a hundred feet from where two totally different worlds had smashed together, and everything looked like the maid had just been in to tidy up and change the floral arrangements.

"Was there any blood?" Lock said to Li.

The question seemed to snap Li out of his reverie. "What?"

"Outside the garage, or inside. Did you see any blood?" repeated Lock.

"No."

They watched as Emily crouched down, placing the knife on the ground. The girl stepped towards her. She bent down, picked up the knife and tucked it down her pants, seemingly unworried about the unsheathed blade.

Lock braced himself for Emily to get the same treatment that Charlie had had. It didn't happen. Instead, the girl reached out and took her hand, as firmly but gently as a kindergarten teacher taking charge of an errant toddler.

One of the gang members flitted past them. Seconds later the Audi reversed out of the garage. Charlie was helped to his feet and, along with Emily, escorted to the Audi. There was some kind of conversation between Emily and the girl, who opened the driver's door. A gang member got out. Emily took his place behind the wheel.

The girl opened the rear passenger door on the opposite side from the driver. Charlie was pushed in. A gang member climbed in beside him. It took off down the drive, disappearing beyond the reach of the security camera's lens. They watched as Emily turned the Audi on the motorcourt and followed it down the driveway into the night. Final destination unknown.

Everything remained still, even as Ty hit fast forward. The screens flickered but didn't change.

Lock didn't move or say anything. He was thinking.

Cars gone. People gone. No obvious signs of a struggle. Nothing disturbed inside the mansion, save a blade missing from the knife block on the marble counter in the kitchen.

Suddenly, with less than three minutes of moving images, it made sense. For the most part anyway.

Questions remained unanswered. But, as with any investigation, it was better to know what you were dealing with than not.

"I need to make a call," said Li.

"Who to?" Lock was done with niceties. This situation was critical enough that they had no place now.

"My boss."

Lock fixed Li with a stare. "That'll be the second call you make," he told him. He had already pulled out his own cell phone. He handed it to Li. "First you're calling the cops."

Li stared at Lock's cell phone, like it was a stick of dynamite.

Lock tapped in 911. "Okay, I'll do it. But it will look better coming from you. First person the cops look at in something like this will be you."

"What do you mean?" said Li. "I wasn't in on that," he said, with a wave at the screen that was still showing the perfectly quiet house.

"You could have set them up," said Ty, stepping easily into the role of suspicious cop. "They have what you want. Didn't work for it. That could make any reasonable person a little jealous."

"Oh, come on," protested Li.

Ty turned to Lock. "He seem kind of touchy to you?"

"He does," said Lock, poker-faced.

An operator had come on the line. Lock held the phone to Li's face. "I need to speak with the Arcadia Police Department," said Li.

14

"You think he's involved?" Ty asked Lock, as they stood in the cavernous front hallway waiting for the cops to arrive.

Li was in the kitchen doorway, breaking the worsening news to his boss in China. It was one call that Lock was grateful he hadn't had to make. If he knew anything about very wealthy self-made men, Li should count himself fortunate that he had an ocean between himself and his employer.

Ty's question was a good one. It had been at the front of Lock's mind even before they had seen Emily and Charlie being jacked and driven off in their own car.

As Li's conversation with Emily's father grew increasingly agitated Lock nudged his partner. "We should get this on camera."

"Already on it," said Ty, who had his cell phone held casually down by his side, the lens tilted toward Li.

"He knows something, and he's not sharing it. But I don't know what that is." Lock shrugged.

"Or we're reading too much into it?"

"That's possible too," said Lock.

Assumptions were dangerous. At any time, but especially this early on. They could send you hurtling down blind alleys and smashing into dead ends without you even realizing it. They ate up valuable time. And in cases like this time was the enemy. The longer Charlie and Emily were gone, the more likely it was that bad things would happen.

"Why did he wait to watch what was on the cameras?" said Ty.

"We need to press him on that."

"Or let the cops?" ventured Ty.

"No, we need to do it. The cops aren't going to share anything with us," said Lock.

"Not with me, you mean," said Ty.

Ty's recent intervention in the armed siege in Long Beach hadn't exactly enamored him to law enforcement. It was understandable.

Despite that, Lock was certain he had made the right call. A crime had been committed and law enforcement had the proper power and resources to deal with it. He and Ty could run something in parallel. Lock was still figuring out what that would entail, if anything.

There was an argument that they had done precisely what they should have done. Perhaps it was enough to work out what had happened and hand it over. It wouldn't pay the bills, but doing the right thing rarely did.

"We should stick around until they get here," said Lock. "We can bring them up to speed. Then I guess it's up to our client here to decide if we stay onboard."

"He wasn't very happy about you making him call the cops."

"I wouldn't read too much into that, Ty. Where he comes from, you call the cops and tell them someone stole your Lamborghini and they want to know where you got the money to buy a Lamborghini."

"Point taken."

They lapsed back into silence. They could hear sirens, first in the distance, then closer.

"You think those kids are okay?" Lock asked his partner.

"I think it all depends on just how smart or dumb those gang members are."

"What do you mean?" said Lock.

"If they're dumb they could try to get an extra pay day. Run a K and R."

K and R meant "kidnap for ransom". It was common in some countries. Big business, even. But not in the United States where law enforcement was way too sophisticated and uncorrupted, and the price was life, without the possibility of parole, if you were caught.

The kidnap part was easy enough, as the gang had just proved. They had stumbled straight into one. The ransom part, the actual collecting, without being detected or the money traced, was far harder. America wasn't fertile ground for that part of the crime.

"This looks way beyond their pay grade," said Lock.

"That's what I'm talking about," said Ty.

"So if they're smart?"

"If they're truly smart," said Ty, "those two kids are already face down in the Pacific."

15

L i could feel his boss's rage radiating all the way from Beijing. His hands were shaking so hard that he had to cradle the phone between his shoulder and his ear.

His boss let rip with a fresh tirade.

All Li could do was wait for the tide of anger to recede.

"How? How could you allow this to happen?" his boss screamed.

"I'm sorry," said Li, for what seemed like the hundredth time.

"Why didn't you check? Why didn't you check the cameras?"

"I don't know. I didn't think anything like this would happen here," he pleaded.

The only consolation he had was that he was in America. If this had been China, there was every chance he would no longer be breathing. Then again, very few criminals in China would have been stupid enough to do this. Not against someone like his boss.

"So what are you going to do about it?" his boss asked finally.

"I contacted Mr. Lock and his associate. They're the best there is. And the police will be here soon."

Mention of the police set his boss off on a fresh rant. "The police? Are you some kind of an imbecile? We can't involve the police in our business."

"I was given no choice. Lock insisted."

"He insisted? He works for us, and you work for me."

"It's not like that here," said Li. "The police will find them."

"And if they don't?" said his boss.

"Then we have our people," said Li.

"I'm coming over. I'll handle this myself."

Li heard him shrieking at one of the assistants to arrange a flight. His boss usually had a jet on standby at all times. China was a big country, bigger even than America, and for a man like him, time was money. "I promise you. This will be resolved quickly."

His boss said nothing. Li had something he needed to ask. But it was delicate. Even more so now. It was a topic his boss had expressly told him not to raise unless they were face to face.

"Have you heard?" said Li.

"Heard about what?"

"What's happened with him? Is he here?"

He waited for a fresh tide of bile. None came. His boss had hung up.

Li put his cell phone back into his pocket and went outside to meet with the police officers.

16

L ock walked back to where Ty was standing by the front door, his re-entry blocked by two patrol officers. They were both giving Ty the death-stare, one with his hand resting on his baton, the other with a palm cradling her Taser.

"I don't think they like you for some reason, Ty," said Lock.

"They're just playing hard to get," said Ty, with a smile. "They know what's up."

"Or, in your case, down," said Lock.

"Whatever." Ty smiled.

He was enjoying his new-found notoriety, Lock could tell. Ty fell into the any-attention-is-better-than-no-attention group of people.

"You get it?" Lock asked him.

Ty held up a tiny key-sized USB drive. "Sure did."

It contained a download of the relevant sections of footage from the security camera. They could review it at their leisure. Lock had already set up a meet with Carl Galante, who worked with Carmen's law firm as an investigator. He was a former San Diego cop who nowadays mostly worked cases in Los Angeles and might have a read on which gang the kidnappers were from.

Not that this gang was necessarily from Los Angeles. The major

gangs were all over California. They had their strongholds and terri-
tories, but they were a lot more spread out over the state, and indeed
the country, than they had been.

"We going to bounce?" said Ty.

"I want to speak with Li before we leave. See if he wants us to stay
on the payroll."

Lock had spoken at length with the local cops, but he hadn't had
any further private conversation with Li. There was every chance
that, now they had made him involve law enforcement, Li wouldn't
want to work with them.

"And if he doesn't?" Ty asked. "You really going to go sit by the
pool until the next call comes in?"

Ty knew Lock well. There was no way on earth that he would
completely wash his hands of something like this. Rich or not,
spoiled or not, Lock would not walk away from two kids who were so
far out of their depth and facing a grisly end, if they hadn't already
met with one.

Neither of them was capable of watching footage like they had
seen, cashing the check, and forgetting the whole affair. It wasn't who
they were.

"We can kick around the weeds a little. Maybe make a few moves
that the cops can't," said Lock.

One advantage they possessed over regular law enforcement was
that they could push the envelope a little more when it came to what
Lock euphemistically termed "investigative methods." In other words,
as long as they didn't get caught, or were dealing with someone who
wouldn't go to the cops, they could do what they deemed necessary to
find the two kids.

"That's what I thought you'd say," said Ty, shooting another grin
at the two female patrol cops. "Ladies." He retreated in the direction
of Lock's Audi. He had some calls of his own to make. specifically to
people he knew who might be able to tell him who in the Southern
California area would be the go-to guy to get rid of a car like a
Lamborghini Aventador.

It wasn't as if those bozos planned on taking it for a joyride before dumping it. It had to be moved on, and only a certain number of people in the criminal fraternity would be interested.

"How'd your boss take the news?" Lock asked Li, as the two men paced the top of the driveway.

Behind them a fresh tranche of CSI had just arrived. Lock had told them they wouldn't find anything inside the house. They had elected not to take his word for it. As far as he was concerned, that was on them.

"How d'you think?"

"So?" said Lock. "You want us to stay on this?"

"I thought you wanted these guys to handle it," said Li, pissy.

"No, I said they had to be informed. Which they are. If you hadn't told them, you could be in a world of pain."

Li laughed. "Like I'm not already."

"Come to America, play by our rules."

"Is that what you plan on doing? Playing by the rules?" Li asked.

A bigger question underlay it. Lock knew that. So did Li.

"I have slightly different rules," he said.

"How different?" said Li.

"Why did you call me?"

"You already asked me that," said Li.

"I forget what you said."

"I needed someone who would do what it takes to find Emily and Charlie."

"Well, my answer hasn't changed," Lock told him.

"Then I see no reason not to continue using your services."

"Good," said Lock. "These guys won't speak to me, so if you hear anything from them . . ."

"I'll let you know," said Li.

LOCK CLIMBED into the front passenger seat of the Audi. Ty could drive them back to Los Angeles.

"What's the good word?" said Ty.

"He wants us to keep working for him."

"Except we're not, are we? Working for him, I mean."

Lock shook his head. He knew what Ty was driving at. This was beyond a standard contract. It had crossed that line as soon as they had watched two young people being driven away by a bunch of gangbangers. Some jobs were business. Some, by their very nature, became something more. This was something more.

"Nope."

Ty buried the gas pedal as they pulled out onto Rancho Road. The Audi took off. "Comes down to the same thing, though," he said.

"So far it does," said Lock.

17

M otel 6
San Bernardino, California

EVEN TIGERS with an empty belly had to sleep sometime. Or, at least, rest in the shade, away from the glare of the sun.

He pulled off I-10 at the San Bernardino exit, found a motel and took a room in back. One night, paid for upfront in cash in case he had to leave in a hurry.

The desk clerk said something to him about no girls. By "girls", the Red Tiger assumed he meant prostitutes. He stared at him. The clerk found a sudden interest in his paperwork and mumbled an apology.

It was good to know that, even here, he could look at another man and scare him. He had always believed it was nothing to do with his appearance. It was something much simpler than that. When he looked into someone's eyes, they sensed that he was capable of killing them.

They sensed it because it was true. He had done it before. He would, no doubt, do it again.

It wasn't something he attached any pride to. Some of the killings he regretted. One or two haunted him. But mostly he viewed them like a slaughterhouse worker would when dispatching cows or pigs.

He moved what he had with him into the room, including the guns. He kept the Mossberg next to the bed. He put down his bag and pulled out the old photograph album.

His shoes were by the door. He lay down and leafed through the album. There were pictures of his grandparents and his parents. He studied those of his grandparents, taken when they were younger. They had been Party members. That was how they had survived. By conforming. By going along with the majority. By not stepping out of line. By being good Communists.

Not to be a good Communist? Not to conform? That was to choose death.

Flipping through, he came to his own baby pictures. He had been a chubby baby. His parents told him he had been happy. Always smiling and content. It was hard to reconcile that with who he was now.

What had happened to him? He guessed it was life. Loss.

A few years after they were married she had fallen pregnant. It was a little girl. The Red Tiger was overjoyed. He refused to be a father who was disappointed by having a girl. Some people killed the child if it was a girl. They denied the pregnancy entirely. Or if they lived in a small town or village where it couldn't be denied, they claimed it was a stillbirth.

Tens of thousands of babies had died like that. All of them girls.

The Red Tiger had vowed that would never be him. He would cherish his daughter. He would give her all that he had.

Once, shortly after she was born, a colleague had teased him about having a daughter rather than a son. This colleague, a fellow officer, had made a crass joke about leaving her out in the countryside to die. He hadn't used those words, but it had been implied.

The Red Tiger had beaten the man to a pulp, thrashed him so

badly that the man's head had swollen to almost double its normal size.

No one ever made such jokes around him anymore. He did not get into trouble or lose his job. Instead he was promoted. It was the first time he had realized the power of his own ability to unleash violence. After that, violence became his narcotic.

A year after that incident, his wife died suddenly. An aneurysm, the doctors said. There in the morning when he left for work, dead by the time he got home.

Family tried to persuade him to let his daughter go. There were still people who would take a little girl. Who were so desperate for a child that it didn't matter their gender. He refused. He found an older lady to look after her. He refused to work beyond his official hours. His boss complained, but not to his face. His boss feared him too.

He did everything he could to transmit the love he had in his heart to his little girl. Then the day had come when it all ended. The day she passed into another life. The day that he still mourned.

Exhaustion finally overtaking him, the Red Tiger fell asleep, the photo album open on his lap, the shotgun next to his head.

18

R yan Lock's Apartment
Marina Del Rey, Los Angeles

LOCK OPENED HIS FRIDGE, grabbed a bottle of beer and handed it to Ty, who opened it using his Gerber and took a sip.

"That's good."

"German. They have a bunch of laws about purity."

"Yeah, I'd heard," said Ty.

"About what they can put in their beer," said Lock. "Not the other kind of purity."

The apartment buzzer sounded. "That'll be Carmen and Galante," said Lock, going to let them in. He had already spoken about the new case to Carmen as they'd driven to Los Angeles from the airport. He had asked her which of her law firm's investigators was strong on organized car theft and street gangs.

Carmen had suggested Carl Galante. He was former San Diego PD but he mostly worked private investigations in Los Angeles. His help had proved invaluable to Lock when Carmen had been kidnapped. Lock trusted him.

Ty took another swig of pure German lager. "Man, first time she gets to see you since you're back from New York, and she's hanging out with us chumps. Shouldn't you two be cozying up together all romantic?"

"There's going to be plenty more time for that. Trust me."

"What you say?" said Ty.

"We're moving in together."

The bottle stopped halfway to Ty's lips. "For real?"

"Yeah, we just have to decide where that's going to be. This is too far out, and her place is too small."

"Damn," said Ty. "Big step."

"Not really. When you know, you know," said Lock.

Ty raised his bottle in a salute as someone knocked at the door. "True dat."

Lock opened the door to his lawyer girlfriend and Carl. He kissed Carmen and shook Carl's hand. "Good to see you, Carl. Go grab yourself a beer."

"Don't mind if I do," said Galante, loping past him in the same shorts and Dogtown T-shirt that Lock remembered him wearing the first time they had met.

Lock and Carmen kissed again. Carmen handed him two brown paper bags full of takeout. Lock held them up to his nose. "Smells good. Thanks. You want a glass of wine?"

"Sure. What you got?"

Lock laughed. "I have what you always drink. It's chilling."

"You're the best," she said, planting a fresh kiss on him. He never tired of her kisses. Couldn't imagine that he ever would. He was a lucky man to have found a woman like her.

"I really am." He smiled.

She walked past him, pinching his butt as she went. Lock put the food on the counter and brought out some plates and cutlery. Ty was on the balcony with Galante.

"You guys hungry?" he called.

"Sure," said Galante.

Ty shot him a what-a-dumb-question look.

It was. Ty was pretty much always hungry. And, much to the annoyance of any woman he dated, Ty could eat a lot and maintain his six-pack. He had a freak metabolism. Plus, and it had taken Lock a while to figure this out, Ty didn't eat very often. It was just that when he did, he ate everything in front of him.

As Lock and Carmen began to unpack the food containers and lay it all out on the island in the center of the kitchen, Ty and Galante wandered in from the balcony.

"Nice place you have here, Ryan," said the investigator.

It was nice. It cost close to four thousand a month in rent, but it was large and airy with a nice open-plan layout, and it looked out over the Marina.

Ty stuck a nose into one of the containers. "Chinese, huh?"

"What? Did I mess up?" said Carmen. "I thought you ate everything."

"Ty's trying to be funny," said Lock. "The kids who've been taken are from mainland China."

"Parachute kids, huh?" said Galante. "I figured that's who it would be when Carmen mentioned Arcadia."

"Different kind of immigrants," said Carmen. "My grandparents came here with nothing."

"Hey," said Ty. "Least it was their idea to come."

Lock decided to call a halt to the game of My Family Had It Worse Than Yours. "Don't go there, Carmen. Ty wins this one every time. Hey, but look at us all now, eating Chinese food, drinking expensive booze and looking out over the Pacific. Not too bad."

They ate, with their plates on their laps, in front of Lock's television screen, and watched the stream of security-camera footage from the USB drive. From time to time one of them would ask to slow something down, or freeze the frame, or full screen the angle from a particular camera.

"Kind of a weird choice for a movie night," Carmen joked.

"Sure. I have a DVD with a Hugh Grant flick around here some-where," said Lock, and Carmen tossed a cushion at him.

"What do you think, Carl?" Ty asked Galante.

He took his time answering, reflecting for a moment on what they were watching. On screen Emily was waving the kitchen knife.

"I'd say she's one tough kid for someone who grew up with a bunch of money," he observed. He took a fresh pull of beer and burped. "Pardon me."

"Anything else?" said Lock.

Carmen slid Galante a coaster as he went to put his beer bottle on the coffee-table.

"Motive seems fairly straightforward," said Galante.

"The car," said Lock.

"Exactly."

"Aren't they hard to move on?" said Carmen.

Ty had spent time talking to an old friend of his in the auto trade in Long Beach. His guy had served time for dealing in what he had termed "vehicles with an unclear provenance." Ty had asked him to repeat it in English. "Stolen cars, bro," he'd clarified.

"It's classic risk and reward," said Ty, passing on his newly gath-ered insight. "They're tough to move, but a whip's a whip. Takes the same time to steal a Ferrari as it does a Honda. I mean, the security's usually tougher, they have trackers fitted, but there are workarounds for all of that."

"It's specialized, though, right?" said Lock.

"Not as much as you'd think," said Ty. "The tough part is getting them back to the 'hood without being pulled over. Couple of kids driving a Lamborghini is an automatic stop. They're either rappers or bangers, and they both dress the same."

It was a good point, thought Lock. Cops got a lot of grief for pulling over certain people. But if you cultivated a look that was synonymous with criminal activity it shouldn't be a surprise if you were treated accordingly. It might not be fair, but then life wasn't exactly fair. As the people gathered in the apartment knew all too well.

"So, they scope out the car," said Galante. "That's easy enough."

"Where you think they saw it?" said Carmen.

"Arcadia's wealthy, lots of cars like that, but I doubt they're prowling around the place. Too risky."

"So how did they scope it?" said Lock.

"These kids go out to clubs?" asked Galante. "That would be my guess. Hang out on Sunset, you're going to blend in. No one's going to pay you no mind. Wait five minutes. You'll see at least a couple of fancy rides. Follow them back, you got your car."

Lock made a note to ask Li about Charlie and Emily's social life. Friends. Places they went.

"Can you look into similar crimes for us, Carl?" Lock asked.

"Already did. Nothing popped. Cars like this get stolen. There were a lot of burglaries in Arcadia about six months ago, but the cops stepped up patrols and they went away."

"They arrest anyone?" asked Carmen.

Galante shook his head. "Nope, I'm guessing the crew involved moved to fresher pastures when the heat got turned up. Burglaries dropped in Arcadia, and around the same time a couple of neighborhoods in Pasadena started getting hit."

"Same kind of vics?" said Lock.

"Funnily enough, yeah. All wealthy Chinese, fresh off their Gulfstreams at Burbank."

"What about kidnapping?" Ty asked.

"That's where it gets interesting. You guys have heard of La Eme, right?"

They all had. La Eme stood for the Mexican Mafia. They were a street and prison gang. Although gang was too small a word for a multibillion-dollar organized-crime outfit with a vertical structure that would shame most Fortune 500 companies.

"They're moving into kidnapping?" said Lock. This was news to him.

"They've always pulled K and Rs south of the border, but from what I've been hearing they've been targeting people on this side too.

Rich Mexicans who've moved. Factory owners, business people. But I don't think this was them."

"They looked Hispanic," said Ty.

"They did," said Galante. "But they haven't taken anyone who's outside their ethnic group. And take a look at that. It's pure opportunism. If they could have gotten in the house, they would have ripped off everything they could and probably left behind two dead bodies so there were no witnesses."

"They could have shot them outside," said Carmen.

Galante picked up the bottle and drained the dregs of his beer. "You have another one of these?" he said, flourishing the empty green bottle.

Lock took the empty, got up and wandered back to the kitchen area to get Galante a fresh beer.

"True," said Galante. "And look at the body language. There's a couple of times they're real close to doing just that."

"But they don't," said Ty. "How come?"

Galante shifted round so he was facing the six-foot-four former Marine. "You grew up in Long Beach, correct?"

"LB do or die," said Ty.

"How many people you see shot?"

"A lot," said Ty.

"And how many times did you see people *almost* get capped?"

"Most weeks," said Ty.

"And the difference was what precisely?"

Ty sighed. "All kinds of reasons."

"Someone's gun jammed?" pressed Galante.

"Maybe saw that twice."

"Someone said sorry and their sincere apology was accepted?"

Ty laughed. "Now you're fucking with me."

"So it was random. The asshole with the gun just decided it was that person's lucky day."

"More like it," said Ty, waving his beer bottle in the air.

"I think it was the same here," said Galante, flapping a hand at the screen. "These idiots in those bandanas are chumps. They live moment to moment. It's all about their feels. They couldn't leave witnesses, so it was either kill or take with. Those two kids right there, they got lucky. They don't know it, but they did."

"But are they still lucky?" said Carmen.

GALANTE AND TY were four beers deep, watching the footage from the house for a third time, while Carmen was helping Lock clear up.

"So, what do you think?" said Lock, scraping a plate into the trash and handing it to her to load into the bottom rack of the dishwasher.

"I think it's what Carl said. They saw an opportunity and took it."

"Not about that. This place. Could you see yourself living here?"

Carmen smiled as he handed her another plate for the dishwasher. "You ever give up?" she said.

Lock feigned thought. "Not really, no. It's kind of my trademark."

"I'll think about it," said Carmen.

Ty stood up from the couch. "You want another beer?" he asked Galante.

"No, I'm good."

Ty reached down to switch off the footage. Galante stopped him. "Let it play out."

Ty shrugged.

Galante got up from the couch. "I need to hit the head."

Lock pointed him towards the bathroom. "Front hallway, near where you came in." Something on screen caught his eye. He stopped what he was doing and walked across to the television. He rewound. Galante had been right: they had watched up to a point where it was all over. Both cars had driven out of frame, leaving only an empty motorcourt.

But that wasn't the final action. Lock hit pause.

Carmen walked over to stand behind him. Ty joined them.

One of the gang members had come back. He was standing facing the garage door. His face was still covered but he was staring straight up at the camera in a show of defiance. He raised his hands, his fingers splaying out.

"Carl, come see this," Carmen called out.

"Let me pee first, okay?"

"What is that?" asked Lock.

"Gang sign," said Ty.

All the major gangs had signs they made with one or both hands. It was a method of identification, and also of provocation. Like flipping someone the bird, only it carried a heavier menace. If, of course, you knew what you were looking at.

"Yeah, but which one?" said Lock. This was not his territory.

Carmen studied the image with a quiet deliberation. "Mara Salvatrucha," she said. "MS-13."

19

Of all the gangs in Los Angeles that Emily and Charlie might have been taken by, Mara Salvatrucha, or MS-13 for short, was one of the worst. *Mara* was the Central American word for 'gang', *Salva* denoted El Salvador, and *trucha* was slang for 'clever', but Salvatrucha was commonly used to describe peasants who had trained as guerrilla fighters.

There were a number of stories about the gang's origins, but it was commonly agreed that it had sprung from El Salvadorian immigrants to LA who'd had to deal with an already established Mexican-American gang population.

Many of MS-13's founding members had either witnessed or participated in the brutal civil war in El Salvador. They were battle-hardened and used to extreme violence.

Kill, steal, rape, control.

A transnational gang, some of its strongest roots were in the barrios of East Los Angeles. That would be a good place for them to focus their search. If MS-13 had taken Emily and Charlie, someone somewhere in East LA would know about it.

One other thing concerned Lock about this latest revelation. While MS-13, like any major organized-crime gang, had numerous revenue streams from an array of criminal activity, it was most notorious for sex trafficking and child prostitution. They had to pray that the gang would be more interested in a fast pay day in return for Emily than deciding she could make money for them in some other way.

Lock, Ty, Carmen and Galante stood around the television screen, the image frozen of the gang member throwing the sign at the camera.

"This just got real interesting," said Galante, with a former cop's understatement.

"We've had some clients with ties to MS-13," Carmen offered. "I can make some calls. Put out some feelers."

"That would be helpful," said Lock. He walked over to the counter and picked up his cell phone. "I'd better let the family know."

Ty picked up his jacket and started for the door. "I'm going to get out on the street. See if anyone knows anything."

"Be careful," said Lock. Normally he wouldn't be overly concerned. Ty had grown up in a bad neighborhood and was well able to take care of himself, but MS-13 prided themselves on their brutality, and weren't exactly known for their progressive attitude towards African-Americans.

"Don't worry, I'm going to roll with my buddies Mr. Sig and Mr. Sauer."

"You think that's wise?" said Carmen.

Ty's outstanding legal difficulties had placed in jeopardy his right to carry a concealed weapon.

"I'd say the same usually," said Lock, "but if we're dealing with these assholes it's better to be walking hot."

Ty patted the gun riding on his hip. "One in the pipe, and nine more for good luck. I'll check in every two hours. How about that?"

"I'll come with you," said Galante.

The two men headed for the door.

"I'll sort out payment for you with Li," Lock told Galante.

"Thanks."

Ty and Galante walked out, leaving Lock and Carmen alone.

"That was a good catch," said Lock.

"That's why we use him. He doesn't miss much."

Lock put his cell phone on the counter.

"You're not making the call?" said Carmen.

"I think I'd rather deliver the news to him in person," said Lock.

He wasn't even sure why he wanted to tell Li to his face. He just did. He still felt like he was missing something in all of this. Then he remembered something from his and Ty's visit to the crime scene. "While we were at the house," he said to Carmen, "we caught Li talking to his boss. Ty videoed it. You have anyone you guys use who'd be able to tell us what was being said?"

"Mandarin or Cantonese?" asked Carmen.

"You're asking the wrong guy."

"Get Ty to email the clip to me and I'll ask. We have a general translation agency we use for clients. They'll have someone. Might take a day or two, though."

"That's okay. Hey, you want to take a drive out to Arcadia with me?"

Carmen put her hands on his shoulders. "I'd love to, but I have work tomorrow, and I should get back to my own place."

Lock looked around. "This could be your place. You could sleep over. Try it out. See how you like it."

"I've already slept here. More than once." She moved in for a kiss. "You don't give up, do you?"

"That's why I make the big bucks," said Lock.

"Oh, is that the reason? I thought it was your charm and good looks."

"Those too."

20

A girl who wanted to join a gang like this had two ways in. She could ride a train and be sexed in, or she could take a beating.

Being sexed in meant spending a couple of hours in a back room having sex with the other gang members, sometimes one at a time, sometimes more.

Even at thirteen, Princess knew that wasn't an option for her. She had two reasons. First, she didn't like boys in that way. She could have done it, just as she could take a beating, but the second reason was always there. She had seen the way that girls who were sexed in were regarded by the others. They were never afforded the same respect. They might be given work to do, but they had no say in decisions. They were looked down upon.

Taking a beating was different. That was what the guys did. Taking a beating meant something. It came with risks attached. More than one prospect had died after a beating. But you were a full member, as good as the men. You had weight. Your voice counted.

There was also a third path. Rarely taken. And never by a girl. Definitely not by a girl who had only just finished sixth grade.

You could kill someone.

That was the path Princess had chosen. When she had mentioned it, and asked for a gun, they had laughed at her, Pony, Joker, all of them. They had howled, and slapped their legs, and pounded each other on the back, and wiped away the tears streaming down their faces. It had been a riot.

"You still got pigtails, school girl."

"What you gonna do? Bring Joker along to help you pull the trigger?"

That one had gotten to her. It had pissed her off. Her answer had almost gotten her killed.

She had looked at Pony. He'd been the one to say it.

"Joker wouldn't be no help. He don't have the balls to pull the trigger on a bitch."

The laughter had ceased as soon as she'd said that. The air had left the room. Joker's hands had balled into fists. Pony had stared at her.

"What you say?"

She had stood her ground. "You heard me."

It had taken Shotcaller to save her. He was older. An old man by their standards. He dressed like a cowboy. All the way down to his boots.

He had stomped a boot heel on the floor and stepped up to her. "Okay, Princess. You have yourself a deal. I'll get you a gat. But you don't make good, I'm going to turn you out. After we've had our fun."

The deal was simple. She had better kill or she'd be taken into the back room. She'd be sexed in, but after that she wouldn't be a gang member, she'd work for them as a prostitute.

As soon as she'd got the gun, she'd regretted her boast. Pony had been right. Pulling a trigger was tough. Not the mental part. She knew she had that down. The actual physical strength it took to pull the trigger. Especially the trigger on the gun she'd been given, which was old and a little rusty.

Princess had got some gun oil. She'd watched a video online and worked out how to strip the weapon down and reassemble it. That was her homework after school for four evenings straight.

But even oiled it was a tough pull.

She had pleaded with Shotcaller for extra time. He agreed, repeating the threat. Pony and Joker had been watching her, like a couple of vultures, eager to get the bed in the back room squeaking.

Princess had gone out and bought something called a Trigger Trainer. It made your fingers stronger, gave you a better grip. She used it every chance she could until one day pulling that trigger was no big thing.

Now all she needed was someone to kill.

The lady at the end of the block was an old African-American woman. She lived alone. She left her home to go to the grocery store, or to attend church on a Sunday. She was the last black person on the block, but because she was old and a church lady, she was left alone.

Princess changed all that.

"You're going to die soon anyway," Princess told the lady, as she begged for her life.

Doing it gave Princess nightmares. She knew it was wrong. Way past wrong. It was evil.

She told herself that was who she was now. She could have found someone else to kill. She could have allowed herself to be sexed in and turned out. But she hadn't. That wasn't the life she wanted for herself.

She wanted to be an equal. And the day after the old lady's body was taken away, and the LAPD robbery-homicide cops walked the block, getting only silence, shrugs and doors slammed in their faces, Princess had joined. No back bedroom with sweat dripping down the walls, no bloody, frenzied beating, only respect, and fear.

A little girl with her hair in bunches doing that? Even in MS-13 that made you someone.

They let her keep her old name of Princess. Shotcaller thought it was funny.

Neither Pony nor Joker had the *cojones* to say anything to her. But the grudge was still there. Even after all these years. When she said black, they said white. They said up, she said down. That was how it was between them. Even now.

Princess checked her make-up in the mirror. She pouted, made a duck face, threw up her fingers into the sign, and took a selfie. She tapped the button to post it on Instagram, adding the MS-13 hashtags that let people know what was up.

She walked out of the bathroom and into the room where Emily and Charlie sat together on an old busted-up couch.

This evening was decision time for them. There was going to be a debate. Princess wanted one thing. Joker and Pony wanted something else. Shotcaller would decide. At the end of it, Charlie might be dead or he might not. The real debate was over what they would do with Emily. Her fate would seal his.

21

The Red Tiger sat in his rental car. The Mossberg was hidden out of sight in the trunk, the Glock pistol concealed under his seat. He stared at the two guardian lion statues that stood sentinel-like on either side of the entrance.

In Japan they were known as *komainu*. In China they were called Foo-dogs.

They were a symbol of wealth. And of superstition. Like so many old parts of Chinese culture, they had fallen out of favor under Communism, but come back into fashion more recently. It was strange to see so many of them standing guard under a full California moon.

The Red Tiger had planned on going straight to the address that would end his journey. But when he was within a few blocks he had lost his nerve. He told himself that, first, he would take some time to explore Arcadia. In truth, he was scared. Scared of the reaction he would receive. This was one meeting where he couldn't force the issue with a gun.

He crisscrossed the neatly manicured streets and avenues. No one gave him so much as a second glance. Why would they? A middle-aged Chinese man in a town full of Chinese. It gave him comfort to be invisible again. He guessed that was why places like Arcadia existed. You could move thousands of miles to be somewhere different and still yearn to be surrounded by the people you had left behind.

He stopped at a restaurant, sat at a bench and ate dim sum. It was hot and greasy and made him feel a little ill. He settled the bill, again using cash, and walked back to his car.

There was no point in delaying this any further. He drove back to the address. Even with the car's air-conditioning running flat out, he was sweating. His heart raced. He turned onto the block. His heart rate quickened even more.

He drove slowly past the entrance to the house in disbelief. Two patrol cars sat outside.

The Red Tiger gripped the wheel with both hands. How? How could they have known?

He laughed to himself, the giggle of a madman. Of course they would know. He had hardly been subtle. He cursed his own stupidity. He had been so careless. His determination had left behind a trail of destruction.

One of the American police officers watched him as he drove past. Any minute now they would pounce. He would be pulled over and arrested.

What would happen afterwards? They could arrange for him to have an accident. Or would they use the guns he had in the car to send him to prison? He could have an accident there. It would be easy enough to pay someone to murder him inside an American prison.

That was what he would do if he were them.

His vision began to tunnel. He felt a pain creeping up his arm. His chest felt heavy.

Somehow he managed to keep driving. He glanced in the rearview mirror.

The patrol cars hadn't moved. Nothing had happened.

They must be waiting for him to be away from the house. Yes, that made sense. Pounce when no one would see him.

A car was driving the opposite way down the street towards him.

It had the four rings that signified it was an Audi. An expensive model from the badge. Fast. Nothing he could outrun.

The driver looked just like a cop, or maybe a soldier. Handsome, clean-cut, tall, muscular. Yes, this had to be it. This had to be the man who would take him down.

Now he had someone tangible to focus on, he began to come back to himself. He slowed his breathing. The pain in his arm and chest began to recede. A panic attack. That was what it was, his body reacting to seeing police officers waiting for him outside the house.

He slowed to a crawl, and reached under the seat, feeling for the gun.

He would not surrender. He would not go quietly. The Red Tiger would show his teeth.

The Audi drove past him. The driver stared at him, but nothing more than that.

What were they doing? Why hadn't he been stopped?

It made no sense. It was almost as if they were playing a game with him. Allowing him to think they hadn't seen him when they surely had.

He pulled over to the curb. He watched as the Audi stopped next to the two patrol cars. The man he was sure was a cop got out.

Maybe they had missed him. Or hadn't recognized him. Maybe this was all a stroke of good fortune and he was passing it up by sitting there.

He placed the Glock on the passenger seat, ready if he needed it, pulled out and kept driving, his mind moving in a dozen different directions all at once.

If the police weren't there to arrest him, what were they doing?

THE WAY the Arcadia cops were staring at Lock, it was just as well that Ty wasn't with him. He understood they had a job to do but so did he. They didn't seem to grasp that inside the house didn't fully qualify as part of the crime scene because the kidnappers hadn't been there.

"Sir, you'll have to move your vehicle."

Lock stood his ground. It was a public street. "I'm waiting for someone. As soon as he gets here, I'll be happy to move."

Just then, he turned around and saw the gate to the house opposite open. Li walked out. A little way behind him, the attractive young woman they had seen earlier was waving goodbye.

Li walked across to the Audi. His face was a little flushed, and he was lifting his jacket to tuck his shirt in. "I was asking her if she'd seen anything," he said to Lock, unprompted.

Sure you were, thought Lock. "I have some news for you."

"Come on up to the house," said Li.

"I can tell you here. The cops are going to need to know in any case," said Lock.

"Don't worry. Whatever it is, I'll make sure to pass it on. And I have something for you in the house. We think it might help with your inquiries."

"Okay," said Lock.

The Arcadia police policy that barred entry to the house lasted as long as it took for Li to make a phone call. The patrol cops stood aside as Lock followed him up the driveway on foot.

"The neighbor see anything?" Lock asked.

"What?"

"You were over there asking her if she'd seen anything."

"Oh, yes. No, she was asleep," said Li.

"Does her property have cameras?"

The question seemed to spook Li. "I've n-no idea," he stuttered.

Lock made a mental note to speak with her. He couldn't imagine that she had any involvement, or that anything she had going with Li would be relevant. Then again, you never knew for sure where a conversation would lead. Li wasn't telling him and Ty everything. That was one thing he was confident of.

∽

"So what did you want to tell me?"

They were in the kitchen. Lock studied the knife block, one still missing. He told Li about the very end of the footage, the gang member throwing the sign and what it meant. Li looked suitably troubled by the news. "If these people are as bad as you say, they may already have killed them," he said.

"It's certainly possible, although somehow I doubt it."

"Why? You just told me that they're very violent and unpredictable."

"Violent, yes," agreed Lock. "The unpredictability is all relative. I don't think they planned on taking Charlie and Emily. That was something that fell into their lap. But if it was a case of eliminating witnesses they could have killed them here. Not that Charlie and Emily could have identified them anyway."

"So they're alive?" said Li.

"I don't know for sure. But I doubt they would take two people only to kill them and dump the bodies. Plus, the higher up you go in these organizations the more measured the people are. They know these two kids come from money. The cars say that much. And they saw the house. So they must realize that someone would pay for their safe return."

"The money's keeping them alive?" said Li.

"Money can make you a target, yes, but it might also be the key to ending this."

Li smiled. "Emily's father would like you, Mr. Lock."

"And why is that?"

"You think along similar lines."

Li walked across the kitchen and opened a kitchen cabinet. He pulled out a black attaché case. Lock watched as he laid it on the counter and snapped open the catches. He held up the open case with a flourish worthy of a Vegas magician.

Lock stared for a second at the contents. "What's that for?"

"It's for you to use as you see fit," said Li.

22

There must have been a hundred thousand dollars in the attaché case, all in hundred-dollar bills, neatly bundled, strapped and fresh from the bank. Lock lifted his eyes from the cash to Li.

"We thought it might help loosen some tongues," said Li, giving the impression of someone who was immensely pleased with himself at having thought of this masterstroke, even though he had admitted only moments before that it had been his boss's idea.

"I'm sure it would," said Lock.

"I sense you're not fully onboard with this, Mr. Lock."

"You kind of sprang it on me," said Lock.

"I'm sorry. I thought it would be welcome."

Lock's fingers tapped the edge of the kitchen counter. He was thinking it through. Cash was a useful tool when it came to gathering information. That was why people offered rewards for missing pets and missing people, as well as for information in other crimes. It was an incentive that everyone understood.

The problem was that offering a reward, even if you didn't publicize it openly, drew all kinds of strange people out of the woodwork. Any major crime, such as murder or kidnapping, attracted psychics, conspiracy theorists, trolls and all manner of society's fringe characters.

Something else troubled Lock about using cash in a case like this. If it got back to the gang holding Emily and Charlie that someone was throwing around dollar bills like confetti, it might raise their expectations.

He put that to Li, who listened patiently.

"I see what you're saying."

"Listen," said Lock. "I'll take it. We'll use it if a situation arises where it would help. And I'll account for every cent. Any of it that's not accounted for, you can deduct from our fee. I want you to make that clear to the family."

"No one has ever doubted your integrity," said Li. "That was why we called upon you."

"I thought you called me because I push the envelope."

"There were many factors," said Li.

He was smooth. Lock had to give him that much.

Li snapped the attaché case shut and handed it to him.

"Make sure you tell the cops about the MS-13 involvement,' Lock reminded him. 'Or would you like me to handle that?"

"No, I'm already serving as liaison between them and the family."

"Yeah, that's probably best," said Lock.

LOCK RANG THE DOORBELL, stood back from the door and waited for the neighbor to answer. He had the attaché case in one hand, and his cell phone in the other. He had just told Ty about Li's gift. Ty was, as Lock had anticipated, pretty excited.

"You know where you can get really good information?" he asked Lock

"Where?"

"Titty bars," said Ty.

Lock sighed.

"Wait, hear me out. Man, people tell strippers all kinds of crazy stuff. When someone has to get something off their chest, it's either strippers or priests. They're the top two confidants."

"Where did you read that? Lock asked him. "The *Wall Street Journal*?"

"Think it was *Forbes*."

Lock couldn't respond to that.

"You're not going to let me drop any of that cash in strip clubs, are you?"

"No, Ty, I'm not. We have two kids in the hands of MS-13, or did you forget that?"

"Come on, brother, I'm just trying to lighten the mood a little."

The door opened to reveal the extremely attractive young lady whom Li had been visiting with when Lock arrived.

"Ty, I have to go now." Lock terminated the call before Ty could say anything else about strip clubs. His partner had the kind of voice that carried, even when he was on the other end of a phone line.

"Sorry to bother you, Miss. I'm an investigator working on the incident across the street. I wonder if I could ask you a couple of quick questions. It won't take too long."

The way she hesitated, he wasn't sure if she spoke English. From what he'd gathered in the short time since they'd taken on this case, Arcadia didn't only house the so-called parachute kids: a whole other section of young people lived in the McMansions.

The other group was composed of young women who served as *ernaicu*, or mistresses. They were stashed in Arcadia and the surrounding area, as well as certain cities such as Shenzhen back in China. A man like Emily's father could come see his kids, then hop next door for some quality time with his young girlfriend. The proximity in age made Lock's stomach churn, but private morals weren't his concern right now. Rich old men had always sought access to attractive young women.

"I don't speak good English," she said, the words perfectly contradicting the apologetic little shrug that accompanied their delivery.

Lock knew he had her. He didn't speak Mandarin or Cantonese, and perhaps she didn't speak English beyond a few key phrases. But none of that mattered. All that did was that she knew what he was saying to her.

"Miss Po, I promise this won't take up much of your time. But it would be in your best interest if you spoke with me."

She seemed startled that he knew her name. It was an old trick. Simple yet effective. Like telling someone you were a detective or investigator and allowing them to assume you were with local law enforcement.

After a flash of unease, she regained her composure. She began to close the door.

"I saw Li leaving," said Lock. "How do you think your sponsor would react to you entertaining at home like that?" It was a low blow, and he didn't feel that great about throwing it into the mix. But desperate times called for desperate measures. At least he had been polite enough to use the word "sponsor" rather than something more literal.

Galante had already run a check of the neighbors, and it had turned up not only her name but something else that had caught his attention. Miss Po wasn't just anyone's mistress. A search of property deeds had shown that this house and the one directly opposite had been purchased six months apart by the same Chinese corporation. On one side of the street Li's boss had a house for his daughter. On the other he had a house where he stored his mistress.

Lock didn't know if it was ballsy, dumb or both. At least the man had the decency to have his mistress live in the smaller of the two properties.

Miss Po glared at him as she opened the door.

"Thank you, "said Lock, walking past her.

She closed the door. "Take off your shoes," she snapped.

He reached down and took them off. She was angry. That was good. Emotional people let things slip that they shouldn't. They didn't have to say anything. A reaction could answer a question more clearly than a simple yes or no.

They sat in the living room. Lock perched on the edge of a couch that was identical to the one across the street. He wondered if the same person had done the furniture shopping for both houses. With this kind of money it was likely an interior designer had selected everything.

Buying a multimillion-dollar mansion for your mistress would seem extravagant, even outlandish to many people, but Lock knew there was a cold logic behind it. For a start it would be what the British termed a grace-and-favor property. Miss Po didn't own it. She was living there rent free. But it was an arrangement that depended upon her sponsor's goodwill. It could be withdrawn at any point. She knew that, which was why she had backed down when Lock had mentioned having seen Li leave.

There was an additional factor. Property was an investment. In Arcadia where prices had climbed year on year, it was an excellent investment with a spectacular return. And it all came down to one thing. Men like Emily's father had purchased property in California for the same reason that Russian oligarchs had snapped up half of central London a few years previously. They were both countries where property rights were respected and the government didn't take it from you on a whim. The same couldn't be said for Communist and formerly Communist countries.

Lock took a better look at the young woman sitting across from him. She was tall and attractive with sharp cheekbones and big eyes. She would turn heads walking into any room. She had won the genetic lottery and leveraged what she had to get herself this far.

"What did you want to ask me?" she said.

She was still irritated. That was fine with Lock.

"I expect the same things that the police asked you. Did you see anything? Hear anything? Did you notice anything out of place in the last week?"

She shook her head. "I heard the cars leaving when it happened. There was shouting too. I didn't think anything of it. I thought Charlie was having a party."

"You knew Charlie?"

"I know his name. I never spoke to them. Chan would talk about them."

Chan was Emily's father, Charlie's uncle. Her sugar daddy. Li's boss.

"Do they know who you are?"

She smirked. "Maybe. I doubt it."

"Do you care?" said Lock.

"Not really, no."

"What about Li? How well do you know him?"

"He was worried about me. That was why he was just over here. He wanted to make sure I was okay."

Lock didn't say anything to that. He let the silence play out. Another old trick that worked more often than it should.

"He's my friend. We don't have sex."

"It's none of my business if you do or don't."

"I like him. He's kind, and . . ."

She stopped.

"And?"

"Nothing."

"My job is to locate Emily and Charlie. That's it. Everything else . . ." said Lock, taking in the room with a sweep of his hand ". . . is beyond the scope of my job. I don't care who you're sleeping with or who you're not. I don't care why you're here or what the deal you have going here is."

"So why are you asking me all these questions?"

"It's my job. I don't know what might be relevant and what isn't until I ask them."

"Go on, then. I'm tired. I need to sleep."

"What has Li said to you about all of this?"

"He told me what happened."

"And what did happen?"

She got up from where she was sitting and walked out of the room into the kitchen. Lock followed her.

She grabbed a glass and poured some wine. "You want some?"

Lock shook his head.

"You know what happened. You're the investigator."

"I'd just like to hear, in your words, what Li told you."

Lock didn't know if there was anything to uncover there. He did know that Li hadn't been entirely straight with him. He also didn't believe for a second that two attractive, ambitious young people, who worked for the same man, and both had reason to resent the power he had over them, might not share more than some late-night talks.

When he'd followed her into the kitchen, he'd seen that there were two wine glasses on the counter, both used, and only one with lipstick around the rim.

"Li told me that some gang was trying to steal Charlie's car. Charlie came out to stop them and they took him and Emily. Li blames himself."

"Why does he blame himself?" said Lock.

"He told me he should have stopped it happening."

Now she had Lock's complete attention. How could you stop something when it had arrived out of the clear blue sky? "Why does he think that?"

"How would I know?"

Lock stepped toward her. "Why does Li think he could have stopped it? Did he know something like this was going to happen?"

"I told you, I don't know. He was upset."

She was staring into her wine glass. Lock reached out his hand. He pinched her chin, lifting her head so she was looking at him. She was scared. She'd slipped up somehow and she knew it.

"What's going on here?" said Lock. "How could Li have stopped this?"

"I swear to you I don't know." She began to cry. "You're going to tell Chan, aren't you?"

Lock kept his own counsel. "What would I tell him?"

"About Li and I."

"That's what you're worried about?"

"Yes. He'd go crazy. He'd kick me out. There are lots of girls like me."

"I don't care who you sleep with, Miss Po. But I need you to tell me why Li thought he could have prevented this."

"I swear to you I don't know. I swear."

Lock reached into his jacket. She flinched.

He took a business card from his wallet. "You should try to remember. When you do, call me."

"You won't say anything, will you?" she pleaded, following him back towards the front door.

THE CASE with the hundred thousand dollars lay on the cream leather passenger seat of Lock's Audi. He stared at it like it contained some kind of secret. He hadn't left Arcadia. He'd been driving around a couple of the wealthier neighborhoods for the past hour. Driving helped him think things through.

He'd been pulled over twice by the local cops. He'd explained to them who he was. He'd fudged why he was there, telling them he'd been called in by some local families who were spooked by the recent turn of events.

The story had satisfied the cops.

The details of the kidnapping hadn't been released or the names of the victims. But it was only a matter of time. It would cause more than a few ripples.

There were two schools of thought regarding how much information you placed in the public domain following a kidnapping. One said the less publicity the better: publicity tended to spook kidnappers and make things more dangerous for captives. The other said that publicity meant more people looking, and more chance of finding the victim.

Having dealt with several kidnaps over the years, Lock agreed with keeping things on the down-low. Most kidnappings were business transactions. Those that weren't, abductions, tended to end badly, even in the cases where the victims came home.

Lock flipped open the attaché cash. He removed the money, bundle by bundle, and placed it on the seat. He reached into the glove box and pulled out his Gerber knife.

He drew the edge of the blade down the side of the interior lining of the case. Peeling back the lining, he put the Gerber down and retrieved a mini Maglite. He switched it on and shone the light into the gap between the lining and the case.

Light reflected off a silver-colored piece of metal the size of a large button that had been glued into place. Lock cut away the rest of the lining. He took a closer look at the silver tracking device. Not big enough to record, but large enough to relay the case's location.

Li knew that where Lock went, the case would go too. He wasn't a man likely to leave a hundred thousand dollars sitting around.

Lock left the silver button where it was. He flicked quickly through the cash bundles and placed the money back in the case. He snapped the case shut and laid it back on the passenger seat as a patrol car swept past him.

He dug out his cell phone and called Ty. "Gimme some good news, Tyrone."

"I was hoping that's why you were calling us."

"Us?"

"Yeah. I'm out here with Carl. Some of these neighborhoods in East LA ain't too friendly for a brother on his own."

"I hear you."

"So what about you? Anything?"

"I'll tell you when I speak to you. I should be back in LA in about an hour. You know that diner on Colefax and Otsego? Let's meet there."

"Okay, dude, speak then."

"Hey, Tyrone."

"What?"

"Be safe."

"You too."

23

P rincess had her turn to speak. She'd been rehearsing. She'd
written down what she wanted to say. She had numbers.
Pony and Joker would roll their eyes. Shotcaller would dig it.
He loved numbers. From hanging with him, she knew he kept spread-
sheets. He was doing a business course at community college. Profit
and loss. Accounts. All that good stuff.

Pony and Joker wouldn't have numbers. They were dummies. The
only numbers they gave any attention to were the ones they played
every week. That was stupid in her eyes. Only poor people played the
numbers. Rich people took that money and invested it. They paid
themselves.

"Princess," said Shotcaller. "What do you think?"

She looked at the two kidnap victims sitting together on the
couch. One of Charlie's eyes was closed, and he sat slumped, his chin
resting on his chest, too scared to look at anyone in case he caught
another beating. He had paid for pulling that gun and not pulling the
trigger. Princess could have told him it was gangster 101. You draw
down on people like them, you'd better do it.

They had cleaned him up before Shotcaller, but he still looked bad. By contrast, Emily was looking good. Princess had made her take a shower and done her make-up for her. Put her in a little skirt, heels and a sparkly top. This was the visual element of her pitch.

"We got the cars. That was what we wanted," said Princess. "The way I see it, these two here are a bonus."

Pony and Joker both nodded in agreement.

"Question is, what we do with them now we have them," Princess continued. "Sure, we could ask for a ransom, but what do we know about running that?"

Pony's top lip curled. "We know plenty."

"We know how to work it with our people. Get a family to send us a few thousand dollars so they can see little Paco again. But this is a whole other level. How we going to collect?"

"We'll figure it out," muttered Joker.

"What you telling me?" Shotcaller asked. "We kill them? Let them go?"

Princess figured she might as well get to her proposal. "Kill him and put her to work."

At this Emily's eyes lifted from the grubby carpet.

"She's a virgin. That's five large to someone right there. First pop. Someone will pay five, easy."

"That's high end," said Shotcaller.

"We know people who know people," said Princess. She had already anticipated the objection.

"So that's five," said Joker. "Then what?"

"We turn her out." Princess took a breath, ready to drop some numbers. "Say ten tricks a night, fifty a trick. Five hundred. Seven nights. That's fourteen a month."

"And how many months before she's all used up?" said Pony.

"A year is a hundred and forty Gs," said Princess. "Tell me that's not real money."

"I like it," said Shotcaller.

Princess felt the warm glow of his approval. She'd known he'd respond to figures.

He turned to the other two. "That's what you call a business plan. Numbers. Revenue projection."

They shot salty looks at her. She didn't care. She had done her homework and made a case. It wasn't her problem if she was smarter.

"But we ain't doing it," said Shotcaller.

Joker and Pony smirked.

Princess couldn't believe it. "How come? Fourteen. A month. Every month."

"You're forgetting one thing, Princess," said Shotcaller.

"What's that?"

"This isn't some regular chava People are looking for her. Him too. People with money."

Joker saw his chance. "People with money who'll give us some to get them back. I say ten million. That's what we ask."

Princess laughed. She couldn't help it. Like someone was going to hand over ten million dollars to these two clowns and let them ride off into the sunset.

Shotcaller cut her off with a glare. "It's an idea. But Princess is right. This is the big league. We need to figure it all out first. How we going to ask? How can we collect without getting caught?"

"Five. They'd give you five," said Emily.

They all looked at her. Even Charlie, with one dead eye.

"I could arrange it. Make the deal," said Emily. "But that would be for both of us going home safe."

"Shut the fuck up," said Princess. "Anyone say you could speak?"

She didn't like where this was going.

She took the three short steps and raised her hand to slap Emily. Shotcaller caught it before she could swing.

"I need to think about all of this. Talk to some people," said Shotcaller. "There's money. No arguing with that. But this is tricky."

"She just said she could speak for us," said Pony. "Five million. Think, how many bitches like this we need to make those dollars?"

"Turn her out? Shit. Small time," said Joker.

Princess could feel her proposal losing traction. "I'm talking about money in the bank," she said.

Shotcaller let go of her arm with a warning. "Any marks on this bitch," he said, with a nod to Emily, "you answer to me. Same goes for him. We keep the produce fresh. I'll get back to you."

24

I t was a blues club with a house band. The sign on the door said it stayed open until two in the morning. He found a table in the darkest corner and ordered a drink from the waitress.

A Chinese tiger drinking whisky and listening to someone sing the blues. He drank it fast, hoping it would settle his nerves, and ordered another. He would have to slow down with this one or he would be drunk, and they would ask him to leave.

The last time he'd drunk alcohol had been at the end of a case that had ended as badly as one of his cases could end. With a dead child. After he'd broken the news to the parents, and watched their entire life implode, he'd bought a bottle of Scotch, drunk half of it on a park bench, gone home, taken a cold shower, and set out to find the men responsible.

That had been a case that started well. It was a hot trail, only a few days old. The kind of case he rarely got. His specialty was cold cases, in some cases so cold that he had to chip away ice to get to the evidence.

Families rarely thought to involve him when a child was taken. They went to the police. More often than not it was a terrible mistake.

So this case had been exciting. He'd gotten straight down to business: interviewing witnesses; speaking with the family; talking to his many contacts and informants.

In less than twenty-four hours, he had a good idea who had done it. Unfortunately, they'd heard he was after them. They panicked, killed the child and dumped her in the river.

It was the closest he had come to walking away from all of this. The gang had killed her because of their fear of the Red Tiger.

He had caught up with them, but too late. He had blamed himself and resolved to stick to the cold cases from now on. To work cases where the crime had been committed, passions had subsided, and he could go quietly about his business.

Now he was drinking again as, a few feet away, a white man tried to sound like a black man as he sang about his baby leaving him. The Red Tiger sipped his second drink, pushed it to the side of the table and reached for a cigarette, then remembered he would have to go outside to smoke it. He tapped the cigarette back into the pack.

On stage, the band finished their last song and people around him applauded. He joined in.

He needed a plan. But first he had to make sense of all of this. Why had the police not arrested him? Why had they been outside like that? If he'd been them he would have hidden, then pounced.

Earlier he had thought that perhaps he had the wrong address. He had checked it. He had even run a fresh search. No, it was correct.

Maybe they had only wanted to scare him off. To let him know that what he was doing was futile.

He took another sip of whisky. Yes, that could be it, he told himself. If they arrested him, and he went to court, all their secrets would slip out. Wasn't it better just to scare him off?

If that was what they wanted they had made a fatal error. They must have known that he wouldn't give up so easily.

He would have to be careful. If he didn't leave, they would have to try something else, something more permanent.

Drinking was a bad idea. He needed to be sober. He pushed the glass away from him.

He would find a motel outside town. He would rest up. Get some sleep. Eat. Exercise. Clear his mind. Plan his next move.

At the bar, he waited to settle his tab, the dollar bills ready in his hand. The bartender was busy, speaking to an older couple. He happened to look up at the television above the bar.

He glanced at it, then away. Then back.

No, it couldn't be.

For a moment he thought it must be some kind of elaborate practical joke, staged just for him.

On screen was the house with the patrol cars outside. Just as it had looked when he had driven past. The only difference was the television reporter standing outside. The dollar bills he had been holding slipped from his fingers onto the bar top.

A hand scooped them up. "Thanks, buddy," said the bartender, seemingly appearing from nowhere. "Crazy, huh?" he added, with a nod towards the screen.

"Could you . . .?"

The Red Tiger mimed someone hitting the button on a remote control.

"Sure thing."

The bartender walked down the bar, grabbed the remote for the television, and increased the volume, then came back with change. The Red Tiger waved it off.

"Thanks, buddy, that's very generous of you."

He had handed the bartender a twenty and a fifty. Not that he cared.

The bartender slid the remote toward him. "Here you go. Knock yourself out. But I gotta close up in a few."

He increased the volume a few more notches and hopped onto a bar stool. It must have looked suspicious, a lone man staring at the television with such intense focus, but he didn't care.

The reporter was mid-way through her presentation.

"So far, local law enforcement are staying tight-lipped about the motive behind this apparent abduction. But they have confirmed that vehicles

belonging to the two victims were taken, they believe at the same time as
the two young people were taken at gunpoint."

The bartender came back. "You know, you can rewind that," he
said, pointing at some buttons on the back of the remote. "Crazy what
they can do now, huh?"

The Red Tiger hit the rewind button until he reached the start of
the report.

"Tonight, news of a shocking robbery and double abduction in Arcadia's
upscale Upper Rancho neighborhood. Two young Chinese nationals taken
from their multimillion-dollar home at gunpoint."

By the time he had watched it twice through, only the bartender
was left. "Buddy, I really have to close up."

The Red Tiger slid off the stool onto uncertain legs. His mind
hovered between disbelief and paranoia. He thought he had anticipated every possible outcome. But nothing had prepared him for
something like this.

The bartender was staring at him. "You know those people or
something?"

"Me?" he answered, a finger pointed to his chest. "No, I don't
know them."

HE DROVE, on auto-pilot, back to the house. He thought about what
he had said to the bartender before he left. It was truth and it was a
lie, all at the same time. He didn't know them. Not really. That, after
all, was why he had come all this way.

As he made the final turn, he had a moment of hesitation. What
was he doing here? Especially so late at night. In his work, he was
bold, but never reckless. This was way beyond reckless. Cruising past
a crime scene. In a car. After drinking whisky. With an unlicensed
firearm.

Still, he kept going, driven forward by the gnawing need he had
hoped would ebb away, but it had only grown.

A sharp sigh of relief as he slowed down. The patrol cars were gone. The gates were closed, the street silent.

He parked on the opposite side of the road and walked over to the gates. His chest felt tight. At any moment he expected to be surrounded and placed in shackles. He stepped back and looked at the wall surrounding the property.

No wonder the house had been a target.

25

Ty held up the piece of paper with Emily and Charlie's photographs. The two boys, both around fourteen years old and still hanging on a corner, although midnight had long passed, looked at them.

"You recognize them?" Ty asked.

The taller of the two boys shrugged. "You crazy?"

"Yeah, I am. That's why I'm going ask you again."

The kids shared a nervous laugh. "You sure you're not Five-O?" By their logic, the old black man out there after dark asking questions would be a police officer.

"I already told you I'm not," said Ty.

"You're a private cop?"

"Something like that."

"What about you?" the taller one asked Galante, who was leaning against the car, arms folded.

"I was a cop."

"We don't like cops around here," said the smaller boy. For a kid who barely cleared five feet he delivered the line with a surprising amount of menace.

"Just as well I don't give a fuck what you like or don't like, then," said Galante.

It wasn't language he would use around kids normally, but these streets were a little different. As Ty kept at it, Galante's eyes swept the block.

It was busy, even at three in the morning. This was a neighborhood that, like many in East Los Angeles, operated on a different timescale. There would have been no point stopping people here in the morning to ask them questions. Anyone out before nine would be on the way to work, and people who worked in these neighborhoods kept their heads down and their mouths closed.

It was only in the afternoon that streets like this sprang to life. Poor, gang-infested neighborhoods operated on an entirely different time zone. East LA time. PST plus five.

A car drove past Galante and Ty, its occupant's eyes heavy with menace. Someone shouted at them in Spanish. Whatever they'd said, it wasn't complimentary.

That had been the car's third pass. They were pushing their luck staying so long. Next time there might be a shotgun poking through the rear window.

"Ty, let's wrap it up," said Galante.

"Yeah, we already told you, we ain't seen any of these bitches," said the taller kid.

Ty's hand shot straight out and grabbed the kid by the throat. He lifted him clean off the ground.

Galante watched. He didn't say anything. He didn't intervene. He knew precisely what Ty was doing, and why.

"You want to try that again, son?"

The kid did his best to shake his head. The smaller kid stared with something approaching awe. Ty put his friend down and let go of his throat. The kid reached up and rubbed at his neck.

"You're crazy. You can't do that."

"Do what?"

"Lift me up like Darth Vader and shit. I'm gunna make a complaint."

"Who to? I already told you I'm not a cop."

"I'll think of someone," said the kid.

Ty dug out some cards. He handed one to each kid. "Here. When you make your complaint to the Department of No One Gives a Fuck, make sure and give them one of these. I hate it when someone can't spell my name correctly."

Ty walked across to the car. "I'll drive."

Galante tossed him his keys. They got in. A couple of younger kids joined the other two on the sidewalk.

As Ty got behind the wheel, he caught the taller kid, the one he'd lifted off his feet, telling his friends, "Another second and I would have fucked him up."

Ty smiled to himself. It was the kind of thing he would have said at that age.

"Guess we know who's going to be playing bad cop," said Galante.

Ty shrugged, spinning the wheel and hitting the gas. "What do you think happens to that kid if he starts talking back to his mom?"

"A lot worse than that," conceded Galante.

"Precisely."

The car that had been circling the block appeared behind them, moving up fast on their rear bumper. Ty watched it in the rearview mirror.

"You strapped?" asked Ty.

Galante patted the bulge under his untucked shirt. "Damn straight."

Ty settled himself back in the driver's seat. "Glad one of us is."

"Oh, yeah – I heard about your run-in with the Long Beach PD."

"Not my first and probably not my last."

"Have to say it was a pretty good exit."

During the siege at the emergency room in Long Beach, Ty had figured that his best chance of not being shot as he surrendered was to walk out front in his birthday suit. "Didn't think you'd approve."

"Oh, I'd have probably shot you. Just on a point of principle for locking a fellow officer in the trunk of his own car."

"I had to get in there, and he was in my way. I did ask politely. It's not like I went straight to putting him in the trunk."

"You mean when you tried to impersonate a police officer?"

"Listen, dude, any man who allows himself to be locked in the trunk of his own car is kind of impersonating a police officer too."

Galante laughed.

They reached the end of the block. Ty checked the rearview. The same car was still following them. "Knuckleheads," he said.

"They probably just want to make sure we're leaving."

"You think we're going to find these kids alive?" Ty asked.

"I'd say it's fifty:fifty. MS-13 aren't exactly shy about killing people."

"I sense a 'but'," said Ty, flicking his eyes back to the rearview. The car had gone. Behind, the road was empty.

"They're also a business organization. If they feel like there's money to be made from keeping someone breathing then that's what they'll do. I'll tell you one thing, though."

"What's that?"

Galante eased back in his seat as they drove down a block of abandoned houses, the front yards overgrown with weeds, windows either broken or boarded up.

"If they do get paid a nice ransom, and walk away without being caught, we're going to see a bunch of this type of shit."

"I hear that," said Ty, lurching forward suddenly, his seatbelt snapping tight, preventing his chest slamming into the steering wheel as something hit them, at speed, from behind.

Ty didn't need to look behind to know what or who it was. Next to him Carl Galante was wiping blood from his nose after he'd bounced face forward into the passenger dash.

"You okay?" asked Ty.

"Motherfuckers," said Galante, reaching down, his gun clearing leather.

"Hold that thought," said Ty, burying the gas pedal, the car lurching forward. "You have insurance on this thing, right?"

"We might have to lie about you driving but, yeah, I do."

"Good," said Ty, spinning the steering wheel, the car spinning around so that it was facing in the opposite direction.

The driver of the gang car threw it into reverse and backed up at speed. Ty could see four people inside. Two in front, two in back, their faces covered by bandanas the same color as those of the people who had taken Emily and Charlie. Ty doubted it was the same gang members, but they were almost certainly MS-13, or affiliated in some way.

"Why don't we just get out of here?" said Galante.

The cars were facing each other, separated by half a block of empty street. The driver of the gang car flicked his headlights onto full power as the passenger door popped open and someone got out.

"Nah, fuck that," said Ty, as a yellow blaze of muzzle flash lit up next to the gang car.

Ty and Galante dived down. Ty hit the gas pedal again, aiming straight for the gang car. He kept his head down, grasping the bottom of the steering wheel as rounds shattered the windshield.

Keeping his foot to the floor, Ty kamikazed his way down the street, occasionally peeking over the dash and adjusting his steering so that he was aimed directly for the open passenger door the gunman was using for cover.

A fresh three-round burst slammed into the engine block.

"Are you nuts?" screamed Galante, as Ty held onto the wheel for grim death.

A final peek through the shattered windshield revealed the gunman throwing himself towards the sidewalk as Galante's car clipped the open passenger door.

The grating sound of metal on metal was accompanied by a shower of sparks.

Ty eased up on the gas pedal and hit the brakes. The car slowed. He yanked down on the steering and turned the car around. Now he was looking at the rear of the gang car as the gunman who'd taken refuge on the sidewalk set off running for a nearby alleyway, abandoning the rest of his crew. "Punk-ass bitch," he muttered, under his breath, at the retreating figure.

He reached over and peeled Galante's gun from his fingers.

Galante offered token resistance. "What are you doing?"

"Hey," said Ty. "They started it. You think I'm going to have a bunch of assholes try to kill us and just let it go? Fuck that noise."

Holding Galante's gun, Ty popped his door open, got out, and squeezed off two shots at the rear of the gang car, shattering the rear windscreen. Inside, the gang members dove for cover in the footwells.

The gang car took off, the hinges of the passenger door giving way, the door dropping onto the street. Ty let off one more round for good measure as the sound of police sirens punched through the quiet.

Galante got out, watching the gang car recede into the distance as Ty stood up and walked to the front of their vehicle to assess the damage. "I think we're going to need another car," he said.

Steam poured out from under the hood. A gasoline smell filled the air.

Ty handed Galante back his gun as an LAPD patrol car turned onto the block.

"Thanks," said Galante. "Do me one tiny favor?"

"What's that?" said Ty.

"Let me do the talking."

"Anything else?"

Galante winced again at the smoldering front of his car. "Try to keep your pants on."

26

———

Holding his shoes, the Red Tiger pushed open the bedroom door, and stepped inside. He moved with all the deliberateness and care of a man entering a temple, which, in his mind, he was.

He stepped into Emily's bedroom, placed his shoes on the thick carpet, and gently closed the door behind him. He closed his eyes, and took a deep breath, pulling every scent that hung in the air deep into his nostrils and down into his lungs, filling himself with what she had left behind.

There was a desk with a computer. There was a large king-sized bed with cuddly toys. Framed posters of Chinese and Korean pop stars lined the walls, many of them signed 'To Emily' by the artists.

On the nightstand next to the bed was a photograph in a gold frame. Solid gold, no doubt. He picked it up. Emily stood with her mother and father. They were all smiling.

He put it back down, not caring for once that he had left his fingerprints on an object.

There were more framed photographs on an armoire by the window. Emily with friends. Emily with her cousin, Charlie, and his parents. He studied that one with care, wondering if there was also someone like him in Charlie's past. Another ghost from Charlie's childhood. Someone else who yearned for what had been ripped from them and given away.

One by one he picked up the framed photographs. He lingered over some more than others. The ones where Emily was a little girl were especially difficult.

The Red Tiger was sobbing now. Tears streamed from his eyes, rolling down his cheeks, and dripping onto the front of his shirt.

He doubted that he was a man people imagined capable of such a display of emotion. For a long time, he would have doubted it himself. Like most men he had been too consumed by business, by the day to day, by fulfilling the needs of others.

Now, alone, the part of himself he had pushed deep down into the very bottom of his heart overflowed. He took one of the photographs and sat on the edge of the bed. In it she was seven or eight. She stood over a cake, a ribbon in her hair, wearing a party dress that was a little too big for her. She was smiling up at the camera. It was the smile of a child. A smile of pure joy that belonged only to that moment.

He closed his eyes. Opened them again. Looked at that smile, imagining it was for him.

In his mind's eye, he stepped back, and scooped her into his arms. She threw hers around him, burying her tiny face in his neck as he spun her around and around, wishing this moment would never end.

The sound of a car pulling up outside. The Red Tiger snapped back to the present, suddenly ashamed of how he'd allowed something as simple as a photograph to pull him down into a pit of maudlin sentimentality.

For all he knew this could be a ruse. Or could it be true, and Emily was already dead.

He put the photograph on the nightstand and crossed to the window. He risked a quick peek down. The man he'd come to learn was called Li Yeng was getting out of his car, and walking towards the front door.

The Red Tiger crossed to the bedroom door. He picked up his

shoes and put them on. He opened the door and stepped out into the hallway, staying close to the wall, out of sight of Li as he came in.

The front door opened. Li walked in. He was alone.

The Red Tiger's hand reached down to the Glock. He put his hand on it. The feeling of the grip was reassuring.

He lay on his front, and belly-crawled forward. He could see Li walking into the kitchen. He was on the phone. He was speaking in Mandarin. Occasionally a word or a phrase would betray his rural origins.

The Red Tiger listened intently to the conversation. He got up as Li disappeared into the kitchen. Inching towards the top of the stairs, he drew the Glock, and began to walk down, stopping every few steps to dial back into the conversation.

By the time he was halfway, he was certain that this was no ruse. Not unless Li was aware of his presence and was staging the conversation entirely for his benefit.

His heart rate quickened as Li's voice grew suddenly louder. He hunkered down, raising the Glock, pushing the barrel through the banisters of the staircase, aiming for the kitchen door. His thighs burned as he held the unnatural position, the alcohol still churning through his body.

He waited for Li to step into the hallway. It didn't happen. His voice fell away again. It was still loud enough that the Red Tiger could hear what he was saying but he must have walked back into the depths of the cavernous kitchen.

Should he retreat up the stairs? Or make a dash for the front door? Or step calmly into the kitchen and confront Li?

He did his best to sort through his three options. His heart pulled him back to Emily's bedroom. But there was nothing to be gained from looking at it again. The emotion it had drawn out of him served no purpose.

What would he gain from confronting Li? Information? He was already getting that by eavesdropping where he was. In any case, it was better to stay in the shadows. Nothing he had seen indicated that they knew he was there. Best to keep it that way.

Li's voice grew louder again. He mentioned a name that had littered the conversation.

Lock. Ryan Lock.

From the rest of the conversation the Red Tiger gathered this was the man they had hired, along with another called Johnson, to find Emily. He was some kind of private security type. Not a policeman, someone who worked for private individuals and corporations.

It was then it occurred to him. Lock was like him. He was his . . . What was the word in English? His counterpart. Yes, that was it.

Who better, then, to help him? Find Lock, and his friend, Johnson, and allow them to take him to her. Then when they had led him there, he could kill them, and claim what was rightly his.

27

T y nursed Galante's car to the diner where they were due to meet with Lock. It was making a series of strange noises that sounded like the automotive equivalent of a death rattle. Whatever humor Galante had expressed about the events of the evening had long since evaporated.

Using fluent cop language, Galante had narrowly talked them out of being taken into custody by the LAPD a few blocks from the scene. Then they had been pulled over by the California Highway Patrol, and again he'd somehow persuaded the motorbike cop to allow them to continue their journey.

Every minute that passed, his temper seemed to deteriorate. Ty didn't blame him. He'd have been way more pissed than Galante if his ride had been shot up. On the other hand, Ty figured, you were way less likely to get emotionally attached to a two-year-old Honda Accord than the lovingly restored 1966 Lincoln Continental that he drove.

They got out. As Galante closed the door there was a loud clang as something fell off the Honda's undercarriage. He hunkered down to see what it was, reached under and retrieved a piece of metal bracket. He opened the rear passenger door and tossed it onto the backseat next to the other pieces of the car that had fallen off.

"Sorry about the mess," said Ty.

"How am I going to explain this to my insurance company?" said Galante.

Now that the high of having survived being shot at had passed, he was really starting to regret signing up to partner with Ty. Maybe if the six-foot-four Marine hadn't been quite so hard with that neighborhood kid they might have got out of there unscathed.

"Just tell them the truth," said Ty. "You were in a bad neighborhood and someone took exception to your presence."

"My premium is going to go sky high."

They looked around as Lock's Audi pulled into the space next to them. Lock got out with Carmen.

"You okay?" she asked Ty and Galante.

Lock took a long appraising look at Galante's car. He'd seen worse. Not much worse, but definitely worse. Then again, the worse he'd seen were vehicles that had been hit by IEDs or suicide bombers. Those tended to melt tires as well as cause body damage.

"Don't tell me. You let Ty drive," he said, knocking a booted toe against the rear of the Honda. Something else clanged to the ground. "Sorry, dude."

Galante bent down to see what it was but stood up again, finally overwhelmed by the whole scene. "Fuck it," he said, straightening. "My insurance company is gonna go nuts," he repeated.

"I can help you deal with them if they get squirrely about paying for the damage," said Carmen, trying to be helpful.

Lock stepped back towards the Audi. He retrieved the attaché case and handed it to Galante.

"What's this?" said Galante.

"It'll cover the cost."

"I thought that was to pay potential informants," said Carmen.

"It is," said Lock.

She looked at him, puzzled.

"I'll explain inside," said Lock, nodding towards the diner. "Anyone else hungry?"

"Damn straight," said Ty.

"There's a shock."

The four headed towards the diner entrance. Galante threw a baleful look back over his shoulder at his shot-to-shit vehicle.

28

Pony finished the call. He opened the back of the cell phone, used his nail to prod the SIM card free, and handed it to Joker. Joker walked over to the coffee-table, picked up a hammer that was lying there and pounded the SIM into tiny plastic and silicon fragments.

Princess walked out of the bedroom. "Put it in the trash disposal, asshole, like a regular person."

Joker lifted the hammer and swung it theatrically, smiling. "Maybe I'll pound you."

"I'd like to see you try."

"She don't like guys pounding her," said Pony, removing the battery from the cell phone, and slotting in a fresh SIM card with a brand-new number.

"Oh, yeah," said Joker, grabbing at his crotch. "Maybe she just hasn't met the right guy."

Arms folded in front of her, Princess made a clucking sound and waggled her pinky finger. "Like the little thing you have would impress me."

"Okay," said Pony, fitting the cover back on the cell phone. "That was Shotcaller."

Princess and Joker looked at him. They had been waiting for this call. It was Shotcaller who had the final say over what happened to Emily and Charlie. Princess had been lobbying hard for keeping Emily. Slow and steady money, an additional revenue stream.

Joker and Pony wanted to explore new territory. See if they could sell them back. Take a ransom. Make a big score. Most of it would have to be kicked up to Shotcaller and those above him, but it would change everything for their little crew. It came with a big risk, but it was a big reward too.

"What he say?" Princess asked, no longer able to contain herself.

"You won't like it," said Pony. He couldn't show it, but he was scared about breaking the news to Princess. She was volatile and, as befitted her name, she didn't like it when things didn't go her way. She had it bad for the Asian chick too. Everyone could see it. Pony figured that was part of the reason why Shotcaller had made the decision he had. This had to be business, not personal.

Princess kicked out at the back of the couch. "Motherfucker."

She started towards him, eyes ablaze. "What you say to him? You been talking shit behind my back, huh, Pony?"

Pony's hand slid back, reaching for his pistol. If he had to, he'd put a cap in her ass. "I didn't say nothing," he told her, standing his ground.

She was up in his face. She jabbed a red-nailed finger at him. "You're a liar. I should have spoken to Shotcaller. Not you."

Joker stepped between them. "Hey, it wasn't our decision. We knew that."

"If it makes it any better, he's not going with what we wanted either."

Now it was Joker's turn to get agitated. "What? We can get seven for them. That's a big score."

Pony grimaced. "It's a big score, but it's not going to be our score."

Both Joker and Princess looked puzzled.

"Someone else is taking them. They're going to run the ransom."

"Who?" said Princess. "She's mine. I took her. So did you. We took the risk getting them back here. And the whips."

"And we're going to see some money," said Pony.

"So who is it? Who's taking them?" Princess pushed.

Pony was getting irritated. Princess had been around long enough to know that there were some questions you didn't ask, and that was one of them. You could ask about what happened down the chain, but not what was going on in the executive suite. Those kinds of questions could get her killed. Not just her either. Him too. And Joker.

"Who do you think?" said Pony. The actual words weren't going to leave his mouth, no way, no how.

If he was asked whether he'd told her that the two people they'd kidnapped were being handed to La Eme, the Mexican Mafia, he wanted to be able to deny ever having said those words.

"Fuck that shit," said Princess. "Fuck them. We're Salvador. Fuck those wetback bitches."

Pony's hand closed around his pistol. He brought it forward, straight into the side of Princess's face, opening up a cut above her eye. "Shut the fuck up."

She went down onto one knee. He followed up with another blow to the top of her head. Her scalp split, blood pouring into her thick tangle of black hair.

He hunkered down so he was at eye level with her. "You want to get us killed? Because that's what will happen. Say they already sent someone. Say they're out on the stoop, and they hear you saying that. What you think they'll do? Say, 'Oh, that's just Princess, she don't mean it'?"

She looked up at him, her eyes still full of righteous anger.

"You know the game," said Joker, handing her a towel that had been lying over the back of the couch.

She took it and pressed it to her head, wincing with the pain.

"How much we getting?" said Joker.

"A taste. That's all I know."

Disappointment hung in the air, like the stench of rotting garbage.

Joker sank down onto the couch. "We could have had real money."

Pony held up the gun, butt first. He wasn't happy about it either. But that was how it worked. "You want a taste of this?" he said to Joker. Their bitching about it was making him even angrier.

Joker didn't say anything.

"Or maybe you want to go tell them yourself?" Neither of them answered him. "Yeah, that's what I thought."

"They coming to collect?" said Princess. "Or are we delivering?"

"What you think?" said Pony.

"Why you think I'm asking?" said Princess.

She was something else, thought Pony. He'd just given her two good ones and she was still talking back.

"They're not going to come here. We'll have to take them."

"I'll do it," said Princess.

That was okay with Pony. He didn't like being around La Eme. He would never admit it, but they scared him. They were old school. They'd seen more blood and death than anyone. They were cold. They looked at you with those dead eyes.

"Okay," said Pony.

"I ain't going," said Joker.

"She can't go on her own," said Pony.

"Then you go," said Joker.

"I have to move the car," said Pony. They'd disabled the tracking devices and stashed them. Today they'd delivered them to the *yonque*.

"I can do that," said Joker.

Pony stared at him. He turned the pistol around, spinning it on his finger so that the barrel was facing Joker.

"Okay, okay, I'll go with Princess."

Princess got up and started for the door.

"Where are you going?" Pony asked her.

She looked at him, the dirty towel still pressed to her head, blood pouring down her face. "I need to get this looked at."

"What you gonna tell them?"

She smirked. "That my boyfriend did it. What the hell you care what I tell them?"

"Go clean up first. Joker, you take her."

"Fine," said Princess.

WITH A TOWEL WRAPPED around her head, Princess climbed into the passenger seat next to Joker. He pulled out onto the street.

"You okay?" Joker asked her.

"I have a headache."

She rested her face against the window and closed her eyes.

"Don't tell them I'm your boyfriend, okay?"

She opened her eyes. "If I was straight, I'd have better taste."

Joker smiled and made a turn onto a cross street. "Fuck you." He was quiet for a moment. Then he said, "This is fucked up. We do all the hard work and they take all the money."

She shrugged. "Always been the same for people like us."

They lapsed back into silence.

"My papa used to hit my mom," said Joker.

Princess didn't say anything to that.

"That's why I don't want anyone thinking I'd do something like that."

"I won't say anything. Don't worry."

He made another turn. Princess sat up straight. She rolled down the window and leaned out, checking the street sign. "This ain't the way to the emergency room."

"I know," said Joker.

She backhanded him in the chest. "What the fuck? I need to get this stitched before I bleed to death."

Joker slowed. He reached down into his pocket, feeling for something. The car wobbled and drifted over the center line. A vehicle coming in the opposite direction honked at him. He threw them the finger and cussed out the other driver. Then he tossed a wallet over the seat and onto Princess's lap. She picked it up.

"Homeboy's wallet with all his cards. I got his pin number too. Made him tell me. Dumb motherfucker uses the same number for everything."

Wide-eyed, Princess began to rifle through the wallet. There were a lot of cards. Bank cards. Credit cards.

Joker turned into a lot. There was a Bank of America dead ahead.

"Pony would lose his shit if he knows we're doing this," said Princess.

"How's he going to find out? How's anyone going to?"

"You know they can track these cards if we use them, right?" Princess was still nervous. They could make some money, and she liked that idea, but it was risky.

"So, what do we care?" said Joker. "You heard Pony, right? They're not staying with us after today. Even if the Five-O track us down, what are they going to find? Nothing. The cars will be gone."

He reached back and pulled up the hood he was wearing. He lowered the sunglasses that had been resting on top of his head. "Wasn't me, Officer."

Princess laughed. "You got it all figured out."

"Come on, let's go get ourselves a taste. Least we'll have something to show for all this work."

Princess stood next to the car as Joker walked up to the ATM. It was quiet, no one else waiting to use the machine. He cycled through all the cards he could, trying for a thousand dollars and working his way down until he found the maximum amount he could withdraw.

A little old white man parked nearby and waited behind Joker. He started to grow impatient. "Are you going to be long?" Princess heard him ask.

It pissed her off. She walked right up on him. "Fuck you, Grandpa. You don't want to wait, go use another machine."

He looked at her, the black eye, her bloodied scalp, and walked back to his car.

She moved in closer to Joker. "How much you get?" she asked.

"Keep your head down, dummy. They got a camera up there."

In the excitement of seeing the machine spit out all those dollars, she had forgotten. She retreated a few steps. "How much?" she repeated.

He fanned out a whole bunch of twenties. "Once we get your head fixed, we should go shopping."

Princess beamed. She had felt bad about losing Emily. This took the edge off.

29

Lock and Carl Galante watched Ty consume a meal that could easily have fed an entire family. Occasionally, Galante threw a glance back over his shoulder at the parking lot.

Every time a new customer pulled up they would give the Honda a long look before walking in. A young couple who seemed like they'd just finished a night of partying took a tour around it, the young man almost admiringly pointing out the bullet holes in the bodywork to his female companion.

Galante, Lock figured, was almost certainly looking at replacing his car rather than having it repaired. Lock's experience with vehicles that had come under hostile fire was that, much like people, they were never the same afterwards. In the meantime, though, Galante's bullet-ridden whip would be a useful prop for at least one part of their investigation.

"So, what do we think?" said Lock.

Ty held up a fork speared with a piece of sausage and a corner of waffle. "Pretty good. I'd hit this place up again," he said approvingly. "Breakfast definitely. Not sure it's a lunch spot."

"Good to know," said Lock. "But I was talking about the reception you and Carl got back there in the 'hood."

Ty smiled. "I know what you meant. I was just attempting to lighten the mood."

"Consider it lightened. Now, what do you think?" said Lock.

"Regular neighborhood static, or someone who thought we were too close?" said Galante, reframing the question.

Carmen's phone chimed. She picked it up. Lock turned to her to see if it was anything case-related. She waved him off. "Go on with what you're talking about," she said, getting up from the table, and walking towards the entrance to make a call.

Lock watched her go with a sudden jab of anxiety. He'd swept her into this without thinking. Now he regretted it. If their relationship was to stand a chance, especially if they were going to be living together, it was better they kept their work lives separate. Too late for that with this, but it was something he needed to be mindful of in future.

"Ty?" said Lock. "What's your take?"

Ty shrugged. "Hard to tell. But if I had to make a call, I'd say we were getting close."

Lock shifted his attention to Galante. "Carl?"

"Same," said Galante. "They took a good long look at us before they made a move. Made sure we knew they were there. Waited to see if we'd leave."

Ty nodded his agreement as he mopped up some maple syrup from the corner of his plate with a piece of waffle. "Exactly. You drive on the block and some cat's going to object to you being there. That shit goes off from the jump usually. Car rolls up behind you, takes its time about it, that's a decision being made."

"So at least we know we're fishing in the right pond," said Lock.

Galante nodded. "I'd say those two kids are within a ten-block radius."

It narrowed it down, but not nearly enough for Lock's liking. A ten-block radius could encompass hundreds of houses. They needed to narrow it down further, and fast. Assuming that the kidnappers hadn't already been spooked, and decided on a move, there was still too much ground to cover.

"So what do we think? Door to door? See if anything pops?" said Ty.

Lock shook his head. "Too risky."

A door wouldn't even need to open. Someone could be waiting for them and fire straight through without even opening it.

"I agree," said Galante. "It's too big an area. It's not like people are going to invite you inside their home so you can check they don't have a couple of Chinese kids tied up in the basement."

Galante was right. To search the area effectively, they'd need warrants. They weren't official law enforcement, so that wasn't going to happen. And even if they'd been cops, they'd still require probable cause for a warrant. All they could do now was poke another stick into the hornets' nest and see if anything broke. Maybe throw some of the cash that Li had given Lock into the mix for good measure.

"So what do we do?" asked Ty. "Keep riding the car angle?"

Before Lock could respond, Carmen walked back to their table, and scooted in next to Lock. "I got a steer on what was being discussed on that clip you gave me."

Lock had almost forgotten about the footage Ty had shot of Li on the phone with his boss, Emily's father, and the heated conversation they'd had in Mandarin. "Anything good?"

Carmen tapped her smartphone and passed it to Lock. An email from the translator gave a rough breakdown of the conversation that had taken place. Or, at least, Li's side of it.

Lock read it over.

"She said that's a rough translation into English. She can be a little more precise if she has more time to go over it, but I'd told her it was priority and that I didn't need the exact wording of everything that was said."

Lock nodded. He read the email again. It would have been useful to have both sides of the conversation, but there was enough from what Li said to give him a handle.

Ty and Galante were staring at him across the table.

"Well?"

"What does it say?"

Lock shrugged. "It seems like they knew something bad was coming but they didn't think it was this."

"What does that mean?" said Ty.

Lock looked at Carmen, then handed the phone to Ty.

"Go ahead," she said.

Ty began to read the email.

The cell rang with an incoming call. He handed it back to Carmen.

A split second later Galante's phone rang. He snatched it and got up from the table.

"Wait. What?" said Carmen. She shot Lock a thumbs-up.

From Galante's surprised reaction, Lock sensed he was getting the same call.

Lock's phone rang. It was Li. He answered as Ty stood up and headed towards Galante. "Can some motherfucker tell me what's going on?" said Ty.

"This is Lock."

"Mr. Lock, it's Li Yeng. The LAPD just called me. Someone used Charlie's cards to withdraw money from an ATM in East Los Angeles."

The cross street was roughly a mile from where Ty and Galante had been looking. That didn't mean much. For a start, poorer neighborhoods didn't have the same number of banks or ATMs. And no self-respecting criminal was going to hit up a stolen card a few blocks from where they lived. The fact that they had done it at all was surprising.

A kidnap for ransom could net a six-figure sum, with the payment made in a manner that was hard to trace. Using a kidnap victim's credit or bank card involved more risk. When it happened, it was usually done immediately after the abduction, not a day or more later when authorities were on the lookout.

"What else did the cops say?" said Lock.

"They have the person who used the cards on camera. That's good, right?"

"For us, probably," said Lock.

"Probably?" said Li, apparently surprised by Lock's on-the-fence reaction.

"Yes, it's good," said Lock, quickly backtracking. "But let's be happy when they're back safe with their family."

For Lock, in these types of cases, it was always important to manage a client's expectations. Things could go wrong at any stage, and fast.

It was good in as much as they had someone they could look for. Dime to a dollar this was an individual who had already been arrested, no doubt more than once. With a little luck a cop working the area would recognize them.

The reckless nature of it was a worry. Ask any law-enforcement official or person who dealt with kidnap for ransom and they almost all preferred to deal with criminals who exhibited a certain level of professionalism. It was much easier to resolve a situation when those involved saw it as a business transaction.

Amateur criminals killed people. So did professionals—but only when they had no other option, or it made business sense. Not on a whim. Not because they were panicked. Not merely because they enjoyed the act of killing another human being.

"What now, Mr. Lock?" said Li.

"I'll keep working on our end of the investigation, and you tell me the second the LAPD give you or the family any kind of an update."

"You think we'll get them back safe?"

Lock thought again about managing expectations. "We're closer to that than we were. But can you do me a favor?"

"Of course. Name it."

"Don't raise the family's hopes too much."

"I understand."

"Oh, and one more thing."

"Yes?"

"I've already had to allocate some of the cash you gave me. Ty and another investigator had a fender-bender and we're not sure if the insurance company will cover it."

"Don't worry, Mr. Lock. It was a token sum. Use it as you see fit. Of course we'll need some kind of accounting, but no one will be looking too deeply at how you use the money."

"Okay. Let me know as soon as the cops update you, and I'll do the same if anything breaks at our end."

Lock finished the call. He was hoping Galante, with his law-enforcement contacts, would be able to put a little more meat on the bones of what was going on. "Everyone hear the news?" he asked.

They all had.

"What do we think?"

"Goddam amateurs," said Ty. Coming from the area of Long Beach that he had, Ty looked down upon badly executed criminal acts more than others around the table.

"Carmen?" asked Lock.

"It worries me."

"Me too," said Galante.

"You don't hit an ATM for a few thousand bucks if you're waiting on a big payoff like this," Carmen added.

Lock turned his attention to Galante. "Carl? What are your cop buddies saying?"

"That was someone I know from Robbery Homicide. They already have a name on the asshole who used the cards, and a couple of addresses for him that they're going to hit as soon as they pull everything together."

"We should back off that neighborhood then," said Ty.

Galante nodded. "Want to know the best thing about it?"

"Go on," said Ty.

"We were about a block away from where his mom lives when we got shot up."

"No wonder you got a hot reception," said Lock.

"I just hope we didn't spook them," said Ty.

"We should know in a few hours," said Galante, getting up.

"I'm going into the office," Carmen said to Galante. "You want a ride?"

"What about my car?"

"We'll take care of it," said Lock.

Lock settled the check as Carmen and Galante headed out to her car, leaving him with Ty. He could tell that his partner felt bad for the potential misstep. It was possible that his and Galante's presence had spooked the kidnappers sufficiently that they had already moved Charlie and Emily.

Or worse.

"Come on," said Lock, slapping Ty on the shoulder. "Let's go see if we can find some auto shops who don't ask questions about bullet-hole repairs."

Ty seemed reluctant to get moving.

"What?" said Lock.

"I'd rather be knocking down some doors."

"Me too," said Lock. "But that's best left to the cops."

Ty rose slowly. He turned his head to look at Lock. "You think they're still alive?"

"I have no idea. But I do know one thing."

"What's that?"

"They're worth a hell of a lot more alive, and that has to count for something."

30

The SUV drove down the side of the house. Hulking. Black. Tinted windows. Shotcaller riding up front. His wraparound sunglasses, steroid-tree-trunk neck and teardrop tattoos matched the driver's. One other man was riding in back, bigger than both of them.

The SUV made the turn and parked directly behind the house. The three men got out, pistols slung low on their hips, and walked to the back door. The two men with Shotcaller held black canvas duffels.

Pony was waiting for them. He pushed the door open and stepped inside.

Shotcaller walked past him and inside without saying anything. The two other men headed straight for the bedroom. Shotcaller dug a brown pill bottle out of his pocket and tossed it towards one of the men. "Two each. It'll take the edge off. Don't want them getting hinky on the ride."

The man who caught the bottle, popped the lid off. He tapped four white pills into his palm.

"You need some water?" said Pony.

"Sure," said the man holding the pills.

Pony started to duck back towards the kitchen to fetch it. Shotcaller caught his elbow. "Where are the others?" he asked.

He had been hoping Shotcaller wouldn't ask him. The rule was that there should always be at least two people in the house in case the Chinese kids tried to escape.

"They had to go out."

Shotcaller's features darkened. He raised his sunglasses so that they were perched on his head. He stared at Pony with coal-black eyes. "Out?"

"Princess hit her head. Joker took her to the hospital."

Shotcaller shook his head. There were sounds of a struggle in the bedroom. Still staring with a deathly menace at Pony, he went into the room.

The girl had her lips clamped shut. Water spilled down her chin. A man held the back of her head, trying to make her take the tranquilizers. He grabbed her hair and yanked at it. She whimpered but kept her mouth closed.

Shotcaller took three long strides over to the boy, Charlie. He drew his gun and pushed the barrel into the kid's temple. "Swallow the pills or I blow his head off. Your choice," he told Emily.

He didn't raise his voice. His tone was even. He had learned a long time ago that sometimes a person would sacrifice their own life before they would that of someone close to them. Blood was a powerful bond.

Emily's lips parted. She stared daggers at him as the pills were forced into her mouth.

She sipped some water. Swallowed.

They made her open her mouth, lift her tongue, and wiggle it around to ensure she had taken them.

"We're moving you," Shotcaller told them.

"Where?" said Emily.

"Somewhere nicer." He turned to the two men he had arrived with. "Get them ready. We're out of here in ten."

Shotcaller walked back into the living room where Pony was sitting on the edge of the couch. He reached into his pocket, pulled out a roll of bills and a bag of weed and tossed them both onto the table. "Don't worry. That's just a down payment. You did good."

"Princess is pissed," said Pony.

"Women are always pissed. She'll get over it."

"So where they going now?"

As soon as the final syllable of the question had passed Pony's lips he knew he'd messed up. The question hung in the air. Shotcaller stared at him.

"Sorry. None of my business," Pony stuttered.

Shotcaller's eyes didn't drop.

"I just––"

Shotcaller took a step towards him. "You just what?"

"It doesn't matter," said Pony. He could feel his throat start to close up. His mouth was dry.

Finally, Shotcaller blinked. "That's right. It doesn't."

"WHERE ARE YOU TAKING US?" said Emily.

Someone grabbed her, pulling her arms behind her back. She heard the rip of heavy silver tape, then felt her wrists being bound together.

Neither of the two men said anything.

She glanced at Charlie. He was staring at the carpet. His eyes were closed. He had started closing his eyes when someone came into the room. She had asked him why. He had told her that he wanted them to think he wouldn't be able to identify the kidnappers. It was safer that way. It gave them a better chance of survival.

Emily wouldn't do it. Every opportunity she had, she stared them down. She was going to let them know that she wasn't scared of what they'd do. She was scared. She was terrified. But she refused to show it. If they wanted to kill her, they could do it while looking into her eyes.

Charlie spoke about Chinese pride. But when it came down to it he was a coward. That was, in some ways, what would linger long after this, that her cousin was what the Americans called a punk.

"Where are we going?" Emily repeated.

She could feel the pills they had forced on her starting to take effect. She wasn't sleepy exactly. It was more that everything seemed otherworldly. As if she were watching herself underwater, and from behind a sheet of glass.

One of the men stood in front of her. He reached into his bag and pulled out a blue bandana just like the ones the kidnappers had worn back at the house. It seemed like such a long time ago. Another lifetime. Completely and utterly separate from the present.

The man started to fold the bandana and place it around her face. She shook it off.

He stood away, drew his hand back and slapped her hard. She felt something crack and pain surged in two lines up her face.

He grabbed her hair and pulled her head back. He was so close she could smell his cheap cologne. He yanked her hair. She could feel her left eye start to close.

This time she let him put the bandana on. He put a ball cap on her head and pulled her to her feet. The other man did the same with Charlie.

They were led out of the bedroom and into the living room. Pain pulsed through her head. She thought she was going to pass out, not sure if it was the sudden blow, the pills kicking in or a combination of the two.

She was dumped on the couch, Charlie next to her.

There were two others in the room. An older man and the younger one who'd been with the three who'd taken them. The younger one looked scared out of his mind.

They had that much in common, she thought.

The older man paced in front of them. From the way the others watched him it was clear that he was in charge.

He crouched down so that he was at her eye level. "What happened to her face?" he said, turning back to the other two men.

The one who had slapped her shuffled his feet and stared down. "She was being difficult."

"That true?" the man said to her.

She looked at him, struggling to keep her eyes open. Still defiant.

"Fuck you," she said.

The man laughed. The others joined in, even the young scared one that she'd heard being called Pony.

"I can see why Princess liked you so much," he said.

He drew his hand back. His fingers were bunched into a fist. Emily braced herself for another blow.

Before it came, the man's cell phone rang. His fingers unclenched. He answered, speaking Spanish.

It was a short call, maybe twenty seconds. He gestured for the younger man to follow him back into the bedroom, telling the other two to stay where they were and keep guard over her and Charlie.

Charlie snuck a look at her. "Stop provoking them," he said to her in Mandarin.

One of the men grabbed his shoulder. "No talking."

IN THE BEDROOM, Shotcaller paced. Pony stood in a corner, one eye on the window. If it wasn't for the bars he would have dove straight through it.

The call. It had been bad news. The kind of call that got people like him killed.

"You know anything about it?" Shotcaller said.

"No, I swear. He was taking her to get her head fixed."

"This is fucked up," said Shotcaller.

"I know, I know, it's bad. I can't believe they'd play me like this."

"They'd play *you*?"

"Play us," Pony corrected himself.

"You know what you have to do, right?" said Shotcaller.

Pony did. Shotcaller wanted him to kill Joker and Princess.

"Me? Can't you get someone else?"

"Hey, you just told me you were the one who got played."

"I know, but they're my homies. Joker and me, we grew up together."

"Makes it worse in my book. A stranger playing you is one thing. But someone that's close, that's family . . ."

Pony's heart sank even further. They should have taken the cars and left it at that. They'd gotten greedy. Moved into territory that wasn't theirs. The two Chinese sitting a few feet away, it was like they'd come with some kind of curse.

There was an inevitability to this. It was inescapable. Pony would have to murder Joker and Princess. If he refused, or didn't follow through, he would be killed, and so would his homies. Double-crossing, Shotcaller demanded it. Those were the rules. Shotcaller couldn't let it pass. If he made an exception, his own life would be in danger. MS-13 was not an organization that allowed for weakness.

"I'll take care of it," Pony said finally.

"I know you will."

31

With a final choking death sputter, Galante's Honda Accord shuddered to a halt a few feet short of the auto-repair shop's metal roll-over doors. A small knot of mechanics had downed tools and gathered outside to witness its final passage.

Lock and Ty climbed out and walked towards them. The mechanics' boss emerged from in back and shouldered his way through his workers. Without saying anything they took the hint and drifted back to work inside.

Lock recognized the squat, steroid-swollen man with the mustache and sideburns from the description Galante had given them. This was Noah Orzana, a forty-six-year-old first-generation Salvadorian immigrant, who was unimaginatively nicknamed El Mecánico.

To the outside world Noah Orzana was a successful small businessman, who owned a number of auto- and body-repair places scattered across East Los Angeles. In truth, he was a leading associate of the Mexican Mafia. Maybe even a full-blown member. No one could say for sure. Membership wasn't something anyone shouted from the rooftops.

The line between associate and member was often a distinction without a difference. Members of La Eme, like those of any proscribed organization, often publicly denied not only their involvement but the organization's very existence. In court they would claim that it had been dreamed up by law enforcement as a way of persecuting members of their community.

Orzana walked over to them. Reaching up, he stroked his mustache as he took in the bullet-ridden vehicle that Lock had somehow managed to nurse all the way there from the diner.

"You get in an argument with someone?" said Orzana, smiling, clearly unfazed by the bullet holes.

"Fender-bender that turned into an argument," said Ty, matching El Mecánico's smile.

"That can happen around here," said Orzana. "Kids, these days. You know what I blame?"

Lock shrugged a "Go on."

"I blame all those video games. You know that Grand Theft Auto. Kids play these games where they go steal other people's property, shoot people, kill cops. It's got to have an effect on a young mind, right?"

"It can't help," said Lock, struggling to suppress a smile. He couldn't tell if Orzana believed what he'd just said, or whether he'd already marked them down as some kind of law enforcement and was teasing them.

This was a man, if the stories and his early arrest record were to be believed, who had built a small empire on the back of handling stolen vehicles, breaking them down, reassembling the parts and selling on the cannibalized vehicles. These days he claimed to be legit, but the word was that his businesses were legit during regular business hours and after dark turned into illegal boneyards or *yonques*, operated either by his employees or leased to others by the hour.

A good crew of car thieves and mechanics could strip down a stolen vehicle into its component parts, including the engine and transmission, and build it back on a different frame within three or four hours. All they needed were the tools and somewhere quiet, like this industrial unit, tucked away at the end of an alley. To the untrained, and even the trained eye, there was no visible difference between the activities of a legal and an illegal auto shop.

"What can I do for you?" Orzana asked them.

"Take a look at our car for a start. Let me know if it's repairable, and if it is how much."

Orzana pulled a greasy rag from the back pocket of his jeans and wiped his hands. "Sure thing."

They followed him over to the Honda. "Pop the hood for me."

Lock tossed Ty the keys. Ty opened up and found the latch. He pulled up the hood. Fumes poured out.

"Not seen you guys around the neighborhood before," said Orzana, as he peered at the engine.

"We needed someplace where people might not ask too many questions about the state of our automobile," said Lock, throwing his first piece of bait into the water. "Bullet holes tend to get people talking."

His hands still resting on the lip of the engine compartment, Orzana glanced back at Lock. "I can take it off your hands. Break it up for spares. That's about all."

"How much?" said Lock.

"Three hundred bucks."

"Get the fuck outta here," said Ty.

Orzana straightened. "Excuse me?" he asked, his features cold.

The amiable auto-shop owner was replaced by the old-time gang-banger who'd done time in some of California's tougher penitentiaries, including the notorious Pelican Bay Supermax, where Lock and Ty had narrowly survived an undercover operation for the US District Attorney's Office.

"You heard me," said Ty, flatly.

Orzana glanced back. Two of his grease monkeys were walking out. They looked ready to start swinging.

Lock and Ty both stood their ground. This was a test. What they called in the penitentiary a heart check.

Lock chose to deal with it by ignoring the tension in the air, and the threat of imminent violence. His manner remained as it had been: matter of fact.

"And to repair? How much?"

Orzana studied them both. If either of them had backed down, or apologized, the situation would quickly have gotten out of hand. "What do you want?" Orzana asked. "And don't tell me you came here because you figured I was some dumbass *cholo* who wouldn't snitch on you."

Lock moved a step towards him. The two mechanics drew closer, taking a position either side of their boss, as the other workers stood ready just inside the workshop. "I'm looking to buy a Lamborghini," said Lock.

Orzana made a point of glancing around theatrically. "A Lamborghini. What? You think this is Beverly Hills? I don't sell no Lam-bor-*ghin*-is," he said.

He was pissed off and wasn't concerned with concealing the fact. That worked for Lock.

"That ain't what I heard. Oh, we're also in the market for an Audi. Should be with the Lamborghini I just mentioned. Oh, and two Chinese nationals. Girl about seventeen, eighteen, and a young man who's twenty-one. They were taken from a house out in Arcadia at the same time as the vehicles I just described."

Orzana regarded Lock with a prison-yard stare. He turned back to his employees and snapped at them, "Get back to work."

The mechanics didn't move.

"Go," he barked.

They retreated inside.

"Put some music on," Orzana added.

Soon rap music was blasting from the sound system of an SUV that was being worked on. Orzana closed the distance so that no one would overhear his conversation with the two visitors.

"If you're cops, I want to see badges. If you're not, get the fuck out of here before someone fucks you up worse than that piece of Jap-crap you're driving."

Tough-guy talk. Lock imagined it would work with most people. He wasn't most people. Neither was Ty. "I'm not a cop, and I'm not leaving," he said. "You might not have those two vehicles I mentioned, you might not know about the two people who were taken in Arcadia, but I'm fairly sure you can find out for me."

"I look like a snitch to you?"

"I'm not asking you to snitch, Mr. Orzana," said Lock, as Ty walked to the back door of the Honda and took out the briefcase.

Just inside the auto shop, Lock saw one of the mechanics lift a gun from a steel workbench and rack the slide. "It's a business proposition," he said. "No one's looking to create any unnecessary excitement." He flipped open the briefcase and turned it around. "We want the Chinese kids returned in one piece. Our employer is prepared to pay. This would be a fraction of the final sum."

Despite his best tough-guy face, Lock could see Orzana's pupils widen as he took in the money.

"Cash. Unmarked and untraceable. No questions asked. No follow-up. Or a wire transfer to the Caymans, if you prefer. We have them returned, whoever has them walks away with the money. That's the deal I'm offering. But it has an expiry date of midnight tonight."

Lock turned the briefcase back around and snapped it shut.

Lock and Ty walked down the alleyway. At the end, Lock's Audi was sitting where they had parked it.

"You think he knows where they are?" said Ty.

"If he doesn't, he can find out."

"So, what do we do now?"

"The only thing we can do."

"And that is?"

"We pray the cops are having more luck than we are," said Lock, settling into the driver's seat and slamming the door.

32

The door hinges peeled from the frame as the Blackhawk battering ram made initial contact. The SWAT team's breacher stepped off to the side as his colleagues poured in, weapons raised, and ready to fire.

"POLICE! POLICE!"

A crowd began to gather on the sidewalk. Additional LAPD patrol cars blazed their way down the block, officers jumping out to establish a perimeter.

More SWAT filtered rapidly down each side of the house, joining the secondary entry team stationed at the rear. The numbers were overkill, designed to send out a very firm message to the kidnappers.

Inside the living room, four body-armored SWAT officers froze in place as Pony emerged from the bedroom, red-eyed and bleary. He put his hands in the air, offering no resistance, as red laser sights danced across his chest.

The lead officer took him down to the floor, pinning a knee hard into the small of his back as he cuffed him.

"Check the bedroom," he said.

Two officers stepped over Pony, returning a few moments later to deliver the bad news.

"Clear, Sarge."

The lead officer turned his attention back to Pony, hauling him up to his feet, and getting in his face. "Where are they?"

"I don't know what you're talking about," said Pony.

He was scared but trying not to show it. Being arrested didn't worry him. Or not in the way regular people would think it should. He might catch a beating from the cops. That was no big deal. He regarded that as an occupational hazard.

No, what worried him was what lay on the other side of the arrest. Jail. The suspicion that he might be marked down as a *chivato*, or informer.

"Yeah, you know who I'm talking about, the two Chinese kids you and your buddies jacked in Arcadia."

Pony sucked his teeth. "I don't know shit, and I'm not talking to no *pinche hura*."

"We'll see."

Two more SWAT officers filtered back into the living room. "He's it."

The sergeant turned his attention away from Pony. "Take up the floorboards."

Pony tried to struggle free. "Hey, this is my home, *hura*."

"The walls too," the sergeant added, his eyes on Pony. "Get some sledgehammers. Punch through every goddam wall in this shit hole. Make sure he's not hiding anything in the cavities."

Tilting his head back, Pony stared up at the ceiling. "Fuck you."

The sergeant grabbed the back of his neck. "No, I think you'll find it's us that are going to be doing the fucking until those two kids are back home safe. So, when you speak to your attorney, make sure he feeds that back to whoever's picking up his tab."

"Hey, Sarge."

The sergeant turned towards a uniform who had walked in from the bedroom with a pair of silk pajama bottoms. The uniform had already placed them in a clear plastic evidence bag.

"These match the description of what the female vic was wearing."

"Oh dear. Looks like your day just went from bad to worse," said the sergeant.

Pony shrugged. "Do what you gotta do."

33

There was a swimming pool. In movies or TV shows in which someone was kidnapped and held for ransom, Emily had never seen them being given access to a swimming pool. The sudden upgrade in their accommodation was surreal and unsettling all at the same time. Although that might have been down partly to whatever pills they had been given before they were hustled into the SUV and driven here.

The house was all on its own on a hillside. She couldn't be sure, but she thought she had glimpsed the ocean, far off in the distance, as they drove up to it. She had taken peeks at the digital display on the dashboard. They had travelled for almost two hours. Definitely west, if she had seen the ocean, but she wasn't sure if they had come north or south.

They had been on freeways, she knew that much. But then they had turned off the freeway and the roads had become quieter and quieter until they had arrived here.

The house was big and modern. A rich person's house.

They were led inside. The tape was cut away from their wrists. Their legs were freed.

One of the men who'd ridden in back with them had taken them into the kitchen. A meal was laid out. Noodles and chicken. Normally she wouldn't have eaten anything like that, but she was starving. So was Charlie, judging by the way he wolfed it down.

The man gave Charlie a beer. She was given a Coke.

She gulped down the Coke without a thought to it being spiked. If they wanted to give them something to knock them out, they didn't need to hide it.

She studied the man feeding them. He was big and muscular with a lot of tattoos. But she didn't find him scary in the way she had found Princess scary. He seemed like a man who was simply doing the job that had been assigned to him. Like one of the bodyguards her father sometimes used on business trips.

As she finished her drink, she got up the courage to speak. "When can we go home?" she said.

The man looked at her, as if surprised she could speak. Or speak English. "Soon," he said.

Charlie picked up his empty beer can. "Hey, can I get another of these?"

The man glared at Charlie. Emily wished he'd stayed quiet.

"Please," said Charlie, unable to keep the hint of sarcasm out of his voice.

The tension of the ride here was back. Emily could feel it.

The man walked to the fridge. He grabbed a bottle of beer from a shelf and closed it again. He opened a drawer and rifled around for a bottle opener.

He popped the top, walked over to Charlie with the bottle, and just as Charlie put his hand out, the man smashed the bottle over Charlie's head.

Emily screamed. She couldn't help herself. The violence had been so sudden, like a storm that whipped up from nowhere.

Charlie went down on one knee, hands raised in a plea for the man to stop.

"Please," said Emily, putting herself between them. "Stop."

The man stared at her, grabbed a dish rag, and threw it at her. She pressed it into Charlie's head where the bottle had opened up a cut.

She leaned down next to him. "Just don't say anything else, okay?" she whispered.

Charlie nodded.

She looked down at the dish rag as blood seeped through. Outside, sunlight sparkled off the surface of the pool.

34

L ock's Audi pulled up in front of the house. Apart from the broken-down door and the yellow crime-scene tape across the driveway there was no lasting evidence that the place had been raided only a few hours before.

"Goddammit, we were only three blocks away from here," said Ty, scanning the street.

As soon as they had gotten the address Lock had known that his friend would beat himself up: he'd been so close to the kidnap victims without having been able to save them. Lock wouldn't have expected anything less from him. It was part of what made him a good partner. It was business, but it was also personal. Not so personal that he got careless, but enough that he went above and beyond.

"Three blocks. Might as well have been three miles," said Lock.

A dark blue Lexus sedan pulled up behind them. Li Yeng got out. He looked nervous as he walked over to meet them. Lock didn't blame him. They were a long way from the multimillion-dollar mansions of Arcadia, never mind Beijing or Shanghai. Not that those had proven much safer than the hard-bitten streets of East Los Angeles.

Lock and Ty shook Li's hand.

"The police told me that they maybe only missed them by an hour or so. Maybe less," said Li.

"They're positive that this is where they were being held?" Lock asked.

"They found some clothing inside," said Li.

"It's not great, but this may not be the worst outcome in the world," said Lock.

"What do you mean?"

Lock paused. He needed to be careful about how he phrased this. "They could have found them here. But not in the way we'd want."

Li was smart enough to fill in the blanks. "Dead?" said Li.

"Yes. I know it's not much of a silver lining, but it's something. Sometimes in a raid like this, if the victims are present, they can be used as hostages. All kind of things can go wrong."

Li nodded. "I take your point."

"If they've been moved, it's almost certainly because the kidnappers want to keep them alive," said Ty. "If they want them alive that's because they want to make a deal."

"But no one's been in touch," said Li.

"We've put out some feelers," said Lock. "Made sure they have a contact point and know that we're amenable to a negotiation. That's okay, right?"

"Yes, of course," said Li. "If we can resolve this peacefully then we will. So, who exactly have you spoken to?"

Lock brought him up to speed with their visit to the chop shop, and their discussion with Noah Orzana.

"This man, he's involved?" Li asked, when Lock had finished.

"Maybe. Maybe not. But with his record and connections he'll be able to feed back the information to the people who are. Now, what about this kid they found here?" Lock said.

They'd already had their own update via Galante's sources but Galante had been a little vague. One person had been taken into custody. A young gang member the cops had placed at the crime scene in Arcadia. But, as expected, he wasn't talking.

His silence was the least surprising development so far. Gang members didn't talk. Period. Even the merest suspicion that they had ratted someone out was enough to get them killed.

HALF A BLOCK DOWN, the Red Tiger watched as Li stood talking with the two men he'd hired. This was where Emily had been taken. This was the house the police had raided.

As the Red Tiger studied Li standing next to his fancy car, he felt nothing but pure, white-hot rage. How could this have been allowed to happen? Emily, taken by common criminals. Still out there, alone and no doubt terrified.

At first, he had wondered if there was something deliberate in this. If it might have been arranged as a way of throwing him off the trail. Sadly, it wasn't. He didn't believe so anyway.

It was just one of life's cruel, random ironies that it would happen now, when he was so close.

Or maybe not. Perhaps Fate had played a part in this.

After all, he was here. A man not only capable of finding her, but a man prepared to do what others would not.

He studied the *gweilo*, Lock, a man who was like him in many ways. Once he caught a scent, he would stay on its trail. And that was all the Red Tiger needed.

LOCK STEPPED over the splintered door and into the house, Ty two steps behind him. Li stood outside.

"Should we be doing this?"

Lock and Ty kept walking. Li followed them in.

The place was a mess. The trash can from the kitchen had been emptied on the living room floor. The couch was still turned over. So was a coffee-table. It lay on its side, one leg broken, in the corner.

"Shouldn't there be an officer here?" said Li, taking in the mess.

Ty looked at him. "What for?"

"I don't know. To guard the place. It's a crime scene."

"They'll have gathered whatever they wanted before they left. The crime-scene tape is there for effect mostly," said Lock. "They'll have called a landlord to secure the place, but you know how that goes in neighborhoods like this."

Ty moved towards the kitchen, scanning the scene as he went. "What would they do with something like this in China?"

"If someone from a family like this was kidnapped? They'd find whoever did it and execute them."

"And if it was someone from a regular family?" said Ty, pointedly.

"The same," said Li. "Kidnapping's a very serious crime."

Lock and Ty exchanged a look. It was obvious that neither of them was buying Li's answer. Not the second part of it anyway.

Lock stopped next to a framed picture hanging on the wall that had somehow survived the SWAT tornado that had swept through the place. It showed a couple of young kids, maybe nine or ten, in Little League baseball uniforms. Lock guessed one had to be the kid whose house this was. He studied it.

Ty came over and stood next to him. "What you thinking?" he said.

"The kid they arrested, there's no way he's going to talk to the cops, right?"

"Correct," said Ty.

Lock ran a hand through his hair, fingertips worrying over an old scar. "But we're not the cops."

"Not sure that's how he'll see it. Not sure the LAPD would appreciate us getting into the middle of this either."

"Not a problem," said Lock. "We're not."

"So how would we offer him a deal if we don't speak to him?" said Li.

Lock dug out his cell phone. He tapped on Carmen's office number. "Everyone's entitled to legal representation, right?"

35

K eep your mouth shut. Wait for the attorney who will be provided for you. Take what you have coming. If you're confused go back to rule one: keep your mouth firmly closed.

Those were the rules that Pony planned on following. Just like he had all the other times he'd been arrested.

This was hardly his first rodeo. By now he was intimately acquainted with all that the criminal justice system in the State of California had to offer. Arrest, detention, trial, incarceration, release and probation were simple inconveniences. Shotcaller had told him to think of them as operating costs, the price of doing business.

However, this go-round was different in two respects. The law would treat him as an adult. And kidnapping was a much more serious offense. Throw the word "conspiracy" into the mix, and he knew he could be looking at a solid dime. Ten years inside. And not just any old ten years. Ten prime years.

The idea scared him. He wouldn't let it show in here, in this jail cell that was designed to hold twelve men but currently held sixteen. He wouldn't let it show to the lawyer the gang would send him. No one could ever know the dread he was feeling. But it was there, right in the pit of his stomach, growing like a tumor.

Pony sat on the edge of the top bunk he had secured for himself, legs dangling over. He rubbed at his wrists, rolled his neck, trying to release the tension from his body.

There was movement out on the walkway. Two county deputies, one of them female, were walking in a new arrival. No matter what the female deputies looked like, their presence always got a reaction. Guys would hoot and holler, and some would wander in back and masturbate, staring at the deputy as she walked past.

This time was different. The initial shiver of excitement was the same. But as the deputies passed each cell, the whooping and cat calls quickly fell away to a whisper.

It told Pony one thing. Whoever they were walking in was heavy. A big deal. A gangster. Someone who commanded the rarest of commodities in a zoo like this: silence.

With what felt like a strange inevitability, they stopped directly in front of Pony's unit. He didn't have a view of the new arrival from where he was. Instead he watched the reaction of the other inmates who could see him.

The vibe was what Pony imagined a lion enclosure would feel like when the rear gate was opened and a huge wild male, fresh from the savannah, padded in to take his place among those that had been born in captivity and had never had cause to kill their own food.

There was a palpable and very real shift in body language. Eyes were cast down, either to the floor, a book or a magazine—one of the anomalies of jail Pony had picked up on was that, without access to their screens, people craved old-school paper. Jail was like a time machine where time didn't just stop, it rolled back a few decades.

One of the deputies made the call, and the door into the unit rolled open. The new arrival walked in, hands still cuffed behind his back. The door rolled closed. With his back to it, he pushed his hands through the slot. A deputy took off the cuffs. They left.

This time, as they walked back down the gangway, the shouts and hollers started up again, full-throated.

"Hey, what's your name, sweetness?"

"Come on in here, Mamacita. I got something for you."

The new arrival moved with a deliberate slowness to the back of the unit, and Pony got a look at him. He was early thirties, a huge mountain of a Latino with serious ink, and some Zapata-styled facial hair.

Something about him was familiar to Pony. Had they met? He didn't think so. Maybe it was that he had met men like this before. Real MS-13 gangsters.

Suddenly, as the man approached Pony, he felt very small. The guy was huge. Block-the-sun big. Only six feet, if that, but three hundred pounds.

The man lying on the bottom bunk opposite stood, swiftly snatching up his belongings, and vacating what was prime real estate. The giant took his place, easing himself down into a horizontal position, hands behind his head,

Without thinking, Pony caught his eye. The giant stared at him. Pony tried to hold eye contact for a second, just long enough to show he wasn't a punk but hopefully not so long that it would be read as a challenge. He found himself unable to break the man's gaze. It was like there was a line between their pupils, a tractor beam drawing him into a void.

"What the fuck you looking at?" said the giant.

Pony swallowed. He looked away. He flipped his legs back up and lay down on his bunk.

His heart was racing. He could feel it in his chest.

Movement. The giant was getting up. Pony scooched himself so that his back was to the wall. His hand felt under the blanket for the shank he'd taken from a bunk while its owner had gone for a shower.

He'd use it, if he had to. Damn straight he would.

The giant was moving towards him. His head loomed over the edge of the bunk. He stared at Pony.

Pony's hand tightened around the weapon. It wasn't much, a piece of melted-down plastic with a razor blade. More for slashing than stabbing and therefore not the tool for taking down a man twice his size. But it was all he had.

The giant's face relaxed into a smile. He reached out a fist. "Chill, little homie. We good."

It was a sensation of relief like he had never felt before. He returned the smile. He let the shank fall back into the fold of the blanket.

He withdrew his hand and bumped the giant's fist. The giant's smile grew into a grin. His eyes crinkled with warmth.

"You're Pony, right?"

"Yeah, dude, that's me."

"Cool," said the giant, conjuring a knife into his hand from the sleeve of his loose jail smock.

Before Pony had the chance to so much as scream, the giant's arm came up and fell, the point of the knife punching into Pony's chest. It felt like a blow, a heavy punch, no more than that. It was only the metallic flash, and the spray of blood that told the real story.

There was a sucking sound as the giant rested an open palm on Pony's chest and yanked out the blade. He lifted his arm three more times as Pony flailed helplessly on the bunk, the blanket growing sticky with blood.

His vision began to tunnel. Darkness folded in around him. The last thing he was aware of was the soft feeling of relief edging out the fear and panic. His eyes remained open as the darkness became complete.

36

"We need to bounce."

Princess tugged at Joker's sleeve. They were standing in the middle of the living room, a breeze whipping in from the front door. Joker stared at the post-raid chaos but didn't move. It was if he couldn't believe it had all unraveled so fast.

"How did they know?" he'd asked her.

It was as much as she could do not to slap him across the face. "We used his bank cards, dummy," was the best she could manage. "You think they wouldn't notice that? They have cameras on all those machines now."

The irony was that, rather than them being arrested, Pony had been snatched up. One more person to wish them dead. Which was why they needed to grab what they'd come for and get the hell out of there, and fast. Before the cops or, worse, one of their own noticed the car outside.

According to the news reports, it was only by sheer chance that the cops had missed the two kidnap victims: they could have swept down when Shotcaller and his buddies had been there to pick them up.

Joker was still standing there, rooted to the spot. Like some kind of *pendejo*, which literally meant a single pubic hair but was commonly used to describe an idiot.

She walked into the bedroom, found a bag, and started throwing clothes into it. She did that until it was bulging.

They had to split. Now. Every second their car was left out front was a second they couldn't afford.

Joker had moved into the kitchen. He was drinking a glass of water. She snatched it from his hand and dropped the glass on the floor. It shattered.

He stared at her like she was crazy. "What you do that for?"

"What you do that for?" she sing-songed back at him. "We have to go. Like now."

"Where? Where are we going to go?"

"Anywhere. Somewhere they won't find us. I don't know. Arizona. Colorado. Oregon. We have the money to get started somewhere else."

He didn't look convinced. She wasn't sure she was getting through to him.

"This is it," she said, digging out a bunch of fresh fifty-dollar bills and fanning them in front of him. "This is our one shot."

"Let me go get some clothes."

She grabbed his wrist as he turned. "I already did that. Anything you need we can buy when we're out of here. We'll need to switch the car too."

"What about Pony?" he asked. "Don't we owe him?"

"He'll be fine," said Princess. "They know this wasn't on him. They'll take care of him."

She didn't want to tell Joker that Pony was dead. She'd been sent that news a few minutes ago, with a warning that they'd be next if they didn't get in touch with Shotcaller and make things right. Like that was possible. She knew that as soon as the others found them they'd be as dead as Pony. Only it wouldn't be as quick. Shotcaller and the others would be looking to send a message. Their deaths would be slow and torturous.

"I don't like this. I don't like running away. Leaving Pony behind to face the music."

"We need to get out of here."

Every minute that passed came with an increasing level of danger. Almost certainly someone had let Shotcaller know they were here. He, or one of the others, would be on his way. If they were caught there would be no escape. At least if they were in the car they had a chance if someone saw them. Right now they were sitting ducks.

"I dunno," said Joker, nudging an empty beer bottle with his toe.

"What is there to know?"

She was losing patience with him.

"Pony wouldn't bail on us like this."

Princess took a deep breath. "Pony's dead."

"What? What do you mean?"

She pulled up the text message and handed her phone to Joker, so he could see for himself.

She watched his expression cloud.

"We're next if we don't bounce. Like right now."

"Okay," said Joker.

Finally, thought Princess. She nodded at the bags. "Grab that one. I'll get the other."

"But where are we going to stay?"

She felt a fresh wave of exasperation. "I don't know. We'll figure it out. The main thing is that we're not here."

He grabbed the bag. "Okay, let's hit it."

She picked up the other. Their two lives didn't amount to much in the end. The contents were easily thrown together. But they'd amount to even less if they hung around.

"We going to be okay?"

Princess squeezed out a reassuring smile. What was it with boys like Joker? They came off tough, but deep down they could be real pussies. "We'll be better than okay. I promise."

A rat-a-tat-tat knock at the front door. The kind of knock that might sound casual on a regular day, but right now carried all the threat of someone leaping out of a closet in the dead of night.

They both froze in place. Princess felt a sudden surge of raw fear. Her nerves pulsed. Her stomach did a back flip.

They were here. Sooner than she'd expected. She stared at Joker with something approaching hate. All these minutes she'd spent trying to talk him round. They could be out on the road by now, merging into the vast ocean of cars and people.

She nodded silently towards the back of the house. It was the longest of long shots, but perhaps they could sneak out that way, climb the fence and make a run for it.

It had to be a better option than sitting here and becoming living, breathing—no, make that living, screaming autopsy practice for some crazy MS-13 *sicario*. Princess knew what they did to traitors.

Joker just stood there. Not moving. She wanted to slap him. But he wasn't even worth that.

She told herself to calm down. Maybe it wasn't who they thought it was. Maybe it was cops, come back to check on the scene. Or perhaps it was a delivery. Or some kind of religious person. If it was, she'd gladly leap into their arms, beg for salvation and a place to hide.

Princess walked swiftly over to the window. She pulled back the edge of the blind, trying to get an angle on the stoop.

No one was there. She scanned the street. Their car was still parked out front where they had left it. Everything appeared normal. Or what passed for normal in this neighborhood. She had a sudden unwelcome flashback to the streets of Arcadia with its trash-free, pristine sidewalks, and empty corners.

Another noise, this time at the rear of the house, brought her back to the moment. The terror that had ebbed flooded back into her as she heard the door being forced open and heavy footsteps fall onto the kitchen floor.

Joker seemed to snap out of it. He moved to the table, and picked up his handgun, a small snub-nosed revolver Shotcaller had given him that had become his most prized possession.

Princess had a moment of clarity. While he dealt with whoever was in back, she could make a run for their car. She could wait to see if Joker made it out. If he didn't appear, she'd take off.

The thought brought her guilt. Did she have another betrayal in her? She was torn. None of what she had done had brought them here. This was all on Joker. But he was still her friend.

A sudden cry of pain from the kitchen. It died away, then started up again, this time as a plaintive sob. "My wrist. You broke my fucking wrist, dog," Joker wailed.

Princess slowly stepped towards the bag she'd packed. She grabbed for the handles.

What was she thinking? She didn't need extra cargo. She needed to make a run for the door. Now.

"Ching chong, asshole."

Joker again.

The words stopped Princess halfway to the door, the bag abandoned.

Ching chong?

It wasn't Shotcaller who'd just broken Joker's wrist. Or any of his crew. It was someone Asian. Either a cop or maybe someone who'd come searching for Emily and Charlie.

Something approaching confidence returned. One Asian person. That she could handle, even if Joker had crumbled.

Choking sounds from the kitchen. They grew louder. The sound of Joker gasping for air.

Princess turned around, her back to the front door. She took a step toward the kitchen as the gasping grew louder.

She had made her decision. She would stand her ground. What had happened back in Arcadia? The two Chinese kids had made a show of defiance. But it had come to nothing more than a bunch of barking.

This would be the same. She felt in her pocket for a blade. She took another step, her hand closing around the handle.

Joker appeared suddenly in the doorway. Or some version of him did. One of his eyes dangled at cheek level from its socket. The other blinked furiously. His feet danced six inches off the ground.

A man's forearm was closed around his neck, the hand cupping his shoulder. The barrel of a shotgun poked out between Joker's arm and his side. It was pointed straight at Princess. The man's head was pressed cheek to cheek against Joker's face.

He was a large Asian man. Over six feet tall and bulky. Late forties. He was wearing a suit and black dress shoes, like someone who worked in an office.

Joker thrashed some more. The dangling eyeball jiggled off his nose, a tiny mirror of the larger, macabre puppet show playing out less than six feet from her.

His one good eye rolled back in his head. The lid stayed open, but she could see that he had passed out. The man didn't let go. He kept holding Joker off the ground.

Finally, he spoke. His accent was strong, but he spoke in English.

"Lie down," he told her, a jab of the shotgun barrel emphasizing that it wasn't a request so much as an order.

She stared at him. It was like looking down into some black abyss. It was the look Shotcaller sometimes had, only deeper and more malevolent.

She knew what she had to do. She should turn, take her chances. A shotgun blast in her back would finish this, or she would make it outside.

That was what she had to do. Only problem was that she couldn't move. The man's black eyes seemed to pull her into him.

Slowly, Princess lowered herself face down onto the floor. As soon as she was there she knew that she had made the biggest wrong turn of them all.

But it was already too late. Hands cinched plastic ties around her wrist. They snapped tight.

She was rolled onto her side. Joker lay a few feet away, his body convulsing with shock, his hand feeling across his face for the eye that had been popped out.

"You can't leave him like that," Princess pleaded, her question directed to the man's sleek black shoes.

She turned another inch, trying to get a better view of him. He drew Joker's snub-nose gun from a pocket, walked over to him, pressed the gun into the empty socket and pulled the trigger twice.

37

"I have bad news," said Carmen.

"That figures," said Lock, staring at the picture of her that had come up on his phone when she called. He glanced at the two patrol cars sitting outside the house. Ty was busy talking to one of the cops as a small group of people from the block gathered on the sidewalk. Carl Galante had called him and Ty a half-hour before to say that something else had gone down at the house where it was believed Emily and Charlie had been held. Something bad. The body of a young Hispanic man who matched the description of the second male kidnapper. The third kidnapper, the female, was still unaccounted for.

"Yeah, I went down to see if I could speak with the kid they'd arrested, but it's a no-go."

That wasn't too bad, thought Lock. A gang-appointed attorney had likely beaten them to the punch. It was one thing you could count on with criminals: they had their attorney on speed dial. In all probability they would have wanted their attorney to speak with the kid to make sure he didn't say anything.

"Well, it was worth a shot," said Lock. "Let me guess, he already had a lawyer?"

"No," said Carmen. "He's dead."

That was what she had meant by bad news. Lock should have guessed from the way she'd said it. "They saying what happened?" he asked.

"Argument with one of his cellies."

Lock rubbed his temple. Ty was still deep in discussion with the patrol cop. A van pulled up behind the cars: a crime-scene investigator got out and began unpacking their gear.

Arguments happened in jail. They often ended in assault, sometimes in one party dying. All it took was looking the wrong way at someone, and sometimes not even that. A person's mere existence could be enough for someone to throw down on the paint.

It was rarer with gang members. More accurately it was rarer that they came off worst. They tended to be more predator than prey. When they were victims it was usually because they had ended up in close quarters with someone from a rival group. It was something that shouldn't happen but did. The system was way past capacity, which made proper segregation tricky.

"Let me guess. Crip?"

The predominantly African-American Crips and Bloods gangs had an ongoing war against most of the major Hispanic gangs in Los Angeles and beyond. They vied for the same territory and drug markets. As the city's racial demographics had shifted, so had the face of organized crime.

"That's what I figured. But Galante asked around. The dude who stabbed him was an MS-13 OG."

OG stood for original gangster, and was a term applied to an older gang member with rank. They didn't necessarily have to be one of the founding members, so much as someone who had stuck around long enough to earn senior rank. The theory behind it was simple. Only the best, most durable and luckiest gang members survived long enough to earn OG status.

The kid who'd just been shanked was more the rule than the exception. Most gang members' luck ran out long before their thirtieth birthday. In the crime trade, forty was a venerable age, the equivalent of a seventy-year-old still going strong in a regular profession.

Lock reflected on the news. "So, they really didn't want him talking."

"Or," said Carmen, "he messed up."

"Using the bank cards?" suggested Lock.

"Could be that, or something else. Maybe they didn't like the fact he went out to steal some cars and came back with two bodies."

One thing was for sure. Pony wasn't about to provide any answers as to what had sealed his fate. Not to Carmen. Not to Lock. Not to anyone.

His death gave Lock no measure of satisfaction. Looking around the block from where he stood, Lock figured that growing up there made a kid's journey into a gang if not inevitable then certainly likely. Some people, like Ty, could escape their circumstances, but it took a lot more determination than most kids possessed not to be sucked into a gang.

"What about Orzana? Any word?"

Lock had kept Carmen and Galante up to speed with his and Ty's visit to the chop shop and his offer to Orzana. "*Nada*," said Lock. "But I wasn't expecting to hear anything this fast."

Ty had wrapped up his conversation with the patrol and had moved down the block to talk with some residents, at least one of whom, a teen mom with a kid in a stroller and one in her arms, seemed to be getting unusually chatty. Ty could offer something in return for information that the cops couldn't. Something that pretty much anyone could understand. Cold, hard cash.

Carmen didn't say anything to that. There wasn't much to say. Finally, she said, "You think they'll be okay?"

"You mean are we going to get them back safe?"

"Yeah, that, and . . ."

Lock knew immediately what she was asking. Carmen had herself been abducted and held captive. Not so long ago. The ordeal didn't end when you were rescued or freed. In some ways that was merely the end of the first stage. Carmen, with Lock's support, was still talking to a therapist about the experience and its aftermath. No doubt that was why she was so eager to see this case resolved. A crime always hit closer to home when you had also been a victim.

"I think the first job is to get them back to their family. We can work on the rest from there."

TY OPENED the passenger door and got in.

"Anything?" said Lock.

"Yeah, but I don't know what the hell to think about it."

"Run it past me."

Ty took a deep breath and exhaled slowly.

"This must be good," said Lock.

"Don't know if good's the right word," said Ty, flattening two huge hands on the dashboard. "Lady I spoke with saw something."

Lock waited for him to continue.

"She was walking past when she heard the two gunshots from inside."

So far that was nothing earth-shattering. It tallied with the information the LAPD had been willing to share: one male homicide vic with what looked like two gunshot wounds.

"Then she saw someone come out."

That had to be the perp. But Ty's delivery told Lock there was some kind of twist in the tale here.

"She get a good look?"

"She did, but that wasn't all."

Ty paused for dramatic effect. He lived for stuff like this.

"You going to tell me what it was or am I going to die of old age?"

"He had the girl with him. Y'know, the third perp from the kidnap. Lady says her street name is Princess."

"Good work," said Lock. They'd share the information with the LAPD, but not now and not here where people might see them. It was never a good idea to look like you were too close to those who many people in a neighborhood like this regarded as the enemy. "And the shooter?"

"Late forties, early fifties, five ten, five eleven, two hundred pounds. No tats that she could see. Cat was wearing a suit and tie."

So far, so predictable, thought Lock. The age alone suggested a professional or at a minimum someone who was trusted to take on such a task. Add in the way he was dressed and that supported the likelihood he was a pro. Run-of-the-mill gunmen didn't show up to work in a suit and tie.

"But that's not the best part," said Ty. "The dude wasn't Latino. He was Asian."

38

A s the Audi sped up the on-ramp onto the 5, Lock called Li Yeng. He didn't pick up. That suited Lock. For what he needed, it was better that he left him a message.

"This is Lock. There have been one or two fresh developments. I don't believe it would be the best idea to discuss them over the phone. We need to meet as soon as you're available."

Lock wasn't lying exactly. He just wasn't being entirely truthful. He could have let Li know what was going on with a phone call, or in a voice message. But he wanted to be looking at his face when he told him about the sudden appearance of a well-dressed Asian man dragging a female gang member out of a house where her buddy had just been capped.

"What you think?" Ty asked.

Lock's eyes narrowed as a rare patch of Los Angeles cloud cleared to reveal a blinding shaft of sunlight. "I think we could be sharing this investigation with someone else, and I don't like it."

"I feel you," said Ty.

When the client was this wealthy it wasn't unheard of for them to hire several private organizations or operatives. Lock had no objection. After all, he had already sub-contracted part of the investigation to Carl Galante. However, etiquette dictated that all parties were made aware of the others. Not only was it good manners, it prevented anyone stepping on anyone else's toes.

This, however, went a little beyond that. Lock rarely shared investigations with someone who was willing to perform executions in cold blood, regardless of how much the victim needed to take a bullet.

At the same time, it was important they didn't jump to conclusions, even if there was only a single obvious conclusion to reach.

Lock's cellphone rang. It was Li. His message had done the job.

"Li," said Lock. "Thanks for returning my call."

"Of course. You said you had some news. It's good, I hope."

"I do have news, but it would be better if we sat down face to face."

There was hesitation at Li's end. It might not mean anything. But if he had hired someone else, and he'd heard what had just happened, it might be that he wanted to avoid an awkward face-to-face with Lock.

"I'm a little pressed for time.Mr. Yan is about to land at Van Nuys and I'm here to meet him."

Ty, who was listening on speaker, shot Lock a thumbs-up.

"That's perfect," said Lock. "We can meet you there. We can give him a full briefing in person as to where we are."

Before Li could argue, Lock continued, "We'll see you there in thirty."

It was moments like this that justified the extra money he had spent on this particular vehicle. He pressed down on the gas pedal, and it surged forward.

∼

LI YENG CLIMBED the steps of his boss's factory-new Gulfstream G650ER. A steward greeted him at the door, and led him back to where Emily's father, Chow Yan, was sitting at a conference table in the middle of a call. Chow Yan gestured for him to take a seat oppo-site, and abruptly wrapped up the call.

He stared at Li across the polished walnut table, a custom addi-tion to an aircraft that had already cost over sixty million dollars. Li could feel a storm coming. There was nothing in the world more precious to his boss than his daughter, and to a slightly lesser degree his nephew, Charlie. His journey here was evidence of that. Chow Yan hated being out of his country. He only ever traveled when it was absolutely necessary, and never, in all the time Li had known him, took vacations.

Like many of China's business elite and newly wealthy, Chow Yan was ever fearful of what he would return to if he left his empire. China wasn't like America. The business climate was subject to the whim of the Party, and so was everyone who operated in it. The polit-ical sands were constantly shifting, and only unwavering vigilance allowed people like him to remain standing.

Li looked down as Chow stared across the table at him. The obvious question, the only question, sat between them, unanswered: *How could Li have allowed something like this to happen?*

It was a question to which Li had given a lot of thought. On the one hand it was a seemingly random crime that couldn't have been anticipated. Crimes of that nature didn't happen in places like Arca-dia. On the other, if Charlie had stayed at home, and not gone out flaunting his wealth in such an obvious way, he would never have come to the attention of the kidnappers.

Li could have been stricter. He should have told Charlie to curb his partying, and perhaps, as he knew Emily had suggested, employ a less obvious display of riches than a Lamborghini. But it was doubtful that Charlie would have listened. And, if Li had pressed the point, he might have complained to his mother, who in turn would have complained to the man now glaring at him from across the table.

No. If anyone, apart from the criminals themselves, bore responsi-bility for this, it was Chow Yan's nephew. But how could he say that?

Charlie was family, and Li was an employee. Worse still, it would look like he was trying to shift the blame.

After much consideration, he decided there was only one path he could take. It wasn't just the most honorable, it was the only path that might possibly allow him to retain some measure of respect in the eyes of the man who had been his mentor.

Li folded his hands in his lap and looked up. "This is my fault. I accept complete responsibility for what has happened. It was my job to look after them, and I failed."

Chow Yan said nothing. Li hadn't expected he would. All that mattered was that Li had accepted whatever blame there was to accept. The idea that a man like Chow Yan would tell Li that he was wrong, and that it wasn't his fault, or that he would try to make him feel better was absurd. Even if he knew the role Charlie had played in his own misfortune, he wouldn't acknowledge that to someone outside the family, and certainly not to someone who worked for him.

"What do we do?" Chow Yan asked. No emotional outburst. No long speech. Just this.

The question lifted Li's spirits. It was the best he could have hoped for. It meant that, regardless of what Chow Yan thought of recent events, he still trusted Li to offer a solution.

Li had also thought about this. He tried to approach it like any other problem: analytically, and without emotion. Shortly after the American, Lock, had called him, Li had learned what had happened at the house where Emily and Charlie had been held captive. The LAPD had informed him that an Asian suspect had been seen fleeing the scene, and asked whether he knew anything about who it might have been. He had told them what he planned to tell Lock. He was as baffled as they were.

"Nothing," said Li. "We do nothing."

Chow Yan shifted in his seat. "And how will that help my daughter?"

Li took a deep breath and told him. Chow Yan listened to him in silence.

OVER THE YEARS, Lock had discovered that the power of asking a question lay in the person's reaction as much as their answer or lack of one. You might not be able to tell if someone was lying, but you sure as hell could gauge their discomfort.

Lock pulled up the Audi beside Chow Yan's Gulfstream. He and Ty got out.

Li Yeng rushed down the aircraft steps toward them. He was clearly flustered. "Unfortunately Mr. Yan doesn't have time to speak with you," he said, before Lock had the opportunity to open his mouth.

"Sure he does," said Lock. "Ty, could you grab the briefcase from the trunk?" Ty opened the Audi's trunk and took out the briefcase full of cash that Li had given Lock. He handed it to Lock. "Thanks."

They started for the stairs.

Li moved in front of him. "He's busy."

"Don't worry, this won't take long," said Lock, side-stepping him.

Rushing to catch up, and prevent Lock stepping onto the aircraft, Li found Ty looming over him. "What's the problem, brother?" Ty asked him. "You worried we're going to tell him something you don't want him to know?"

"Don't be ridiculous."

"Well, then, chill out," said Ty, clapping a hand on Li's shoulder.

Li trailed Ty up the stairs and into the aircraft where Lock was making a beeline for Chow Yan. Li squeezed hastily past Ty to catch up with Lock. By the time he did, Lock had his hand out in greeting.

"Mr. Yan, I'm Ryan Lock. This is my business partner, Tyrone Johnson. I'm sorry we've had to meet under such trying circumstances."

Chow Yan shook Lock's hand, but looked past him to Li as if to say, *Why am I dealing with the hired help when I pay you to do that?*

Lock decided to deal head-on with any question of propriety. "Because of the personal nature of your daughter's abduction, I thought you might appreciate an in-person update."

"I'll have to translate," said Li, his hand resting on Lock's elbow.

Lock turned his head. "I just watched an interview at *Business Insider*. Your boss's English seemed more than passable to me."

Li shot daggers at him. Lock gave him nothing back. This wasn't a time for respecting people's feelings or any kind of corporate pecking order.

He turned his attention back to Chow Yan. "Your daughter and your nephew are in the hands of some very dangerous individuals. I want to get them home safe as quickly as possible."

"So do I, Mr. Lock. So do I," said Chow Yan, motioning for everyone to take a seat. Ty sat across the aisle, his long legs still an obstacle to comfort, even on a private plane. Lock and Li were opposite Mr. Yan.

Lock didn't speak. He allowed the silence to build.

Li started to speak to his boss in Mandarin, no doubt apologizing for the intrusion, but Chow Yan abruptly cut him off.

Mr. Yan's chin fell to his chest. He looked exhausted. There were dark circles under his bloodshot eyes. "Mr. Lock, there is nothing more precious to me in this world than my daughter and, of course, my nephew." He waved a hand at the plush interior of the jet. "I would give up all of this to have her back with me."

Lock believed him. "Then allow us to do our job unhindered," he said.

Li blanched as Chow Yan stared at him, then returned his gaze to Lock. "You've been obstructed in some way?" said Chow Yan.

"Not directly, no," said Lock. "But one development has made us question whether we're being kept entirely in the loop."

"In the loop?" Chow Yan queried.

"Not being fully informed. Can I be blunt?" said Lock.

"Please do."

"Do you have someone else helping you find your daughter?"

Chow Yan's gaze darted to Li. A tell that was as good as a spoken yes in Lock's book.

"What would make you think that?" asked Li.

Ty leaned across the aisle. "Because there was an Asian dude seen taking one of the gang members out of a house where Emily and Charlie had been held."

"Middle-aged, suit and tie, some kind of enforcer by the sound of it," added Lock. "It's an entirely Hispanic neighborhood, which was why we wondered if he might have had some connection to you."

"So does he?" said Ty.

"No, he doesn't," said Li, pointedly. "I didn't know anything about some *Asian* man being at that house until you just told me. Never mind him taking someone."

Lock knew that the emphasis Li placed on the word was there to indicate that, somehow, they were being racist. Lock knew better than to engage with that kind of bullshit.

Chow Yan leaned forward. "Mr. Lock, you are the only people we've hired to help us with this. I give you my solemn word on that. But if you don't trust that we're being entirely honest with you then perhaps we should reconsider our current arrangement."

Lock had anticipated something like that. "Mr. Yan, I'm not for a second questioning your desire to have Emily and Charlie returned safely. But I've worked many kidnap cases, and if they're to be resolved it's vital there aren't any secrets between us and the client. Secrets are what get people hurt."

Chow Yan stared across the table at him. "That we can agree on."

39

The Red Tiger drove one-handed, the Mossberg shotgun resting on his lap, his free hand near the trigger, the hot end of the shotgun pointed at the young Latino woman in the passenger seat.

She was bunched up, knees pulled almost into her chest, her back against the door. Eyes narrowed to slits, she glared at him. For the past hour they'd been driving west and south. Moving in entirely the wrong direction.

Princess had planned on driving east with Joker, away from LA, away from Shotcaller, away from her old life. Only now Joker was dead, executed in cold blood with two shots by the crazy asshole next to her, and all because he couldn't grasp that 'Let's get out here *now*' meant just that. Now. This second. Not two or three minutes later.

She shifted her glare from the barrel of the Mossberg to the man holding it. Who the hell was this guy? He wasn't a gangster. Not like any gangster she'd ever met anyway. Or not here in California. He wasn't a cop either.

Not a cop and not a gangster. More some kind of natural force.

He'd moved through the house like a hurricane, sweeping all before him, including her. She'd never thought she'd live to see the day where she'd be taken by a man without so much as a peep. Today had been that day.

She'd been so shaken by what he'd done to Joker she'd pretty much checked out. Like she was in a daze. It wasn't seeing her friend murdered. It was the way it had gone down. No threats, no warnings, just two smooth trigger pulls. Five pounds of pressure per square inch, applied twice.

Whoever he was, he was on some other level. Which, going by the questions he'd been asking her, was bad news for Shotcaller and the others.

Out of nowhere, he hit the brakes, and steered the car into the breakdown lane. It bumped to a stop.

Was this it?

The road they were on now was quiet, long and straight. You could see the approach of other vehicles long before they got to you. He could have her open the door, get out, then shoot her in the back of the head and be on his way.

Part of Princess was already resigned to it ending like this. In a way it made sense that her joke of a life would finish with this kind of a punchline. Mere minutes away from the chance of a new life, a fresh start, only to die face down by the side of a highway, her brains spilling out of her skull.

The man looked at her. "Call your friends. Tell them you want to meet," he said.

"They're not my friends, and the next time they see me they'll kill me."

Slowly he raised the shotgun so it was pressed into the side of her neck. "Then give me your phone."

"Okay, I'll do it." She moved her head to the side. "You mind?"

He lowered the Mossberg. She fumbled in her pocket, pulled out her cell phone, thumbed down to the number she had for Shotcaller. She hoped it still worked. Shotcaller changed his number every few weeks and Pony was usually the one who gave them the new number.

It was ringing.

He picked up almost immediately. "Why ain't you dead yet, bitch?"

She hadn't had any time to think about what she would say to him. She knew that if she came straight out and asked to meet he'd be suspicious, and might not go for it. Or he'd be on his guard and, no matter how much she resented the man who'd murdered Joker, she didn't hate him any more than she hated Shotcaller. There wasn't enough real history between them for her to have developed that kind of feeling.

She didn't say anything. Let Shotcaller fill the silence.

"You still there?"

"Yeah, I'm here." She tried to gather up a lump in her throat. She needed the hitch in her voice that suggested she'd been crying or was about to.

Her sounding scared would be like throwing a bucket of blood off the coast of Catalina. All you had to do was wait for the sharks to pick it up.

"It was Joker's idea to take the money," she said. "I swear."

At the other end of the call—nothing. She felt bad blaming Joker, even though it was the truth.

"But you went along with it," said Shotcaller.

"I've made it right," she said.

Shotcaller laughed. "How? How you done that?"

A deep breath. She'd already weighed what she was about to say. Now the moment had arrived, the words were harder to get out of her mouth than she'd anticipated. It wasn't the lie that bothered her as much as the betrayal.

"I took care of him."

She had chosen the phrase carefully. *Taken care* rather than *killed*. No one in their world would ever say 'killed' during a phone call. There was no ambiguity in the word.

"Bullshit."

The disbelief was genuine. That worked for her. Shotcaller would know that there was no way she would choose to murder Joker. And, of course, he'd be correct. But then—

"You don't believe me then go take a look for yourself. He's at the house."

There was a rustling sound as Shotcaller covered the phone with his hands. She could hear him barking orders at someone in the background. He was verifying what she'd said. He came back on the line. "So?" he asked coldly. "You want a medal?"

"No. I wanted to make things right between us. I don't want to live my life always looking over my shoulder."

Another silence.

"I have the money he took. I can bring it to you."

Now she had laid the ground, he would go for it. If she had offered to meet straight off the bat he would have been suspicious.

He would still want her dead. She knew that much. But she needed his guard lowered, even if it was only a little.

Who knew? Maybe she could find a way to play off the two men against each other. She didn't know how that would work. Not yet. But it had to be an option. Two stone-cold killers who both wanted the same thing. It had possibilities.

"You'll bring it to me, huh?"

"No, meet me somewhere. Somewhere public. With people."

He made a cooing sound. "You think I'm gonna do something to you, Princess?"

"I don't want to take the chance."

This was good. If she had any kind of a play she had to be close. And, crucially, Shotcaller had to be off guard. Something that wouldn't happen if they were in a crowded public place.

"I give you my word. Come with the money, and we can talk."

She hesitated.

"Okay," she said. "Where?"

"I'll text you," he said. "But if you don't show ..."

40

Lock's cell phone rang as he stepped from the Gulfstream. He recognized the voice, if not the number. It was Orzana, a.k.a. El Mecánico.

"You found me a car yet?" said Lock.

"No, but I have located the other packages you were interested in."

Lock turned, Ty at his shoulder. They walked back into the cabin. Lock waved at Li and Chow Yan and sank into the closest seat.

Chow Yan and Li hurried from the back of the aircraft to stand next to him. Lock put his finger to his lips, hoping the gesture of calling for silence was universal.

Chow Yan shifted his weight from one foot to the other, the billionaire tycoon gone, replaced by a concerned father.

"That's good news," said Lock. "What are they going to run me?"

"Ten," said Orzana. "A piece."

Lock didn't miss a beat. "That's absurd."

Chow Yan must have caught enough of the conversation. He half lunged for Lock's cell phone. Ty placed himself between him and Lock, and patted his shoulder as Lock hit the mute button.

"This is what I do," said Lock. "Let me do it."

"But I can pay that. It's nothing."

So much for the hard-headed oligarch, thought Lock.

"Hello? You there?" said Orzana.

Lock unmuted the call. "Give me a second. I didn't realize I was dealing with a bunch of amateurs."

He hit mute again, and shifted in his seat so that he was facing Chow Yan.

"If we take the first offer they'll be suspicious. They'll assume that we either have no intention of paying it or, more likely, that we're working with the cops. It has to be a manageable number."

Chow Yan puffed himself, taking in the luxuriously fitted cabin of the plane. "It's manageable."

"In their mind, not yours. They've pulled a number out of their ass here. It's a test. You accept the first offer and it sends the wrong signal."

"This is my daughter's life we're talking about," he pleaded.

"I know, but to them it's business. That's how we have to deal with it."

"And if you're wrong?" said Li.

It was the question guaranteed to screw a negotiator. Lock wasn't going there. He couldn't allow himself to go there. This was a situation where you couldn't allow yourself to contemplate being wrong. As soon as you did, you were as good as dead.

"The only thing you have to decide is whether or not you want me to handle this," Lock told them. "Yes or no?"

All eyes settled on Chow Yan.

He nodded.

Lock went back to the call. "Ten's too rich. The insurance company won't cover that kind of exposure," he said.

There was a pause. Lock was almost certain that this was the first time the assholes had heard the word 'insurance' in relation to kidnapping.

"So what will they cover?"

"Maximum payout is five hundred K per package," said Lock, deliberately low-balling.

"Get the fuck out of here."

Lock smiled. That was a fast counter. It was a good sign. They had begun the negotiation without Orzana even knowing that was what he was doing.

"What can I tell you? That's the ceiling."

"Then I guess someone will have to cover the excess," said Orzana. "If you don't want them damaged in transit."

Lock said nothing.

"We know you have access to money," Orzana followed up. "A lot of money."

"Maybe we can go higher. Cover it out of our own pocket."

"You'd better," said Orzana.

"Call me back in five," said Lock. "Oh, and before this goes any further, we'll need POL."

"POL?"

Lock suppressed the urge to roll his eyes. Chow Yan and Li were still watching him from a few feet away. "Proof of life."

"What? You mean like a picture with today's *LA Times*?"

Lock swiped a hand over his face. He was going to ask Orzana if he'd ever heard of Photoshop, but he didn't strike Lock as a man who dealt well with sarcasm.

"I was thinking more of a video call. Skype. Facetime. That kind of thing."

"I'll see what I can do, but you're going to have do a lot better than that chickenshit offer. We'll need at least two. Each."

"Call me back," said Lock, killing the call.

"GIVE THEM WHAT THEY ASK FOR."

From Li's agitated body language, Lock could tell that he was not used to seeing his boss like that. Chow Yan stalked up and down the aisle of the plane, his fist pounding into an open hand.

Lock stood with Ty near the exit, and waited for him to settle. "We will, as soon as they decide what they want."

"They told you," said Chow Yan, raising his voice.

Lock gestured for Chow Yan to sit down. Reluctantly, and with a loud sigh, he did so. Lock squeezed in across from him. "This may sound counter-intuitive . . ." said Lock

Chow Yan looked confused. Li provided a quick translation of the phrase into Mandarin, then indicated with a nod that Lock should continue.

". . . but it's important that the kidnappers feel like there's been a process. People in their circumstances get jumpy if you give in too readily. Both parties have to work towards the resolution. But we're very close. We get a phone call, you confirm that Emily and Charlie are alive, we negotiate the final terms and then we make the exchange."

The man opposite him seemed to be aging in front of Lock's eyes. His skin was sallow and the bags under his eyes were growing darker as the minutes ticked by. He spread his hands, palm down, on the table. "Okay," he said. "Do I need to gather the money?"

"No," said Lock. "We'll do it electronically. Guys like these don't like touching cash unless they have to. Cash takes laundering, and laundering cuts into their profit margin."

"And how do we know they'll let my daughter go when they have the money?"

It was a good question. There was no definitive answer. Beyond the initial abduction, the exchange was the tensest part of a kidnap-for-ransom case.

"Leave that to me. We can organize it so that it's as close to simultaneous as it can be."

"I hope you're right about all of this," Chow Yan told him.

So do I, thought Lock. The truth was that there were no guarantees. The only guide was human nature. Or, rather, the worst part of human nature. The part that focused on greed.

Li watched Lock and Ty get into their car, and drive away. When the

Audi was out of sight, he walked back into the plane's cabin. Chow Yan was still slumped at the table. Somehow, rather than giving him hope, the meeting with Lock had deflated him. The phone call between Lock and kidnappers had made the situation real.

Chow Yan looked up as Li approached.

"If this works, it's better," said Chow Yan.

Li agreed. A ransom payment for their return was simple. There was less to go wrong. But what they had talked about still hung in the air.

"What about the Red Tiger?" Li asked.

"What about him?"

"He's still here."

"So?" said Chow Yan.

Li didn't understand how his boss could be so matter-of-fact. The man they thought might solve this seemed to be nothing more than a minor detail. But he wasn't. How could he be?

"You're not worried about what he might do?"

"The only thing that concerns me is my daughter."

"But what if he finds her first? Before Mr. Lock can make this arrangement."

Chow Yan appeared to take a moment to consider the possibility. "They could be anywhere, and this isn't home. How could he possibly find her here?"

"He's already found some of the people who took her," said Li.

41

They turned onto a fire road. The Red Tiger moved the Mossberg from his lap to shove it between his seat and the door. Out of the girl's reach.

The road surface was too bumpy to risk keeping the barrel pointed at her. All it would take was a deep pothole, and a lapse of concentration on his part, and her innards would be spread all over the inside of the rental car.

He had no intention of harming her. Not unless he had absolutely zero choice in the matter. And not that he wanted her to know that. It was safer, she was safer, if she assumed he was some kind of crazy Chinese psychopath.

She glanced across at him as he moved the shotgun. "Where are we going? Why aren't we staying on the road?"

She held up her phone screen for emphasis, and jabbed a red-polished fingernail at the Google Maps screen. A blue dot showed the address she'd been sent: 17786 Yerba Buena Road. Another dot signified the location of her phone as it inched, pixel by pixel, across the map.

"We arrive on that road, they can see us. This way, they don't."

"But they already know I'm coming."

For a girl with such obvious street smarts, she missed things. It surprised him.

"Yes, they know you're coming. But they don't know that I'm with you."

As soon as the address had arrived, the Red Tiger had done a quick search, pulling up the details of the house from an old sales listing on the Zillow website. Unless it had been remodelled since its last purchase three years ago, it was a six-bedroom, single-story ranch-house set on seven acres of trees. It was positioned near the top of a slope with an excellent 180-degree view of the surrounding area. The closest property was close to a quarter-mile away.

In other words, it was the perfect location to kill someone such as Princess without anyone knowing about it. That also made it the perfect place to stash a couple of kidnap victims out of sight.

The Red Tiger guessed that although the people involved were professionals they wouldn't have all that many multimillion-dollar Malibu homes at their disposal for delicate matters like this, which required a degree of isolation and privacy.

Princess blew a stray strand of black hair out of her mouth. "They'll fuck you up. You know that, right?"

He didn't say anything. There was no need.

"It ain't like you're walking in on me and Joker. They're different."

The road narrowed. A stand of trees closed in on them, branches whipping across the windshield.

"How are they different?" he asked her.

"They're hardcore. Y'know, OG gangsters."

"Gangsters," he repeated.

He'd seen all of the American movies about gangsters living in places like Los Angeles. He found the idea comic. Laughable.

She bristled at the smirk he hadn't managed to keep off his face. "Yeah, gangsters. MS-13, motherfucker."

"You know how many people were killed in my country after Chairman Mao came to power?" he asked her.

"I don't even know what country you're talking about. Who is this Mao dude?"

This Mao dude. His smile broadened. "Two and a half million killed. Another two million committed suicide. *That's* a gangster."

Her eyes narrowed. "So what? You ain't no Mao, or whoever." She lapsed back into her sulk.

The road opened up again. The track evened out a little.

If the satellite view was correct, they would soon reach a rise that lay above the house. He planned on leaving the car there and hiking the rest of the way at twilight. He still didn't know what he was going to do with the girl. She had been part of what had happened, he had figured that much, but he didn't have it in him to punish her, like he had punished her friend.

Was it because she was female? That was part of it. He found it more difficult to hurt a woman than a man.

But that wasn't the only reason. She was around the same age as Ji Chi would be now. She was someone's daughter. He wasn't sure if he could wrench a daughter from someone else, like Chow Yan had done to him. He knew that pain. He had lived with it all these years. He had no reason to wish it upon someone else.

"So, what's up with this anyway?" Princess asked.

"Up with?"

"Yeah, up with. Why are you doing this? You working for this guy?"

"Which guy?" he said.

"You know, their father."

They began the climb to the top of the rise. The car struggled with the steepness of the incline, the engine whining in protest.

"Something like that," he said, as the car rolled to a halt. He put on the parking brake, and got out, taking the Mossberg with him and walking to the very apex of the rise so he could take a look at the ranch-house below.

～

PRINCESS WATCHED HIM GET OUT. He had been careful enough to take the gun with him. But a sunburst glint below the ignition revealed the car key with the rental fob still attached.

Her heart almost stopped when she saw it. All she could do now was sit there, and wait, counting his every step. Halfway up the slope, he turned and looked back at the car.

She made a show of studying her nails, playing the role of a disinterested teenager on the world's weirdest road trip. He turned back, and began to climb again.

He took four more steps. Then five.

She did a quick calculation. As soon as he heard the engine start, he would react. He would be running back down the slope. That would be faster.

How many seconds did she have from that moment. Five? Six?

Would he try to catch the car? Or would he shoot?

A shotgun had a wide spread that could easily catch the rear tires.

What was her alternative? Stay with him?

And what then?

Either his mission, whatever it was, would fail, and she'd be facing Shotcaller. Or it would succeed and she'd be surplus. He hadn't hesitated to kill Joker. Why would he behave any differently with her?

This was her one shot. And it was a gift.

He was almost at the very top of the rise. She leaned over, making sure her hand was on the key.

She pulled her knees up, clearing the gear shift, and scooted into the driver's seat.

She pressed down on the brake pedal, and turned the key. She slammed the transmission into drive, hit the gas pedal, and turned the wheel.

She didn't look back until she'd completed the turn and she was heading back down the dusty, dirty track. Then she allowed herself a single glance in the rear view. He was scrabbling down the slope, the shotgun in his hand.

The car picked up speed. She braced herself for a blast shattering the rear windscreen.

It didn't come.

A fresh peek in the rearview revealed that he had stopped. He was standing, the shotgun at his side.

Two thoughts followed in quick succession. The first: why wasn't he shooting?

The second came almost immediately. He wasn't shooting because a shotgun made one hell of a noise. Especially on a hillside overlooking a canyon.

The final time Princess checked the rearview, he had turned around and was trudging back up the slope.

A FEW MINUTES LATER, as she turned from the fire road back onto blacktop, Princess glanced down at her cell phone. It lit up with an incoming message.

WHERE ARE YOU?

She reached over and powered it down.

Nowhere you'll ever find me.

A perfectly open road stretched out before her. She glanced at the gas gauge. The tank was almost full. More than enough to take her well out of reach of Shotcaller. And this car? It had no link to her.

Unless she drove back into East LA, there was no way they would find her. Not if she stayed careful.

Okay, Joker hadn't made it with her, but it hadn't been her fault. She had tried to tell him there was no more time.

She looked back at her cell phone. Anger rose in her. She powered the phone back up, opened the text and hit reply.

No, she told herself. That was chicken shit.

She hit the call button and waited for the call to connect.

"Yeah, that meeting. I ain't gonna make it. Nice crib, though. Oh, and good luck holding our two friends. Someone's coming for them. In fact, he's outside the house now, watching you, and believe me, he's super-pissed. I gave him all your details too. Where to find you, all that good stuff."

At the other end of the line, Shotcaller started to curse her out.

"Good luck. You're going to need it."

Now, with a feeling of real closure, and a line drawn, she lowered the driver's window and tossed the phone out. She drove east, a smile spreading on her face.

42

S hotcaller looked down at his cell phone. She was bluffing. She had to be. He tried to call back. There was no answer. He tried again with the same result.

What was she talking about? Some guy outside the house?

But he had given her the address. That much was true. She could easily call it into the LA County Sheriff's Department.

He pulled up another number. This call was answered immediately.

"Move them."

The man at the other end began to question him. Shotcaller cut him off.

"Just do it. Now."

43

The automated ranch-house gates of 17786 Yerba Buena Road slid open. A hulking black Suburban barreled through, waved in by two guards toting semi-autos. Gravel sprayed from under the wheels as the driver beat a path to the front of the house.

The instant the Suburban came to a stop, side on to the front door, the rear passenger doors popped open. The driver and front-seat passenger exited. Both were armed, the passenger with the same semi-automatic rifle, and the driver rocking a pistol on his hip.

The main entrance door of the house opened and two men guided Emily and Charlie, blinking, into the sunlight. Their hands were cinched behind their backs with plasti-ties.

The two men hustled them down the steps towards the Suburban. They helped them up into the rear of the vehicle. The front-seat passenger climbed in with them. The doors slammed. The driver got back in, turned the Suburban in a wide circle, and headed out through the open gates.

From arrival to departure had taken less than sixty seconds. The two men on the gate walked slowly back to the house to begin the clean-up. Their task was to remove any trace of its most recent guests in case the LA County Sheriff's Department made an unannounced visit.

44

L ock palmed his cell phone to Ty, who took it, angling the screen so he could get a better look at the pictures. He winced. It wasn't something Lock had seen him do all that often. Like most men who had seen active duty on the frontline, it took a lot to get a reaction from him.

Ty swiped the screen, working his way stoically through the pictures.

"That's some ISIS-level shit right there," said Ty, handing back the phone.

Lock pulled up to the valet stand. He and Ty got out. Lock passed the key fob to the valet with a twenty-dollar bill. "Keep it close. We may not be staying all that long."

"Yes, sir," said the valet.

The two troubleshooters hustled up the red-carpeted stairs of the hotel. A man in livery held open the door for them. They walked into the lobby, and headed to the desk.

"We're meeting with Mr. Chow Yan."

The receptionist lifted the phone and made a hushed phone call. "If you could take a seat for a moment, someone will be with you presently."

As he put the phone down, Lock leaned over the desk and snatched it from his hand. "Excuse me." He held it to his ear. "We're coming up."

He returned the phone to the startled desk jockey. "Which room?"

The receptionist struggled to regain his composure. "It's not our policy to—"

Ty cathedraled his fingers and cracked his knuckles. "The man didn't ask you about hotel policy, he asked what room."

The receptionist hesitated. Lock slid a fifty over the desk with his fingertips. "We're kind of in a rush here."

"Penthouse suite," said the receptionist, the fifty disappearing.

They turned and made for the elevator.

"Remind me never to recommend a principal stay here. Their security sucks," said Lock.

"Word," said Ty.

THE ELEVATOR DOORS opened directly into the suite's private foyer, another hefty tip having secured the attendant's cooperation. Lock knocked at the door.

"He's going to be pissed," said Ty.

"Too bad," said Lock.

The peephole darkened. Lock and Ty stepped back so whoever it was could see them clearly. They could make out a muffled conversation. It sounded like a young woman and a man. Lock couldn't tell if the man was Li or Chow Yan, but the slightly deeper timbre suggested Chow.

The door opened to reveal Miss Po, the attractive young woman, with no visible means of support, who lived opposite Emily and Charlie. Her hair was wet, and she had a fluffy white hotel bath sheet wrapped around her. Her expression hovered halfway between embarrassment and resignation. At least, thought Lock, it wasn't Chow Yan's wife who was the unannounced visitor.

"May we?" said Lock.

Without a word, she held the door open, and he and Ty walked in.

The suite was cavernous and suitably plush. It ran about five thousand square feet and ten thousand dollars a night, two dollars per square foot per night. Miss Po padded away and disappeared into one of the three bedrooms as Lock and Ty walked past the kitchen area and into the lounge.

Chow Yan walked out of one of the other bedrooms. He was wearing trousers but no shirt, his belly spilling in rolls over his belt.

From what Lock knew of *ernai*, mistresses in China tended to focus entirely on money and power. Aesthetics didn't come into it, which was just as well for Chow Yan. He wondered if the tycoon was aware of Li Yeng's closeness to Miss Po. It was something he could deploy, but only if he had to. Right now, his focus was clear. To find out what the hell was going on.

Chow grabbed a white silk-blend dress shirt from the back of a couch and began to put it on.

"Who let you up here?" Chow said, buttoning the shirt, and opening a jewelry box to reveal a pair of diamond-studded gold cufflinks.

Lock tossed the briefcase onto the couch. It slid off. "I'm returning this. It's light the money we gave to one of our associates to get his car fixed. My not invoicing you for our fee more than covers it."

"I don't understand," said Chow.

"The hell you don't."

Chow stared at him.

"Do you remember the last thing I said to you?" Lock asked.

"When we last spoke you were negotiating."

Lock advanced on him as Ty hung back.

"Secrets," Lock said, now within touching distance of Chow Yan. "They get people hurt." He dug out his cell phone, opened the photograph folder, and tapped on the first of the images he'd received an hour before from Noah Orzana.

The image was of a kidney-shaped swimming pool. But the water was not so much azure blue as muddy brown-red. Four men floated in it, face down, limbs splayed out like starfish.

Lock passed the phone to Chow Yan. He looked at the image, his expression shifting instantly from irritation to shock.

He looked up from the cell phone. "Who are these men? Why are you showing me this?"

"They're MS-13 gang members. Or soldiers from a cartel linked to MS-13. Or they're freelance muscle of some kind. It doesn't really matter. What matters is that they work, pardon me, they *worked* for the people who have your daughter and your nephew. Someone killed them and dumped them in the pool of a house between Hidden Valley and north Malibu."

Chow Yan stared at him, disbelieving.

"I know I didn't do it. And I've been around long enough not to believe in coincidences. So that leaves you."

Chow glanced around the suite. "I've been here the whole time."

"That I don't doubt," said Lock, with a glance to the closed bedroom door his mistress had disappeared through. "Interesting coping mechanism, by the way. A shrink would have a field day. Anyway, I'm not suggesting you did this. But you know who did, don't you? Just like you knew when we spoke last who the man coming out of that house in East LA was."

There was a knock at the door. Ty went to answer it, his hand falling to the butt of the Glock riding high on his hip. If Chow Yan had other people on the payroll there was every chance they wouldn't appreciate this unscheduled meeting.

Ty checked the peephole and opened the door. Li Yeng walked in.

"Good, I'm glad you're here," said Lock. "Take a seat."

"What's going on? Have they been back in touch?" Li asked.

"Oh, I almost forgot." Lock reached into his pocket and pulled out the silver button tracking device he'd found planted in the briefcase. He tossed it at Li. "This is yours. It was hidden inside the lining of that."

Li caught it one-handed. He looked sheepish. "I'm sorry."

"You and me both," said Lock. "Yes, they've been in touch. Your boss can bring you up to speed."

Chow Yan said something to Li in Mandarin. He walked over and handed the younger man Lock's phone with the picture of the four dead men floating in the swimming pool. Their conversation continued. It grew heated. Lock couldn't follow it, but he didn't need to know Mandarin to catch the general drift. Dollars to donuts, they were arguing over whether or not to let Lock cut himself loose or tell him some version of the truth.

A minute of rapid-fire back and forth later, Chow Yan held up his hand and Li Yeng fell silent.

"I told you secrets got people hurt," Lock said to them. "Now, I don't know if you care about what happens to your daughter and your nephew. But if you do then you have to cut out all the BS, and be honest with me. Completely honest. Whatever you tell me now stays in this room, but I need the truth. I need to know what's going on here. What's *really* going on."

Chow Yan bowed his head. Finally they glimpsed a real man.

"You're right, Mr. Lock. What you said about secrets, it's true."

Lock walked across and hunkered down so that he was at eye level with him. "So, tell me. I don't want to walk away from this." He glanced back over his shoulder at Ty, who was standing with arms folded. "Neither does Tyrone. Not when two young people are out there at the mercy of these people. But you have to trust us. It's the only way we can help you."

Chow Yan nodded. "I know." He took a deep breath. "Can I ask you something?"

Lock gave a nod. "Go ahead."

"Do you think that, after this, they are still alive?"

The truth worked both ways. Lock knew that. And he guessed that Chow Yan knew it too. He didn't know if this question was a test or not. In a way it didn't matter. All that mattered was that he extended the same respect to his client that he wanted to receive.

"Honestly, I don't know. They won't have taken the deaths of four of their men lightly, I'll tell you that. On the other hand, if they kill them, this will all have been for nothing. Orzana has probably said enough that we could have him arrested. He won't want that. On the other hand, with a good lawyer he'd likely be able to wriggle free."

Chow Yan sat perfectly still, staring at the rug. He seemed to be shrinking inside himself as Lock spoke.

"Let's just say that this guy you hired, the man who did this, he hasn't helped matters."

"I didn't hire him. I wasn't lying about that."

"But you were lying?" said Lock.

"It was . . . What do they call it in your language?" He looked to Li Yeng for assistance.

"A lie of omission," said Li.

"Yes," said Chow Yan. "I didn't lie. But I didn't tell you the whole truth either."

"Then maybe it's time to do that," said Lock.

~

LOCK AND TY watched as Li Yeng ushered an immaculately dressed and made-up Miss Po out of the suite. On the way, she stopped by Chow Yan, and gave him a kiss on the top of the head, almost like he was her grandfather. The gesture ratcheted up the creepiness factor even further, thought Lock, and it was already close to off the chart.

Ty leaned in to him. "This is some weird scene, even by LA standards," he said.

"They're not from LA," Lock reminded him.

"No kidding. We're having to import our weirdness now. Seems like they do that better than us too," said Ty.

Li Yeng walked back into the room and sat down in an armchair opposite. Chow Yan gestured Lock and Ty to seats.

"Miss Po makes me happy. I know you may not understand that. But it's the truth. She listens to me. I can talk to her. Confide in her."

"Never heard doing the nasty called that before," said Ty, with a glance towards the bedroom door.

"Ty," Lock reproached him, as both men sat down.

"Just saying," said Ty.

Silence settled over the room. Chow Yan took a deep breath. Lock hoped that this really was it, that the time had arrived for their client to tell them the truth. He couldn't spell it out any more plainly than he had. The lives of two young people rested on this. If, that was, they weren't already dead, which they very likely might be. Organizations like MS-13 operated on business lines, but when it came to violence, especially violence visited upon them, they didn't always behave like a business. Pride was involved, and they couldn't risk being seen as weak. Someone else killing their members or associates was seen as a direct challenge, and one that was usually met with equal or greater levels of brutality.

That was the circle Lock would have to square. But first he had to know what was going on.

"Allow me to start at the beginning," said Chow Yan.

"That's usually the best place," said Lock.

Chow shifted in his seat. He still seemed to be experiencing some kind of internal struggle. Finally, he appeared to compose himself. He leaned forward, placing his hands in his lap.

"You're aware of the one-child policy in my country?" he asked them.

"We are," said Lock.

"The Party was concerned about over-population. They had the best of intentions. But . . . What's that saying you have in the West about good intentions?"

"'The road to Hell is paved with good intentions,'" Lock offered.

"Yes," said Chow Yan. "Exactly that. When you try to impose your will on human nature it can make things worse rather than better."

Chow Yan snuck a glance at Li Yeng as he spoke. Lock could guess the reason. Criticism of the Communist Party, and its decisions, was risky.

"What does this have to do with your daughter?" Lock prompted.

"After we got married my wife was desperate for a child, but there were problems. We tried everything we could, but with no luck. When families could have more than one child, poor families often allowed the third or fourth to be taken in by someone else. But that had stopped. Except, of course, for little girls."

Lock had a feeling where this was going. "You adopted Emily?"

Chow nodded. "Every family wanted a boy. Girls were often abandoned, or worse."

"So why the big secret?" said Ty, reading Lock's own thoughts. "Lots of kids are adopted. You did a good thing."

"There was more to it than that," said Chow. "Official adoptions were difficult. They took a long time. There were lots of questions. I was starting my business."

"You didn't want the intrusion?" said Lock.

"Precisely," said Chow.

Lock figured he would help his client along. "So, you went through unofficial channels?"

"You have to understand the desperation of wanting a child when you've been told you can't have one. The pain it causes. Especially for women."

Lock's life had never allowed him much time to think about having kids. He wasn't opposed to the idea, and he hoped that, one day, he would have them. Maybe with Carmen, if things worked out between them. But he had never been at the point of needing to bring someone into the world. He could imagine, but not feel, the burning desire Chow was describing. He knew, though, that any great passion often led people to do things they wouldn't normally. Including breaking the law. He guessed that was what was coming next.

"We got the baby home, and we couldn't have been happier. My marriage, it was better than ever. She was a beautiful little girl."

Here came the 'but', Lock said to himself.

"Then we received word that Emily's family hadn't given her up freely."

Ty leaned forward. "What do you mean when you say, 'hadn't given her up freely'?"

Chow Yan swallowed. "I mean she had been taken."

"Abducted?" said Lock.

Chow looked at Li, as if for guidance.

"It doesn't matter what you want to call it. I think we get the general drift."

"I didn't know. I swear to you," said Chow. "It was only later that I found out the circumstances. And by then she was settled with us. She was a happy little girl. She had a family who loved her, my business was doing well, and I could give her a life that she would only have been able to dream about."

Lock didn't blame Chow Yan for his justification of himself. In some ways he was correct. Emily had won the lottery. That didn't change the fact she had a family somewhere. A family who had been robbed of a child. Their only child.

"You've never told her?" Lock said.

"I did my own investigation. Discreetly. It took time to get answers. We had to move carefully. By the time my investigator tracked them down, the mother had died. An accident while she was working in the fields."

In that context the word 'accident' jumped out at Lock but he decided to let it go. Accident sounded convenient under the circumstances.

"And the father?" said Ty.

"He was still alive. We located him, but . . ."

Lock waited. Chow Yan seemed to be struggling to find the words.

"But?" said Ty.

"He was a dubious character. Someone capable of tremendous violence. Emily was still too young to understand. I decided it was better to let her live her life. What she didn't know couldn't possibly unsettle her, and she was doing so well with us."

"This man who was capable of tremendous violence, do you mean the kind of violence I just showed you pictures of?"

"He had tracked us down."

"And the kidnapping?" said Ty.

"A terrible coincidence," said Li Yeng, who had held his own counsel while his boss told them the story of how he had come to be Emily's father.

"Terrible or lucky?" Lock asked.

"I don't follow you. I promise you that those people kidnapping Emily and Charlie aren't in any way connected to what I just told you."

"So you hire us to fix it," said Lock. "But then you have this maniac as backup, ready to do the dirty work. Except you didn't figure on him being quite as reckless as he's been."

"And you weren't lying when you told us that you hadn't hired anyone else," said Ty.

Chow Yan gave an uncomfortable shrug of agreement.

"But you weren't telling the truth either," said Lock, sharply.

"I'm sorry, I truly am," said Chow.

"So are we," said Ty.

"Emily's father—her biological father," said Lock. "Does he have a name?"

45

Lock's Audi peeled away from the hotel, hung a right on Wilshire, and turned onto Rodeo Drive, the shopping street made famous by people with more money than taste. He'd already called Carmen and asked her to see what she could hunt down about Emily's biological father from the very limited information that Chow Yan had provided.

"You buying all that?" Ty asked.

"Some of it."

"Which parts?"

"The parts that make sense and make him look good," said Lock. "Those are usually the parts that hold together when anyone tells you something that's had to be dragged out of them."

"So, wanting to keep his wife happy, loving the kid?" Ty said.

"Yeah, I bought all that," said Lock. "The mother's accident—who knows? It might be true, might not. It's kind of convenient, but accidents do happen."

"And the father?" said Ty.

"He could have told her about him. If it went down like he said it did."

"You mean if Chow didn't know she'd been abducted?"

"Exactly," said Lock. "A lot more difficult to explain to a kid how they were taken from their real family, but right now that's tomorrow's problem."

"Agreed," said Ty. "What now?"

"Let's go see our friendly neighborhood auto mechanic. See if we can't pull something out of the wreckage of this complete shit show."

46

Lock turned into the alleyway. The doors of the auto shop were open. A couple of guys were out front working on a Camaro. They stopped when they saw Lock's Audi. One walked inside, trying to come off casual and doing a bad job of it.

Lock had figured that everyone even remotely connected to this mess would be amped up after what had happened. These people were unaccustomed to being on the receiving end of that type of violence, at least on this side of the border. In Mexico, four dead gangsters in a pool would barely make the local newspaper.

The mechanic who had gone inside reappeared, walking heavy, a Glock tucked into his waistband. Lock did a quick scan of the others. He looked like the only one carrying, but that didn't mean other guns weren't stashed nearby.

"Your boss around?" Lock asked the mechanic with the gun.

"Nope," said the man with the Glock.

"Know if he's going to be here any time soon?"

The question was met with a shrug.

"That thing loaded?" said Lock.

The mechanic grinned. "Wanna find out?"

"Any idea where we can find Orzana?"

"Sure."

"Want to share that information with me?"

"Nope."

The other mechanics had begun to drift back to work. Only the one with the gun was still talking, and even he was starting to look bored.

Ty wandered casually over to the Camaro. The hood was up, and a man was fiddling with something, doing his best to look busy.

"Nice car," Ty said.

The mechanic turned his head. "Fuck off."

Ty reached over, grabbed the hood support rod, and yanked it out of the holder. The hood slammed down hard, catching the mechanic's fingers. He let out a scream.

His buddy went to draw the Glock, but Lock already had his SIG aimed at him. "Don't even think about it," he told the man. "I do this for a living."

The mechanic dropped his hands to his sides.

"Now let's start again, shall we?" Lock said.

47

Ty, his weapon drawn, watched each mechanic drop his cell phone onto the work bench.

"This is bullshit," the last man muttered, as he put his down.

Ty picked it up and turned it off. "It's way less bullshit than the LAPD coming in and asking questions. You fellas know what conspiracy is, right?"

The question earned him more surly glances.

"Conspiracy means that if you work here you're going to be held accountable for whatever shady shit has gone down on these premises. Now if anyone wants to drop a dime, go right ahead," said Ty. "Yeah, figured that would be the answer."

He settled himself against the bench where he had a good view of everyone. Thankfully, one of them had coughed up an address only a few minutes away. An apartment where Orzana entertained a female friend.

Lock had gone to check it out, while Ty took babysitter duties and ensured no one gave El Mecánico a heads-up about his incoming visitor.

AS AN ELDERLY MAN hefting some bags opened the main entrance door into the small two-story apartment block on Guirado Street, Lock slipped in with him. "You want some help with those?" he asked.

The man smiled, and gratefully passed over his shopping.

Lock followed him past a broken elevator and up a flight of stairs to his apartment. As the man fumbled with his key, Lock checked out the numbers. The apartment he'd been given was at the end of the corridor.

Lock helped the man inside and set the groceries on a small kitchen table. The man thanked him profusely in Spanish. Looking around the tiny, slightly disheveled apartment, Lock felt a pang of something. An echo of loneliness. A glimpse of a possible future. He had to set things straight with Carmen as soon as the case was resolved. He had an idea about how they could settle the argument over whether she moved in with him or him with her.

Back in the corridor, Lock opened the jacket he'd thrown on to conceal his SIG. He walked the forty feet to the apartment and listened at the door.

There was music. Some kind of slow, sultry number from a singer who sounded like the Hispanic answer to Barry White. He guessed he had the right place.

He gave three sharp knocks and stepped to the side. Twenty seconds passed and he knocked again.

Inside, someone turned down the music. He heard a voice that he pegged as Orzana's, and the pad of footsteps toward the door. He'd be answering gun in hand, nothing was surer.

"Orzana, it's Lock. I've come to talk. I'm alone."

"Gimme a second. I've got to put pants on."

Although they had met only briefly, he hadn't struck Lock as the modest type. Lock moved back down the corridor to the stairs. He hustled down them two at a time and pushed through the door.

Outside he took a moment to get his bearings before skirting around the side of the building. He stayed close to the wall, and watched as, above him, a window opened, and Orzana clambered out.

Lock waited, remaining tight to the wall. Orzana landed with a thud, and Lock tackled him to the ground while he was still off balance from the jump, taking him at the knees, both arms wrapped around his hips.

He pinned Orzana beneath him. He grabbed his wrist, snapping it back so that he dropped his weapon. Orzana did his best to wriggle out from under him, but Lock scooted up so that his knees were forced into the man's armpits. His legs rested on Orzana's hips, making sure that he stayed where he was.

Orzana bridged, trying to shuck Lock off him. Lock shifted back slightly, staying heavy, and allowing Orzana to tire himself out. Lock worked his hand under the back of the gangster's head. Keeping his hand palm down, he locked in a gable grip with his other hand, switched his hips and drove his shoulder into the side of the man's neck, a move colloquially known as 'the shoulder of justice'.

Orzana's struggle continued, but he was growing weaker with every attempt to get out from under. As he bucked and bridged, Lock talked to him, keeping his voice calm and his tone even.

"If I wanted to shoot you, I could have done it by now. If I wanted to have you arrested I could have called it in. A felon with a gun is about the easiest PV there is."

PV stood for 'parole violation' and in this case it would have meant a direct trip to jail.

"So why you jump me like this?" Orzana managed, through deep gulps of air.

"Why'd you run?"

Lock eased up the shoulder pressure a little before Orzana began to pass out from the pressure on his carotid artery.

"You kidding me? People like me run from people like you. Or we shoot them."

"All I came here for was to give you a message," said Lock.

"I think we got it already. And payback's gonna be a bitch, homie."

"It wasn't us killed those men. Not me, and not Emily's father or anyone working for him," Lock said, rolling out the same careful choice of words that Chow Yan had deployed with him.

"You expect me to believe that bullshit?"

Lock sat up and rolled off in the direction of Orzana's gun. He picked it up, and made it safe, ejecting the mag, and dry firing it into the ground to make sure, then handed it back to Orzana.

"The person who killed your men."

"They weren't *my* men."

"Whatever. I don't care if they were OGs or mercs or Boy Scouts gone wrong. Whoever they were, they were killed by someone who's going to keep coming at you until those kids are released. He's not going to stop, which makes him your worst nightmare."

"How you figure that?"

"Because a man who just keeps coming, regardless of the consequences, is everyone's worst nightmare. You should know that better than most people. Isn't that MS-13's secret? You're relentless."

"I don't know anything about that. But this guy you know all about, he's nothing to do with you."

"No, he's not."

"Then why's he doing this?"

"I can't tell you that."

"You're going to have to, because otherwise it makes no sense."

"Let's just say it's personal."

"Personal, how?"

Lock took a moment. Orzana was correct. It made no sense without the missing piece of information. What possible motive could a man have for such slaughter unless he was being paid or had a motive that went deeper. He remembered what he had told Chow Yan about the danger of secrets. It was time for Lock to take his own advice.

"He's her father," he said.

"Wait. What?"

"She was adopted," said Lock, fudging it slightly. "The man who took out four of your guys is her biological father. The man I'm working for is her adoptive father. And the good news for you is that he still wants to make a deal, and he has the money to make all of this go away."

Orzana got to his feet. Lock took a step back, maintaining distance in case he did something dumb, although that moment seemed to have passed.

"But if you don't then, like I said, this other guy is going to keep coming. And if anything happens to them, if they die, he's going to have some serious backup and all the resources he needs to finish the job he already started at that house in Malibu."

"Aren't you assuming something?" said Orzana.

"What's that?"

"Well, what's to say they're not already dead?"

"Are they?" Lock asked.

Orzana let the question hang unanswered. He smiled. "No, last I heard, they're not. But it was a close-run thing."

That Lock could believe.

"We're going to need some compensation on top of what we already agreed," Orzana continued. "Those men had families, kids of their own."

Lock hadn't considered it in those terms, but it was true. Even hired killers and kidnappers had responsibilities. He wasn't going to argue about who was liable. They just needed this done, and fast. Before anyone else got hurt, including Emily and Charlie. "I'm sure we can factor that in."

"There's no 'sure' about it, you're gonna have to. And my broker's fee just went up too. I want twenty per cent of whatever's agreed. On top."

"Five."

"Ten."

"Done."

Lock holstered his weapon. He extended his hand. In the end, money had won out. It usually did.

48

I t was remarkable how quickly a few hundred thousand dollars could transform the relationship dynamic between two people. Especially when one was a scumbag criminal like Noah Orzana. Now Orzana had skin in the game, things should run more smoothly. And, crucially, Lock had made sure that Orzana knew he wouldn't see his finder's fee until the exchange had taken place, and Emily and Charlie were safe.

That alone made Lock feel better about the whole deal. He made a mental note to try to build that extra failsafe measure into any future kidnap-for-ransom cases. There would be more, he knew. In a world of ever-tightening security the two growth areas in the past decade had been cybercrime and kidnap for ransom. One high tech, one distinctly low tech, they both offered guaranteed high returns, albeit with different risks.

Lock pulled the Audi to the curb four blocks away from the auto shop. Orzana had assumed Ty's regular shotgun position in the passenger seat.

The two men shook hands.

"Let's just get this done," Lock told him.

"Fine by me," said Orzana, exiting the car.

Their financial agreement would stay between them. It was in neither party's interest to make Orzana's colleagues aware of it. That suited Lock. It gave him additional leverage over El Mecánico, should he need it.

TY WALKED toward Lock's car and got in. The mechanics would be hustling to the bench to collect their cell phones and power them up. There would be a scramble on to see who could be first to alert their boss. Lock wondered if it would secure any of them an Employee of the Month ribbon.

"How'd it go?" Ty asked, as Lock floored it down the alleyway and hung a right.

"Better than I could have hoped. I brought Orzana on board to broker the deal."

"Thought he was doing that already."

"He was, but now he has a direct financial incentive to make sure it all goes down as it should. They also want compensation for the four guys who were killed. I just need to sell the additional expenditure to our client."

"Damn, Ryan, can't see that being an issue. He was going to give them ten a piece before you intervened. Good work, brother."

Ty reached over to hit the button to push his seat back and accommodate his long legs. They bumped fists.

"Yeah, let's not count our chickens just yet, though. We still have a tiger on the prowl out there."

"No kidding," said Ty. "He's about the only thing that could screw up this whole deal right now."

"I already have Carl working that angle," said Lock. "I messaged him on the way over to Orzana's place. He's checking with a contact at Homeland Security, seeing if we can't figure out when he landed on US soil and if he left any clues."

"Why don't we just inform LAPD or the Feds?" Ty asked. "They have the resources to track him down."

"I thought about that, but it'd involve a lot of questions. Questions we don't want to answer just yet. Or, at least, not until we've made the trade."

"Yeah," mused Ty. "That makes sense."

Law enforcement tended to treat kidnappings as purely criminal. The aim was to track down the culprits and bring them to justice. Lock, like a lot of people in private security, came at it from a different angle. He saw his primary duty as ensuring the safe return of the victim or victims. The crime and punishment part came after that, if at all.

Just as law enforcement didn't want ransoms paid because it encouraged repeat offending, Lock saw hunting down a kidnapper after the deal as creating a problem for future transactions. It wasn't exactly welching on a deal, but kidnappers or kidnap gangs liked to stay at liberty to enjoy their ill-gotten gains.

As a general rule, Lock thought it better to let sleeping dogs lie. As long as the kidnapper understood that what had just transpired was strictly a one-time deal.

They headed west, away from the grinding poverty of East LA, and back toward the near-obscene opulence of Beverly Hills: America's great paradox laid bare in a journey of less than ten miles.

Lock wanted to return to the penthouse suite. The negotiation would be easier to conclude quickly if he was in the room with the man who'd be authorizing the ransom payment. But first they'd need proof of life.

"Live stream," said Lock.

"You think they'll go for it?" Ty asked him. "That stuff is easy to track."

"Not if they're clever about it. They can use a bunch of proxies, route it through half a dozen different countries before it gets to us. Plus, if they have any sense, they'll move them immediately after they do the stream. Or they can just move the device or destroy it entirely."

Lock doubted it would get that complicated. Digital communications left an electronic trail, but those trails were usually time-consuming to unpick, even for governments.

"And what if they've anticipated that and pre-recorded some footage?"

"I'm going to have Chow Yan talk with them in Mandarin, ask questions. If they've pre-recorded video footage, we'll know."

"Okay," said Ty, apparently satisfied. "Sounds solid."

It was. Without getting carried away, Lock felt they were close to wrapping this up. Cutting Orzana into the deal had given him renewed confidence. Once they had confirmed that Emily and Charlie were still alive, they could agree the terms and make the exchange.

Ty was looking pensively out of the passenger window.

"Something bothering you?" Lock asked.

"I was just thinking about the kid, Emily."

"What about her?"

"Well, lots of kids don't have one father who gives a shit about them, and she's got one who'll pay ten million dollars to keep her safe, and another who'll kill for her."

Ty had never had a relationship with his father. As with a lot of kids from his community in Long Beach, it had been left to his mother to raise him. Lock had been fortunate in that respect. He'd been close to both his parents.

They turned onto Rodeo Drive. Lock was turning over in his mind what Ty had just said. Something about it bothered him.

"Kind of begs the question, though, doesn't it?"

"What question's that?" said Ty.

"If you have someone on deck who's prepared to hand over a pile of cash to get your kid back, why not let them handle it? Why take all these risks?"

Ty shrugged. "I dunno. Maybe he feels like he has a point to prove. If you had a child, and someone kidnapped them, what would you do? Especially if it wasn't the first time."

Lock knew the answer. Things would get very ugly, very quickly. "I'm not buying it. The guy gets on a plane, and comes all this way, goes and takes out a bunch of MS-13 associates, when all he needs to do is let someone else make a payment. There's something more going on here."

"Like what?" said Ty.

"I don't know." He couldn't put his finger on it, but something felt off.

"Look, Ryan, we're talking about the man's flesh and blood. Maybe it just is what it is."

"And that's?"

"The man's violent. No one can argue that. His kid is taken from him. He tracks her down after all these years only to find she's in a world of trouble. You really think he's going to leave it to the man who took her to make things right?"

Lock didn't reply. Ty was right. Of course he was. What he'd just said was all the explanation that was needed. But the niggling feeling that they were missing something didn't leave him.

His cell phone rang. The number had been withheld. Lock tapped to answer.

"We're ready to go with this whole proof-of-life deal," said Orzana.

Giving Orzana a direct financial interest was working beautifully. With good will on both sides, they might just be able to wrap up the nightmare today.

"Okay, I'm about ten minutes from the client," said Lock, checking the time on the car's display. "Give me about thirty and we can do this."

"We can't do it now?" Orzana was agitated. "I have everything set up."

"Thirty minutes," said Lock, killing the call.

LOCK STOOD with Chow Yan and Li Yeng in front of the large display screen in the living area of the opulent suite. Ty pressed a button to lower the blinds and the room dimmed, cutting down on any screen glare and ensuring that no one in the building opposite would be able to catch even the tiniest glimpse of what they were about to watch.

On Lock's instructions, Li had set things up so that the live video feed would play on a laptop computer. A dongle plugged into it would cast the video onto the screen. Lock had also had Li install software that simultaneously recorded the feed so that they could review it later. Everything told him that they were on the home stretch, and ready to wrap things up, but it was crucial never to take anything for granted.

Ty adjusted the lighting in the room, using the Creston panel sitting on the coffee-table, and joined them in front of the screen. It was displaying the desktop view from the laptop computer. Skype, video-conferencing software, was open.

Chow Yan glanced at his watch, a Patek Philippe that would cost the guts of two hundred thousand dollars down on Rodeo. The seconds were dragging for everyone in the room, but more for him than anyone else. He was doing his best to look composed and in control, but Lock could tell from his body language that he was barely holding it together.

You could be one of the richest men in the world, but family and those closest to you being in pain or under threat was the great equalizer. No amount of money could relieve emotional pain.

The Skype icon pulsed, signaling an incoming call. Lock placed a reassuring hand on Chow Yan's shoulder as Li stepped back toward the laptop, ready to accept the call at Lock's signal.

"You ready?" said Lock.

Chow Yan took a deep breath. "Yes."

Lock had already warned his client about the state hostages can be in after even a short period. They may look disheveled. They may have signs of physical abuse: bruising; abrasions; visible wounds. Worse, they may demonstrate signs of having suffered psychological trauma. Eye contact, speech patterns, their body language may all be different.

"It's going to be upsetting." Lock had told him. "There's no way for it not to be. But the most important thing is that you remain calm for their sake. And, remember, the kidnappers will be watching your reaction. The more distress and emotion you show, the more likely they are to think they have additional leverage."

It was for all those reasons that this part of the negotiation was best handled by a third party. But that wasn't an option this time: professional hostage negotiators were thin on the ground, and those who could speak English and Mandarin or Cantonese even more so.

That meant this part would have to be handled by Chow and Li, while Lock would take care of the next stages of the process.

As the Skype window opened, Li adjusted the position of the laptop so that its camera was facing Chow Yan. Lock and Ty both stepped to the side, staying out of the direct line of sight but ensuring they had a good view of the screen.

There was a brief pause and then the screen mounted on the wall lit up with a video image of a sun-splashed room filled with natural light. Emily Yan was perched at the end of a queen-sized bed. She looked tired, frayed around the edges, and at least a decade older than her tender years. There were dark circles under her eyes, and hastily applied make-up appeared to conceal bruising on one side of her face.

Lock watched as Chow Yan dredged up a smile, taking the advice Lock had given him. *Even if you don't feel strong, give the appearance of strength for them.*

He started to speak with Emily in Mandarin. Ty leaned in next to Lock.

"Where's Charlie?"

Lock had been wondering the same. They needed evidence that they were both alive. Assuming, of course, that they were.

Lock waved Li Yeng over. "Get him to ask where his nephew is."

Li Yeng flitted back to Chow Yan and whispered in his ear. Lock lasered all his attention on Emily. Her eyes kept flitting from the screen, where she could see her father, to the left, where presumably one or more of the kidnappers were stationed.

As Chow Yan asked Emily about Charlie—Lock picked out the name in English—she looked back to the same spot.

"My father wants to see Charlie," she said in English, to whoever was standing off camera.

There was the sound of staccato chatter in Spanish, and of a door opening. Emily snuck nervous glances toward it.

Lock stiffened. There had to be a reason that Charlie hadn't been in front of the camera. After all, from the kidnappers' point of view this was a simple matter of showcasing the goods before a price was agreed and they were exchanged for money.

Chow Yan said something else to Emily in Mandarin. She was midway through her reply when a hulking figure in black sweats whose face was covered with a mask, entered the frame, grabbed her arm, and pulled her to her feet.

A door slammed, and Charlie was shoved roughly onto the bed. His face was badly bruised, and his nose was squashed to one side. One of his eyes was almost completely closed. He sat on the edge of the bed and stared at the floor.

Chow Yan gazed at the screen, frozen. He opened his mouth to speak but nothing came out.

Lock walked over and took his place as Ty guided the business tycoon to one of the couches.

"Charlie," Lock said to the laptop camera. "Charlie, look at me."

Charlie looked up, terrified.

"Charlie," said Lock. "This is all going to be over soon, okay?"

"Okay."

"Until then I want you to do what you're asked by these people. Don't create any problems for them. Don't resist. Don't attempt to escape. I'm going to have you back with your family very soon."

Reassurance was all that Lock could offer. It was clear that Charlie had taken at least one beating. All they could hope was that, between now and his release, he didn't catch another. The best way of achieving that was by being compliant.

Charlie reached up with one hand and rubbed his face. "My head hurts."

"Just hang in there for me, buddy," said Lock, before the screen went blank.

Li tapped at the laptop keyboard. "They're gone," he told them.

Chow Yan started to speak, but he was interrupted by the chirp of Lock's cell phone. Lock answered.

"You satisfied?" said Orzana.

"What happened to Charlie?" said Lock.

"Kid has a big mouth. Not a good quality to have if you can't back it up," said Orzana. "Don't worry, he'll be okay."

"And you know that how?" said Lock. Charlie's comment about his head hurting was worrying. He'd looked concussed. Head injuries were always a cause for concern. Left untreated they could prove fatal.

"Listen, do you want them back or not?" said Orzana.

"We do," said Lock.

"Then let's stop screwing about."

He gave Lock the new figure. Four and a half million dollars for Emily's release and the same for Charlie.

"Two million each. Four total," Lock countered.

"Five," said Orzana.

"Hang on," said Lock.

He hit the mute button on his phone and ran the amount past Chow Yan and Li Yeng.

Chow Yan nodded dumbly. Lock had the sense he could have given him any figure and he would have nodded. Seeing Emily and then Charlie had left him in a state of shock

Li Yeng seemed a little more composed. "That should be fine," he said.

Lock unmuted the call. "Fine. Five. But you take your finder's fee out of that."

"I'll need to get final approval. I'll call you back," said Orzana.

～

CHOW YAN SAT on the couch, and obsessively reviewed the video footage of his call with Emily. Tears streamed down his face. Li Yeng stood by the window, seemingly embarrassed by his boss's show of emotion.

It had been ten minutes since Lock's call with Orzana. He was on edge, but not overly so. Most deals involving five million dollars took longer than ten minutes to sign off.

It was a decent score for the kidnappers. Not major-drug-shipment big, but large enough to merit proper attention from the higher echelons of MS-13, and certainly enough to warrant all the hassle and corpses. Orzana had made a big play of compensating the four dead men's families, but Lock doubted they'd see more than a hundred thousand each, if that. Loyalty was how the gang sold itself to new recruits, but the reality was often very different, especially when it came to sharing the spoils.

Lock walked over and sank onto the couch next to his client. "It'll be okay," he said. "The worst part is over. They'll take the deal, then Ty and I will go collect them."

Chow Yan pulled a silk handkerchief from the top pocket of his suit and dabbed at his eyes. He smiled apologetically at Lock. "I'll come with you," he said.

A warning klaxon went off in the back of Lock's head. Family was usually kept well away from hostage exchanges. The last thing anyone needed when they went down was an emotional family member. In almost every case Lock had worked, loved ones were kept at a safe location and reunited with the kidnap victim there. Sometimes medical checks of the victim took place first.

"That's not a good idea."

Chow Yan stared at Lock, the emotional father pushed out by the hard-edged businessman. "It's my decision."

Lock decided against arguing with the man. There would be time for that once the deal was agreed. He was confident that he could finesse it so that Chow felt involved and the delay between Emily and Charlie's return and reuniting them was kept to a minimum.

"Does she know?" said Lock.

"About?"

"That she's adopted? That her biological father is looking for her?" *That her mother's dead? That she was illegally taken from her family?* he wanted to add, but didn't.

"No," said Chow Yan. "And I have no intention of telling her."

"You don't think she's owed the truth?"

Lock knew he was outside the bounds of the job he'd been tasked with. But after everything that had gone down, he didn't really care.

"I think she's already had enough to deal with."

Lock accepted that. But he didn't think Chow Yan maintaining the lie had much to do with Emily's welfare. "So what happens with her biological father?" he asked.

Chow Yan raised his head. "That's not for me to decide."

Lock's cell rang. It was Carmen. "Excuse me, I'd better take this," he said, getting back.

Chow Yan got up too and began to follow him.

"It's not them, but they'll still be able to get through on my line if they need to," Lock reassured him.

He stepped away so he could listen to Carmen without anyone else overhearing. "Hey, I think we're almost there with this," he said.

"That's great."

"Yeah, we're just waiting on final acceptance of the offer before we move to exchange."

"You make it sound like a real-estate deal," Carmen said.

"That's harsh, but it's not a million miles away. We can deal with the human side once we have them returned safely. They're both going to need some heavy-duty counselling and support."

"Speaking of the human side . . ." said Carmen.

"Yeah?"

"The father. I have some details."

49

T he elevator opened and Lock stepped into the hustle and bustle of the lobby.

"You know how you told me once that the only coincidences you believe in are the bad ones?" said Carmen.

Carmen had a habit of reciting Lock's beliefs back at him, which admittedly tended toward the pessimistic, when the need arose.

"I only told you that once?"

"I was trying to be polite," she said, trying to keep the laughter out of her voice.

"So, what you got?" said Lock, steeling himself.

"The biological father. He's a badass, all right. Just maybe not the kind your client was telling you he was."

"Go on."

"His name's Tang Bojun. From a poor family in a poor province. He got that part right."

Carmen hesitated.

"And?" Lock prompted.

"So little Tang grows up and, just like here if you don't have much going for you but want to change that, he joins the military."

"Which is where he learns to kill?" said Lock.

"Which is where he learns that he's very good at a lot of things. Doesn't climb the ranks, but does win a bunch of military honors, and becomes a kind of go-to guy for the more dangerous missions. Then when he's overseas his young daughter goes missing."

"Emily?"

"Exactly. One day she just disappears into thin air. He's stuck out somewhere in East Africa, doing God knows what for his government, and by the time he gets back, the trail is cold, and it wasn't all that warm to begin with. His wife is bereft and takes her life, because she blames herself for what's happened."

Lock felt himself stiffen. Another lie.

"Tang's a mess. His wife's dead, his kid is gone. He hits the bottle and crashes out of the army. When he finally dries out, he starts helping other families who've had kids kidnapped. And there's plenty of them. For the most part, the cops aren't a lot of help, so he fills the vacuum. Gets pretty good at it, too, because in a way every case he takes on is personal. So let's just say his methods aren't exactly by the numbers."

"Violent."

"If he has to be. It's a whatever-it-takes approach," said Carmen.

"And no one stops him?"

"He has some friends in high places. Not high enough to find out what happened to his own child, but sufficient to keep him out of jail. Plus, he's a highly decorated military veteran going after scumbags. The authorities turn a blind eye. And a lot of officials are pissed that their one-child policy is being made to look bad by infanticide of girls and all these abductions." Carmen took a breath. "He's like some kind of Chinese superhero. They even give him a name, the Red Tiger."

"What about what's happening now?"

"About a year ago Tang starts getting a lot closer to the truth of who has his child. Your client, Chow Yan, didn't abduct her. He bought her from the people who did or, rather, the people who got her from the kidnappers. There was quite a complicated supply chain going on."

"So, Chow Yan moves her out of the country," said Lock, piecing it together.

"Might have done it anyway. Lots of wealthy Chinese send their kids here for education."

"And the kidnapping?" said Lock. "This kidnapping?"

"Random, as far as Carl Galante has been able to tell. Okay, maybe not entirely random because the kids who took Emily and Charlie have been working robberies in Arcadia for months. This was just a step up."

Lock took a breath. He was trying to figure out what, if anything, this changed. Chow Yan had been lying. Not much of a surprise there. He'd done what most people did and only revealed as much of the truth as he had to in order to keep Lock on board. It was unlikely, but possible, that he didn't know how the people from whom he'd received Emily had come to possess her.

There were still two young people in the clutches of MS-13. That hadn't changed. The task remained the same. Finish the job. Make the exchange. And after that?

Should they tell the LAPD what they knew? Probably.

But where did that leave Emily? Fresh from the trauma of having been kidnapped she'd discover that her life to this point had been one long abduction story. The man she'd thought was her father was a liar, and her real father was some kind of . . . Some kind of what? Lock didn't know. Dumping a bunch of MS-13 muscle face down in a swimming pool might be considered a public service by some. It wasn't anything that he or Ty would mourn.

"What are you going to do?" Carmen asked him.

It was a good question. One to which he didn't have a complete answer. Not yet anyway. There was a lot to digest. "For now?"

"Yes."

"I'm going to do my job."

50

The California Highway Patrol's Los Angeles headquarters was located near downtown Los Angeles, close to the intersection of the 10 and the 110 freeways. The 10 ran east to west, the 110 north to south.

The intersection of the two major freeways offered the quickest access to the Greater Los Angeles area. Lock had selected a parking spot directly across from the Seventh-day Adventist Church on Georgia Street, on the other side of the 110, for the same reason.

Neither he nor Ty knew yet where the exchange would take place—east LA, downtown, on the Westside, or out in the San Fernando Valley—but the interchange would allow them access to those areas of the city and more. Now all they had to do was wait for the call agreeing the final deal and providing them with the location for the exchange, which, for obvious reasons, was the kidnappers' call.

Lock shot Ty a look as he noisily sucked up the last of his shake.

"Sorry, dude, don't like to waste any," said Ty, shaking the paper cup.

"Why don't you just take the lid off and lose the straw?"

"Too much risk of spillage," said Ty. "This shirt cost me like a hundred and fifty bucks at Nordstrom's."

"Really?" said Lock. "Someone would have had to pay me that much to wear it."

Ty pinched at the fabric. "What's wrong with it?"

"Where do you want me to start?" said Lock, taking in the eye-blindingly bright yellow and red patterned shirt.

Ty responded with another loud straw clearance. "What do you think our client is going to tell his daughter? Assuming we get her back in one piece."

"About being adopted?" asked Lock.

"And the rest."

Lock took a moment. It was "the rest" that would present the problem. Whatever relationship Chow Yan had with Emily could be blown apart. At worst she might never forgive him. At best it would cause untold upset and emotional turmoil. For both of them.

Lock's cell phone rang. He answered. It was Orzana.

"We're agreed on the final figure. You can transfer it now and I'll set everything else in motion."

Lock looked across the road at the church. "You must be new to this," he said to Orzana. "There is no way you can get the ransom upfront."

At the other end of the line, Orzana sighed. "No harm in asking. Okay, half now, half when you see them at the exchange."

That was more like it, but Lock wasn't satisfied. With the kind of money involved it was smart to minimize the upfront payment and load the back end. That way there was more incentive for MS-13 not to go back on their word, and deliver Emily and Charlie to him in good condition.

"Twenty per cent now, the balance on delivery."

"And what guarantee do we have that you'll pay the eighty?"

"You have my word, although I also want a guarantee that they won't be having any more of these negotiations."

"I think it's fair to say that this was a one-off."

"Good. Just don't go getting any ideas. That's friendly advice.

We're handling this privately, but the LAPD and the Feds are going to be all over you after this. You make a habit out of this, especially with these people, and it'll end badly."

"What? You mean Chinese?"

"No, I mean wealthy people," Lock clarified. "This isn't South America."

Orzana chuckled. "We know that. So, forty per cent now?"

"Thirty, and that's my final offer."

"Okay."

Lock gave Ty a thumbs-up to signal that the deal was done. "So where do you want to meet?" he asked Orzana.

"All in good time. Just make sure your phone line stays clear," said Orzana, before terminating the call.

It was a reminder to them that, right now, Orzana still held all the cards, or at the very least the two that mattered. Lock tapped on Li Yeng's number and waited for it to connect.

As soon as Li answered, he outlined the agreement. There was a hasty, muffled conversation, and Li came back on the line. "That's all fine. I have an account set up that will allow us to make an instant transfer into whatever account they want to receive the money."

"Good," said Lock.

"And you're confident that they'll deliver?"

"As confident as I can be. These situations are always delicate, but we've established some trust now, and that's what counts. As long as nothing else happens to upset them, I'd say we should have Emily and Charlie back with you by midnight."

"That's great."

There was more muffled talk and then Li said, "Wait. Mr. Yan wants to speak with you."

"Mr. Lock, I wished to thank you myself for this. I can't tell you how relieved I am."

"I appreciate that, but we're not there just yet."

"I'm sure everything will be fine."

"I certainly hope so."

Ty must have sensed something in Lock's manner as he finished the call.

"What is it?"

"Even if we get them back safely, this isn't going to be over. Not after what happened at that house out in Malibu," said Lock. "MS-13 aren't exactly the forgiving kind. They won't be happy until they have this particular tiger by the tail."

Ty raised his milkshake cup, peeling the lid back and swirling it around to make sure he hadn't missed any of the dregs. "In that case," he said, "there won't be anything to tell the kid."

51

Shotcaller blinked as the car's trunk opened. Dazzled by the shift from total darkness he squinted up at the man who loomed above him, his squat body silhouetted against the bright, unrelenting sunshine.

The MS-13 boss was still struggling to come to terms with what had happened. It was his people who dished out the beatings. His people who stuffed their battered bodies into the trunk of a car before driving somewhere quiet to dispose of the evidence.

But not this time.

His body was a mass of pain. He had been dropped by a heavy blow to his liver that had left him writhing on the ground in his backyard when he had gone to investigate a noise outside. What had followed was brutal and relentless. He had been hit so hard and so many times, with such targeted ferocity, that it had been hard to believe it was one man hitting him and not half a dozen.

The last thing he remembered before blacking out was looking down at his blood lacing the lawn, scarlet splashed over the vivid green, like an old painting. He'd come to a short time afterwards in the trunk of what he was sure was one of his own cars.

It wasn't the first time it had been used for such a purpose. But he had never imagined that he would be the one taking the ride.

He had survived, though. He was breathing. It was time to gather himself. To show this man what Salvadorian pride was all about.

Shotcaller tried to move his hands to grip the lip of the trunk and haul himself out. They wouldn't move. It took him a second to realize that his wrists were bound together with thick black tape.

The man leaned into the trunk. Shotcaller cleared his throat, gathering an oyster of phlegm and launched it at the man, who stepped back, laughing.

Shotcaller waited for the beat down to start again. It didn't. The man stood there, looking at him, his expression neutral.

"Where are they?" the man said.

"Who?" said Shotcaller. If that was what this was about, those two Chinese kids, then this man who had beaten him was going to be very disappointed. He'd die before he snitched on his fellow gang members and gave up that information.

"It's okay," said the man. "You're going to take me to them."

Shotcaller smiled up at the man. There was zero chance of that happening. The man was crazy.

"No, I won't. I promise you," he told him.

The man shrugged. "We'll see."

"Yeah, we will. Anyway, why are you sweating this? Those two are going back to their family as soon as the money's paid. All this is a waste of effort."

The man's expression shifted. His eyes narrowed. His features darkened. Shotcaller had pushed some kind of button. If he'd pissed the guy, then good. "Relax," he continued. "Let their family deal with it."

"Their family?"

"Yeah, the father," said Shotcaller. "He has money. He'll pay a ransom. It's not a problem."

"And a father would do anything for his child?" the man said, stepping to the side so that Shotcaller couldn't see him.

There was the sound of someone else struggling. A car door opened, then closed again. Feet scuffed on the ground.

The man reappeared. He was dragging someone with him. They were about five feet four inches, wearing baggy jeans and a blue plaid shirt. A hood had been placed over their head.

Shotcaller screamed as he realized who it was. "You motherfucker! He has nothing to do with this."

The man reached to the back of the teenager's neck, and undid the twine securing the hood. He yanked it off with a flourish, like a magician performing a reveal.

Shotcaller's son stared at him. His face was drawn and pale, and he was crying. "Alex," he said. "Listen to me. It'll be okay."

It was only then that he noticed the man had gathered something else from the car. It was a gallon-sized container.

The man swept the boy's legs out from under him. He landed face down. He pulled him onto his knees and pulled his head back by the hair. He held up the container so that Shotcaller could see the label.

One Gallon

Hydrochloric Acid Solution

"Don't do it, man," Shotcaller said.

The boy must have picked up the panic in his father's voice. "Dad, what is it?"

The man slowly unscrewed the top from the container. His manner was what unsettled Shotcaller the most. He was perfectly calm. He tossed the container top to one side and hefted the container above the boy's head.

"Okay! Okay! I'll find out."

The man's arm stopped in mid-air. He reached into his pocket with his free hand, pulled out a cell phone and held it up.

"What's the number?"

Shotcaller gave him the digits. The man punched them in. Holding the container in his other hand, he walked over to the trunk and held the phone up to Shotcaller.

"Yeah, it's me. I need to know where they are."

He paused. This wasn't going to be information given freely. "No, listen, I don't have to explain myself to you. Just tell me."

Another pause.

"Okay, okay."

He gave the man the location, adding, "But they won't be there for another hour. That's the exchange point."

The man put the cell phone back into his pocket.

"Let him go," said Shotcaller, trying to sound like he was somehow back in charge.

The man lifted the container high up above Shotcaller's head and tilted it. The liquid poured out onto his head and ran down his face.

He let out a scream of horror before he realized there was no pain. Gingerly he prodded his tongue out between dry, cracked lips and tasted only water.

Rage took over, and he screamed, this time in fury. The man stepped back, and began to laugh. He slammed the trunk down on Shotcaller. The darkness returned.

52

Lock's Audi slowly squeezed through a freshly cut gap in the chain-link fence into the parking lot. He made a sweeping turn and stopped so that the hood of the car was facing the gap.

He switched off the Audi's engine, and placed it in park. He reached under his seat for his SIG Sauer, ejected the mag, checked it was full, and snapped it back in, ensuring he had a round racked in the chamber. Next to him, Ty ran through the same procedure.

Like his partner, Lock believed that the more prepared you were, the less likely you'd be called upon to use a weapon. It wasn't so much the deterrent factor as some glitch in the cosmos that seemed to dictate that the one time you weren't carrying was the one time you'd need your gun.

Not that Lock fetishized firearms. They were simply a tool of his business. He'd happily never touch a gun again if he could be guaranteed he'd never need one.

He scanned the area. It was more fenced-off waste ground than parking lot. There were only a half-dozen vehicles there, and at least four of those were missing tires. If he'd had to guess, he'd have said that the owner of the land was waiting on some sort of re-zoning to take place so he could open his parking business or sell it for condos.

"Guess this is when we find out how professional these guys are," he said, taking in the traffic on the nearest street.

"How's that?" Ty asked.

"How many kidnappers do you know who make the exchange at the first location?"

"I hear you."

In Lock's experience, those who were used to running kidnap-for-ransom operations did their best to keep the other party off-balance before the exchange took place. It wasn't unusual for a negotiator or exchange team to be sent to a half-dozen different locations before the swap took place. Frequent changes of location made it easier for a kidnapper to spot law enforcement. And, looking around, this was far from an ideal exchange site. It was too open, too public, and overlooked by any number of nearby office buildings.

A beat-up silver Toyota Corolla edged tentatively through the gap in the fence. Lock could only make out the driver, an elderly Hispanic lady, who was hunched over the wheel as she drove at a snail's pace toward them. She didn't look much like an MS-13 gang member, and there was no sign of either Emily or Charlie. In any case, they still hadn't been given details of where the first part of the ransom was to be transferred.

Perhaps, Lock speculated, she had simply seen them parked, and figured she could save a few bucks by leaving her car there.

She pulled up about ten feet away, opened her door and, with a great deal of effort, hauled herself out, assisted by a cane. In her free hand she clutched a large brown purse. Lock kept hold of his SIG, just in case. After all, this was still LA, a city where even the grandmas were capable of packing heat.

He tensed as she closed in on them and reached into her purse.

"What's up with this?" said Ty.

"Guess we're going to find out," said Lock, hitting the button to lower his window.

The old lady's hand cleared her purse. She was holding a white envelope.

"Señor Lock?" she asked.

"That's me."

She handed him the envelope. "This is for you."

Lock reached out and took her arm at the wrist. She startled. "Who gave you this?" he said.

"Let go of me."

"Answer my question."

She tried to shake him off, but he held onto her wrist, his grip just tight enough to make sure he kept hold of her but not to hurt her.

"I dunno. A young man at the market. I'd never seen him before. He gave me a hundred dollars if I drove down here and gave you this."

"Where was this market?"

"Boyle Heights."

"You know who he was? Had you seen him before?"

"No, he was just one of those young kids."

Lock believed her. The story made sense. He let go of her wrist. She turned and tottered back to her car. They could catch up with her quickly enough if they needed to.

He opened the envelope. A cop would have put on gloves and handed it to Forensics. He and Ty had no need for such careful procedure. They already knew who it was from, and he had a rough idea of what it contained.

He wasn't disappointed as he pulled out the single sheet of paper. At the top was an address. The next stop on their human scavenger hunt.

At the bottom of the piece of paper, carefully printed out in black ink, was a series of letters and numbers. It was a bank-account number with the corresponding SWIFT code. Almost certainly it was for an account outside the United States, an offshore tax haven, one of those places where the authorities didn't ask too many questions.

"We'd better call this in. They can make the initial payment," he told Ty.

As Lock reached for his cell phone to call Li Yeng, the screen lit up with an incoming call from Carl Galante. He passed the note to Ty. "Here, call Li and give him these account details. I should take this."

He tapped the screen. "Carl, what's up?"

"A whole world of pain is coming our way, that's what's up. You're not going to believe the call I just got from a buddy of mine at the LAPD."

53

L ock threw the car into drive, and hit the gas pedal, aiming straight for the gap in the fence. With the cell phone cradled between his shoulder and his ear, he bounced out of the lot and back onto the street. Whatever the bad news was, they still had to make an appearance at the next location, and he'd recognized the address as soon as he'd seen it. He'd been there with Carmen, and it fit the bill of somewhere you might want to trade two human beings for cash.

"Lock, you there?"

"Yes, so what's the world of pain we're looking at?" he asked Galante.

"There's been a report of an armed abduction at an address in Boyle Heights. Victim is an Ernesto Flores, and his fifteen-year-old son, Ernesto Junior. Flores is a local shotcaller for Mara Salvatrucha."

Lock's heart sank. He had a feeling he knew what was coming next, but he asked the question anyway.

"Suspect?"

"Asian male, late forties, early fifties."

Lock cursed under his breath, and bit down on his lower lip. The Red Tiger. It had to be. No one else had the motive or, for that matter, the sheer balls to go to an MS-13 shotcaller's home and kidnap him and his son.

"Anyone hurt?" said Lock.

"Not that we know of. Looks like he got hold of the son first and used him as leverage to get the father."

"Taste of their own medicine," said Lock.

"That's what it sounds like," said Galante.

"Do his associates know what's happened?"

"The LAPD are keeping it as quiet as they can for now, but someone could easily have seen something or picked up the address from a scanner," Galante said.

MS-13, like most street gangs, used scanners to monitor law-enforcement communications in their area. They also had people on the streets. It was fifty:fifty whether they'd know what had happened.

"One of their boys gets snatched up, they're going to hear about it sooner or later," Galante added.

Lock was less convinced by that part. Criminals like Ernesto Flores lived chaotic lifestyles. They could drop off the grid for days at a time, and not even their closest friends would know why or where they were. It was better to assume they would know, but it wasn't certain.

His cell phone buzzed. With one hand on the wheel, he pulled it away from his ear and checked the screen. His heart sank a little further as he looked at the number.

54

"Where are you?" Orzana asked Lock.

"We're almost there."

"Okay, well, hurry up. We're not going to wait around forever."

"You're there now?" Lock asked.

No response.

"Orzana? Hello?"

He looked again at the screen. Orzana had hung up.

Lock spun the wheel, turning left from Hill Street onto South Broadway, and dodging around an LA Metro bus.

"So, I gave Li Yeng the bank details," said Ty. "What was the call from Galante?"

Lock told him.

"Goddammit. This guy's going to get these kids killed if he keeps this up."

"I'm not sure that's how he sees it. He's probably thinking he has some leverage now."

Ty made a tutting sound. "If he thinks those guys'll prioritize one of their own over a couple million dollars he's dreaming."

Lock nodded. "No kidding." From his own experiences with criminal gangs, including time undercover in a Supermax prison, he knew that gangs might use solidarity and family as a hook to get people on board. But when it came down to it, the color green trumped any other.

He turned into an alleyway across the Grand Central Market. There was a prominent "No Parking, Tow Zone" sign. They would have to risk it.

"Weapons?" said Ty.

Lock nodded. They grabbed jackets and put them on. Both he and Ty looked sufficiently like cops that people rarely questioned why they had a firearm, but it was good practice not to make it too obvious.

Although they were entering a crowded public place they still had no idea what they were walking into. Innocent members of the public didn't count for much in the world of MS-13. If the gang had gotten word that one of their own had been taken, there was every chance Lock could be walking into an execution rather than a hostage exchange.

"You ready?" said Lock.

They dodged through the traffic on South Broadway and into the dimly lit hustle and bustle of the Grand Central Market. They wove through the flower stalls, a riot of scent and color, toward the food stalls that sold everything from some of the city's best tacos to ice cream, ramen noodles to bento boxes.

The smells were making Lock's stomach rumble, so who knew what effect they were having on Ty, with his vast appetite? Lock focused back on the task in hand. He scanned the shoals of people sitting at benches eating, or waiting in line at one of the stands, or simply cruising around, paralyzed by the sheer variety of options. He was looking for someone who stood out, or someone who was watching them, but it was close to an impossible task. The place was jammed.

He looked down at his cell phone, hoping for a text message, or some kind of signal about what they should do next.

There was nothing.

"Goddam that smells like good barbecue," said Ty, as they strolled slowly past a stall called Horse Thief BBQ.

"You want to get something?" said Lock.

While they were waiting, they might as well blend in. Walking around the place staring at people wouldn't achieve that.

Ty seemed taken aback. "You sure?"

"Yeah, go ahead."

Ty stepped forward to order. Lock stood with his back to the counter and swept the area around them, looking, as he always did, for something, or someone, that was off. He caught a likely candidate sitting alone on a bench about twelve feet away, a teenager, maybe fifteen or sixteen. Hispanic. He had a baseball cap pulled down low, and he was hunkered over a plate of tostados. Lock caught the kid glancing straight at him. He was going for casual and doing a bad job of it. He quickly looked away.

Lock stayed where he was as Ty placed his order, handing over the money at the same time in case they needed to make a swift exit. "Yeah, gimme the fried-chicken sandwich." He turned to Lock. "You want anything?"

"No, thanks. I'm good."

"Okay. Don't change your mind and be asking for some of mine."

"Yes, Mom," said Lock, catching sight of the kid's sneakers.

They were blue and white Nike Cortez, as good a giveaway that he was Mara Salvatrucha as a flashing neon sign around his neck. A middle-aged person might wear the sneakers not knowing what they signified on their streets, but a teenage kid in this part of town would know for definite that they were a symbol of gang allegiance.

In this situation, they were more than that. Galante had told Lock and Ty that word had come down from MS-13 high command about a year ago to ditch those sneakers. Their meaning had become too well known among law enforcement.

Now they were reserved for certain situations. When you wanted to flaunt affiliation. Or let someone else know who you were with.

As Ty waited for his food, Lock decided to move things along. The kid watched Lock coming toward him. He didn't get up, but he did take a last forkful of food.

"Where you going?" said Ty.

"It's cool. Just checking something out."

Lock reached the bench. He pulled out a chair and sat down close by, careful to keep an eye on the boy's hands in case he reached for a weapon. The kid's body language shifted. He turned his plastic fork over in his hand. He threw it down on his half-finished meal. Finally, he picked up his plate, and stood up. He slid the tray over so that it was in front of Lock, the white paper receipt from his order turned over.

On the back an address was scrawled in blue pen. Lock picked it up as the kid dumped his plate in the trash and took off.

Lock got up and walked back to Ty. "Let's go."

Ty looked pleadingly at the young man who was making his sandwich. "Hold that for me, would you?" he said.

"Sorry, dude," said Lock, as they walked back past the flower stalls and out onto the street.

"This job's going to give me an ulcer," complained Ty. "It's not good for your stomach to think it's getting some food and then it doesn't. All those juices floating around with nothing to digest."

Lock was checking the address. It was four blocks away. He dodged across the street back toward the alley where he'd left the Audi. The good news was that it was still there. The bad news was that two teenage hood rats were already scoping out the rims.

"Sweet ride," said one of the kids, seeing Lock walk up on them.

"Thanks," said Lock, shouldering past them.

One of the hood rats must have caught a glimpse of Lock's holstered SIG. He nudged his buddy. "Let's bounce."

They swaggered off down the alley, fading into the concrete gloom of the nearby buildings.

The Audi chirped, and Lock opened the driver's door. Looking over the top of the car, he saw Ty's stance change. He had one foot planted behind the other, and was standing side on to the street, like he was ready to throw down.

The kid who'd left his tray for Lock was walking toward them. He had a posse of four others with him. They looked like they meant business.

Lock reached for his SIG, ready to draw. The kid held his hand up.

"Chill, *ese*. We're your escort."

"I think I can find it," said Lock.

"No car," said the kid. "We have to walk there."

Ty took a step forward. The kids visibly shrank back. Ty had that effect on people.

"I wouldn't mess with him," Lock told them. "He's pissed that he didn't get his chicken."

The kid looped his thumbs into his pants. "I don't make the rules. Don't worry about your car." He turned to one of his compatriots. "You stay here. Make sure no one messes with it."

One of the kids peeled off, and took up position next to the Audi, arms folded.

Lock didn't like that. He wanted to have his car to extract Emily and Charlie when the time came. But he wasn't in a position to dictate terms.

This was a power-play. An effective one.

He took in the kid standing sentry over the Audi. He clapped a hand on his shoulder. "So much as a scratch when I get back and I'll find you. You hear me?"

55

The Red Tiger sat in the backseat, next to Shotcaller's son. He had felt bad about the trick he'd played with the water in the acid container. Then he had thought about the people he was dealing with. The man at the steering wheel, the one they called Shotcaller, would have used acid and thought nothing of it.

He packed away his guilt and eased back into the seat.

It was a good trick. He used it sparingly, saving it for people he suspected would be difficult to break down. Those who were used to dealing with fear and intimidation.

With those people, the secret was to find what they cared about. Usually it was a child, or children. Most people would withstand a threat to themselves. They would be able to work through their own physical pain. But hurting someone they loved more than anything? That was a different proposition.

He leaned forward. "This is where they'll be?" he asked.

Shotcaller glanced at him in the rearview. "That's what they told me."

"How close are we?"

"Close. It's just down here," said Shotcaller.

The Red Tiger sat back, satisfied, as Shotcaller made a right turn.

This street was quieter. Abandoned warehouses ran either side.

"This was the old garment district," said Shotcaller. "We use these places a lot."

A car honked behind them. The Red Tiger twisted round, his gun still aimed at the man's son. A huge steel grille loomed behind him, and the vehicle passed them at speed. It was a large black SUV, like the one Red Tiger had seen at the ranch-house.

Just before it pulled out to pass them, he glimpsed the people sitting in back through the front windshield. One was a young Asian man, the other a young Asian woman. They were sandwiched between two large Hispanic men with tattoos.

His heart surged. Panic, recognition and longing swelled in him all at the same time.

The girl. It was her. It was his daughter.

Even though he had seen her for less than a second, he had recognized some of her mother's features in her face. He struggled to compose himself.

When he looked forward again, the SUV was slowing down, and Shotcaller was studying him.

"That's good. Pull over," said Red Tiger.

Shotcaller pulled to the curb.

"Can we go now?" Shotcaller asked him. "That's them," he added, waving at the SUV and confirming what Red Tiger had just seen. "All you need to do is follow it from here."

Red Tiger made a quick calculation. He didn't need a driver. That was true. But he couldn't let the man leave. Not when he could alert his friends. And he didn't have time to put him back in the trunk.

"Leave the keys in the ignition," he told him. "Then get out."

"What about my son?"

Red Tiger opened the passenger door and got out. He held it open for the man's son, who clambered out, still shaking.

All three stood on the sidewalk for a moment. Shotcaller tossed him the keys. He took out his phone and tossed that to him too.

"We can go?" he asked Red Tiger.

"Yes. Go."

Shotcaller turned and started in the direction they had just come from. His son fell in next to him.

Six steps later, Red Tiger raised his gun, and aimed at Shotcaller's back. He squeezed the trigger twice.

"Papa," his son shouted, as Shotcaller fell forward, arms wide, his face planting hard on the concrete.

The boy looked back, crying, anticipating more gun shots—for himself.

Red Tiger climbed behind the wheel, started the engine and took off, leaving the boy on the sidewalk.

56

As Lock and Ty walked up the loading ramp and into the warehouse their juvenile escort melted away. Cresting the top, they walked down a long dock that smelled of mould and motor oil, and into a cavernous warehouse, long since abandoned.

At the other end of the building was a set of large swing doors, one of which had been wedged open. Through the open door, Lock could see an alleyway. On one side of the warehouse a set of metal steps led up to a gantry that ran half the length of the building. Behind it were several offices, presumably where the warehouse and factory managers would have been able to watch the workers below.

Lock's cell phone rang. He answered.

"You ready?" said Orzana.

"What is this? A scavenger hunt?"

"Just wanted to make sure you hadn't called in any LEOs."

"Listen to me. We want this deal done clean as much as you do. Speaking of which, where are you?" Lock asked, as Ty walked over to the steps and began to climb. The height of the gantry made it a strong strategic position. Plus the offices behind would offer some kind of concealment and cover.

Lock hit the mute icon on his phone and shouted up at Ty: "Check the offices. Make sure they're clear."

Ty shot him a thumbs-up as he bounded up the steps. "On it."

"We're almost there," said Orzana. "Less than a minute. By the way, one of my *carnals*, Ernesto, has disappeared off the radar. You wouldn't happen to know anything about that, would you?"

"I don't even know who he is," said Lock.

"Just wondered," said Orzana. "Talk soon."

Lock started walking the length of the warehouse, scoping out any other entrance or exit points. So far, they had only the loading dock they'd walked in through and the doors at the other end. Two exits didn't give Lock a happy feeling in a situation such as this.

As he did his recon work, he called Li Yeng. "We're at the exchange point."

"Emily and Charlie are there?" asked Li.

"Not yet, but I'm assured they'll be here soon. You good to go?"

"All we need is the word from you to make the next transfer."

There was more muffled conversation at Li's end. Then Chow Yan was on the line. "Mr. Lock, do you see them?"

"Any minute now is what we've been told."

"But you're at the location?"

Lock did not need this right now. He understood Chow Yan's anxiety, but he and Ty had to focus on what was in front of them. Things could change at any second.

He looked up as Ty appeared back on the gantry and flashed him an OK. "Clear!"

Lock hit mute again. "Stay there for now. Give me cover if you need to."

"Lock?" Chow Yan was saying.

He unmuted the call. "Yes, I'm here."

There was the sudden sound of engine roar from the alleyway. The noise echoed through the warehouse. Lock guessed this was it.

Game time.

Car doors opened and slammed.

Two men wearing ski masks appeared at the swing doors. They

both had long guns slung over their shoulders, and handguns on their hips. Lock noted their lack of body armor. A good sign under the circumstances. They had come armed, but not anticipating any kind of pushback or fire fight. He hoped they were correct.

The two men pushed open the other door, and a black Suburban drove slowly through, tires squealing on the poured-concrete floor.

"Stay on the line, and await my command," said Lock, switching into operation mode.

Chow Yan was no longer a client, no longer a worried father or uncle: he was the man Lock was relying on to hold up their end of the bargain. Lock reduced him in his mind to a functionary, just as he was.

For this to be finished it was important to tune out any remaining vestige of emotion and function on the mechanics. It was a transaction. One weighed down by greed and distrust and a lot of other ugly human factors, but a transaction nonetheless.

Chow Yan continued to jabber questions in the background. Lock tuned him out as he walked towards the vehicle. At the very edge of his vision, he could see Ty hunkered down, weapon drawn, ready to lay down fire.

Not that it would be of much use. Lock was standing dead center of a warehouse. The MS-13 didn't need to shoot him. All they needed to do was have the driver of the Suburban stomp on the gas pedal and Lock would be so much road kill.

The only thing he had going for him right now was that they didn't have the balance of the ransom.

The solar system must have bounced the thought all the way to Beverly Hills because the next thing he heard Chow Yan say was, "Should I action the transfer?"

"No," Lock barked into his phone. "Not until I say we're good."

"Can you see them? Are they there? I heard something."

"There's a vehicle. They may be inside," said Lock, taking a few more steps. "I'm approaching it now. Don't do anything until I tell you."

He stepped off to the side. As he moved, the rear passenger door popped open. Instinctively, his right hand fell to his SIG.

Another MS-13 heavy climbed out, revealing Emily and Charlie on the backseat. "Okay," said Lock. "I see them."

Now the front passenger door opened, and Noah Orzana got out. Lock hadn't expected to see him. He figured that, like Chow Yan, he'd leave the actual physical exchange to the lower ranks.

Orzana stayed next to the vehicle, his door still open.

"What's the delay?" he asked Lock.

"I see them," Lock answered, with a nod to the backseat. "But that's not the same as having them with me."

"What?" said Orzana. "You don't trust me? You think we'd take your money and drive off?"

"You have that option," said Lock. "I don't."

"You want me to have someone bring your car round?" Orzana smirked.

"No," said Lock. "Just let them out of the vehicle. Soon as they're with me and I'm walking out, I'll say the word and you can have your money."

"You want to know the problem with this world? There's no trust anymore," Orzana said, nodding for Emily and Charlie to be let go.

A cell phone rang. It was Orzana's. He looked at the screen and there was a flicker of something across his face that Lock didn't like. He held up his hand in the direction of the heavy who was in the process of helping Emily and Charlie out of the Suburban. "Wait."

As he took the call Lock did his best to tune in to what was being said. He could only catch Orzana's end.

"What? . . .Where? . . .You're sure?"

His expression was darkening with every question. Whatever it was, Lock knew it wasn't good. And it looked like bad news that couldn't have come at a worse time.

"That *carnal* I asked you about earlier," he said to Lock. "Ernesto?"

Lock shook his head. "Never heard of him before you brought him up."

"He's been shot. Three blocks from here. In front of his son," said Orzana, eyes dead.

"And your crew have been with me this whole time. They walked me down here, remember. I think they'd have noticed if we'd stopped to put a hole in one of your associates."

"What about him?" said Orzana, with a nod to the gantry where Ty had his gun aimed square at Orzana's back, the message unambiguous—*Kill Lock, and you die too.*

"Same. He was with me. Ask your junior crew if you don't believe us."

"Even so," said Orzana, "price just went up a million, and this time I mean it."

He turned back to Emily and Charlie. "I'll kill them both right here in front of you."

"Deal's agreed. It's too late for renegotiations," said Lock, his tone even, his voice calm.

"Fuck you," Orzana countered. "Too late? What does that mean?"

Lock had hoped not to play this next card. It was open to his bluff being called. But things could spin out of control fast if he didn't talk some sense into the man facing him.

"It means that when we got here I texted this location to my buddy Carl Galante. I told him that if he doesn't hear from me in the next . . ." Lock theatrically checked his watch ". . . three minutes he's to call LAPD. So, we have three minutes to do this and get the hell out of here. Because I don't want to explain to them what we're doing here anymore than you do. So, dead *carnals* or not, it's time to either piss on the pot or get off."

Orzana said nothing at first. Seconds passed. Lock looked past him to Emily. Her head was down and her eyes were closed. Her nails were dug hard into the palms of her hands. She was holding on, but only just. She must have been able to sense that this was it. In the next minute she could be free, or dead.

"Okay," said Orzana. "But if I find out you had anything to do with it then this isn't over."

Lock kept his own counsel. He'd be happy to discuss any of this one-to-one with the man in front of him at a later date but telling him that wasn't going to get this done.

Orzana gave the signal for the second time. Emily and Charlie were helped out of the back of the Suburban on shaky legs.

"You mind removing their restraints?" said Lock.

A nod from Orzana, and one of the men took out a knife. He cut the ties from around their wrists and ankles.

"You can make the transfer," Lock told Chow Yan.

Everyone waited. Lock motioned Emily and Charlie to walk over to him. Emily had to put a hand out to steady her cousin. He'd need medical attention, but first Lock had to get them out of there. And for that to happen, Orzana had to get confirmation he'd been paid. Then Lock had to hope the money clearing would push any thoughts of revenge or double-cross to the back of his mind. In his experience, a few million dollars tended to have exactly that effect. People found all kinds of forgiveness in their hearts when they saw seven figures lined up in a row. Even hardened criminals, like Orzana.

Orzana's cell rang again. This time he seemed to respond to the news a little more positively.

"Okay. Thanks," he said, his mouth threatening the barest of smiles.

Lock stayed on guard. He wasn't about to turn his back on anyone. He moved so that he was in front of Emily and Charlie, and made sure he had one hand on his weapon. Above him, Ty held his position, ready to move on Lock's signal.

"We'll let you guys leave first," Lock said to Orzana.

"You don't want a ride?" Orzana asked.

"Think we'll pass," said Lock as, out of the silence, another vehicle roared down the alley, and seconds later all hell broke loose.

57

The vehicle, a red sedan, powered through the swing door, tires squealing. The driver must have yanked on the parking brake because it slid across the warehouse floor side on. The man was a blur, but Lock saw enough to know who it was.

The Red Tiger had made his entrance. It was a one-man cavalry charge that had come too late.

Tang Bojun bailed out of the sedan before it had come to a stop. He tucked in behind the car, using it as moving cover. A second later he popped up from behind the trunk, and took aim with what looked to Lock like a Mossberg.

He squeezed a shot off at the back of the Suburban, blowing out the back windshield. Glass fragments flew everywhere.

Lock, meanwhile, was already on the move. His SIG was drawn, and pointed toward the MS-13 heavies, who were clambering out of the Suburban, guns in hand, and beginning to return fire at the Red Tiger.

Orzana had flung himself to the ground, and crawled under the hulking SUV—a wise decision, assuming no one moved it, in which case he'd be squashed like a bug.

Declining a conventional shooter's stance that would narrow his body, Lock spread himself out, trying to get as much of his body between the fire zone and Emily and Charlie. He held fire, his finger ready on the trigger of the SIG. In the wild early exchanges of a gun fight, firing drew return fire.

He glanced up at the gantry. Ty was nowhere to be seen. Then he spotted him working his way down the metal steps. Lock put out his free hand and waved Emily and Charlie to the rear as he started to back up.

With all the action at the other end, and shots still being exchanged between the Red Tiger and MS-13, their best bet, maybe their only bet, was an exfiltration via the loading dock where he and Ty had come in.

He twisted his head round so he could look at Emily and Charlie without sacrificing the cover he was offering them. "We're going out that way," he said, jabbing a finger toward the loading dock.

Neither of them moved. They seemed frozen.

The sound of the gunshots echoed at ear-shredding volume around the empty warehouse. Lock turned back to see one of the MS-13 gang members take a shotgun blast straight to the chest, blood blossoming in a crimson flood.

One down. Three to go, including Orzana, who was still hiding under the Suburban, a gun drawn, desperately belly-crawling in an attempt to get an angle on the Red Tiger.

The Red Tiger racked the Mossberg again and took aim at another of the MS-13 escort. Lock was struck by the sheer calmness of the man as he pulled the trigger and found his target for a second time.

The round struck the man's throat. His arms frantically wind-milled, his hands clasping at what was left of his neck, blood spraying.

Ty cleared the last few steps in a single leap. Lock backed up a few more steps.

He caught movement from underneath the Suburban just in time to see Orzana aiming his pistol toward them. Lock squeezed off a single round. Ty hunkered down and did the same, their two shots making Orzana's round go high and wide.

Lock risked another quick glance behind him. Charlie had his hands clamped over his ears and was hunkered down in a near-fetal position.

"Get him up on his feet, and start moving back there," Lock shouted at Emily.

She grabbed her cousin's arm and hauled him upright.

Ty scrambled over to them, a fresh shot from near the Suburban whizzing so close to Lock's head that he felt it pushing through the air. If they stayed any longer it was only a matter of time before one of them caught a round.

The Red Tiger moved out further from behind the sedan. He was shouting at Emily. Lock couldn't understand the words, but the tone, the plaintive plea, was unmistakable.

Orzana had broken cover. He was at the side of the Suburban. He popped open the door and seemed to reach down into the footwell.

Lock kept backing up. Now both he and Ty were standing in front of Emily and Charlie as the four of them backed towards the loading dock.

All they needed to do was make it outside to the street. There were no sounds of sirens yet, but Lock had to believe that gunfire so close to downtown would draw some kind of a response. If it didn't, one of them could make the call to 911 as soon as they were clear of the kill zone.

The Suburban's door slammed. Orzana reappeared hefting a rifle. He fired an immediate shot toward the Red Tiger who dove for the ground, kissing the concrete just in time and crawling back toward the sedan.

Lock grasped the moment, turning his back on the gunfire and grabbing Emily as Ty swept up Charlie. Together, they ran for the loading dock.

As they made it, Lock saw Orzana heading for them with another of the MS-13 men. Orzana stopped, and raised the rifle.

Lock grabbed Emily around the waist and took her down to the floor, falling on top of her as the shots rang out overhead. He spun round, staying on top of her, making sure that his body covered hers, punched his arm out and took aim.

Next to him, Ty was doing the same, protecting Charlie with his own body as he fired back into the warehouse.

The Suburban's engine started. One of the other remaining MS-13 heavies piloted it slowly toward the loading dock, as Orzana used the open passenger door as cover. At the back of the Suburban another masked man fired toward the sedan, keeping the Red Tiger pinned down.

Lock's heart sank. They were outgunned, and the Suburban was good cover.

The SUV inched forward, getting closer to them by the second. Orzana kept pace with it from behind the door, a boxer walking down an exhausted opponent, closing the distance, ready to deliver the final knockout punch.

They were trapped. Lock knew it, and so did Orzana.

Stand up and make a run for it, and they'd be shot in the back. Stay where they were and the result would be the same.

"What you wanna do?" said Ty.

Lock looked around. "I'm not seeing many options here. Make the call," he told Ty.

Ty dug out his cell. Fresh fire split the concrete in front of him and he ducked his head back down. He tapped at the screen and waited for the call to connect.

Lock glanced up. He could see the grille of the Suburban looming larger with every second that passed. He took aim at the portion of Orzana's lower legs that he could glimpse between the bottom of the vehicle door and the ground and fired. His shot fell short, skittering up from the concrete and into the door.

The Suburban picked up pace. It was maybe forty feet from them now.

Ty was screaming their location into his cell phone. He looked up at Lock. "They're going to be here, just not fast enough." His expression wasn't one of fear so much as resignation.

"Listen we gotta make a move here," Lock shouted to Ty. "Back down there," he said, waving his hand at the loading dock behind them.

"There's no way, man," said Ty.

"That's all I've got," said Lock. "We can't stay here."

"Okay then," said Ty. "On three?"

The Suburban rolled forward another foot. Orzana's head popped up. He had a smile plastered over his face. "Thanks for the cash."

A voice from behind the Suburban. The Red Tiger had broken cover again. He was walking toward the rear of the Suburban, the Mossberg tucked in against his shoulder.

He and Lock made eye contact. The Red Tiger flicked his head, indicating that if Lock and Ty were going to make a run for it then now was the time.

The Red Tiger began screaming at the Suburban. He fired at the masked man standing at the back. His shot found him, hitting the man in the leg.

He broke into a jog heading straight toward the SUV.

"Three," shouted Lock.

Both he and Ty hauled Emily and Charlie onto their feet. Lock grabbed Emily's collar and spun her round so that they were back to back. He backed up, still facing the Suburban. Ty did the same. They alternated shots as they crested the dock and began to edge down it.

Lock watched as Orzana moved toward the back of the vehicle. The Red Tiger was still jogging, heading directly for it, out in the open, with no cover.

Orzana waited for him to fire. As the Red Tiger threw the Mossberg to the ground and reached for his hand gun, Orzana took his chance. He lifted his rifle and calmly took aim.

With Orzana no longer aiming at them, Lock turned and scooped Emily up into his arms. He sprinted down the dock, Ty next to him, both of them making a mad dash for the street.

Behind them, he heard Orzana's rifle fire. There was a mangled scream and the sound of a body hitting the concrete.

Lock didn't look back. He didn't have to.

They kept running, reaching the street. A patrol car was headed toward them. Lock swiftly holstered his SIG and waved it down as it came to a stop and the two officers bailed out.

Lock put Emily down, his arms and legs burning from exertion as the adrenalin dump subsided. More LAPD units were headed into the street.

Lock and Ty raised their arms, palms open, making clear they weren't a threat to the responding officers. Two hundred yards down the street, the Suburban appeared suddenly, driving in the opposite direction and immediately drawing fire. It kept going, clipping a patrol car and sending it spinning out of the way.

Emily was standing next to him, hands on her thighs, gasping for air, as cops rushed toward them.

"You hurt?" Lock asked her.

She shook her head.

"It's okay," he reassured her. "It's over."

She reached up, swiping her hair from her eyes. "Who was that back there?" she asked.

He knew whom she meant. The avenging angel who had arrived out of nowhere and bought them just enough time to get the hell out of there before they met the same fate he just had. The man who had sacrificed himself, not for Lock or Ty but, Lock knew, for her.

He wanted to tell her. *That was your father. Your real father.* It wasn't his place.

"I don't know who that was," he told her, as uniformed bodies swarmed in around him and Ty, and he was taken to the ground.

58

The three men, Lock, Ty and Li Yeng, stood side by side on the apron and watched as the cabin-crew member, a young woman who looked like she'd stepped straight from the cover of Chinese *Vogue*, closed the aircraft door. Lock could glimpse Emily Yan at the window, staring mournfully out of the window, her life of freedom cut short.

The Gulfstream's engines shifted up a notch from low roar to sharp whine. It began to taxi, making a slow, sweeping turn as it headed toward the runway.

"Not a bad way to travel," said Ty.

Lock agreed. But the kind of money Chow Yan had was a double-edged sword that he had seen before. With wealth came the constant fear of losing it or being targeted by those who wanted some of it for themselves.

That was why the smart wealthy either kept their lifestyle simple, like Warren Buffett, living in the same house for forty years in Omaha and eating at McDonald's. Or, if they enjoyed a more lavish lifestyle, they lived it behind closed doors, and kept social media to the accounts set up to promote their charitable foundations.

Charlie, and Emily had learned the lesson the hard way. Shove your wealth into people's faces and expect some blowback.

Lock didn't doubt for a moment that places like Arcadia would be the scene of more crimes like this. He and Ty had already fielded dozens of calls from wealthy Chinese and Chinese-Americans from up and down the west coast who were seeking their expertise on how to make themselves, their families and their property safer.

The Gulfstream took its place in the line of aircraft awaiting clearance to take off.

"You're not heading home?" Lock asked Li Yeng.

He shot Lock a diplomatic smile. "Mr. Yan still has investments he wants me to oversee here in Los Angeles."

"Can't kidnap an office building," said Ty.

"One of the many advantages of real estate," said Li. "Speaking of which, Mr. Yan has asked if you'd like to oversee security for his properties here." He dug into the inside pocket of his perfectly tailored Hugo Boss suit, took out a piece of paper and handed it to Lock.

Lock unfolded the paper and read what was written. Ty snuck behind him and took the paper out of his hand.

"Are those zeros after the decimal point?" Ty asked Li.

"No, that's the figure," said Li.

It was an eye-watering sum. Too eye-watering.

"A security review?" said Lock, taking the paper back from Ty.

Chow Yan had already proved very generous, giving them both a substantial bonus for securing the safe return of his daughter and nephew.

"And, perhaps, some work to ensure that certain people are disincentivized from harming his family in the future," Li Yeng added, his expensive American education beginning to show through.

"You mean he wants payback, and he wants us to deliver it?" said Lock, cutting to the heart of the matter.

It wasn't a question that would be answered with "Yes." Li wasn't stupid, far from it.

"Consider it," he said.

Lock handed the piece of paper back to him. "I don't know if it's worthy of a fortune cookie, but you ever hear the saying 'Let sleeping dogs lie'?"

"Of course," said Li.

Ty leaned in to Lock and whispered, "You ever hear the saying 'That's a twenty-five percent down payment on a condo'?"

Lock shook him off.

"We did what we had to do when we had to do it," he told Li. "Poking at an organization like MS-13 is rarely a good idea."

Li nodded. "Excellent advice."

"Make sure and pass it on to your boss," said Lock. "Come on, Tyrone, we have a housewarming to get to."

59

Lock pulled out of the exit from Van Nuys airport in his Audi, Ty next to him in the passenger seat.

"You know you don't have to come to this thing, right?" said Lock, as Li Yeng overtook them in his blue Lexus, both cars headed for the 405 freeway.

"Wouldn't miss it for the world," said Ty.

"You bummed about me shooting down that last proposal?"

"Nah," said Ty. "You're right. Better to let sleeping Salvadorian street gangs lie."

"Listen, we're going to have enough work to keep us going for the next year. Easy work too. Domestic-security reviews. We can charge top dollar too."

"I know, but it wasn't just the money. Know what I'm saying?"

Lock did. Revenge was always tempting. The problem was, it rarely ended where or when you wanted it to. It had a habit of turning into a feud, and Lock had settled one not too long ago. He didn't want to get sucked into another.

"It's done. Best that we leave it like that."

Ty was staring at the mirror on his side of the car. "Maybe somebody should explain that to these guys."

Lock's eyes flicked to the rearview where a beaten-up silver Ford Mustang with two young Hispanic males inside was closing in on them. Everything about their appearance and demeanor screamed "gang member."

The driver of the Mustang sped up, and whipped suddenly around Lock's Audi, almost colliding with a pickup truck headed down Haskell Avenue in the other direction. Lock slowed so they could pass. He was happier to have the Mustang in front of him where he could see it.

Ty had already drawn his weapon and was wearing his game face.

The Mustang was moving away from them. For a second Lock thought it might just be a coincidence. It wasn't as if gang members were a rare sight when you drove around the Valley. If you were on the lookout, you'd see them.

The Mustang drew out again, pulling around another car. It was then Lock spotted their actual target, Li Yeng's dark blue Lexus, about a hundred yards ahead. The Mustang slowed now, tucking in behind it.

"You see what I see?" he said to Ty.

"Uh-huh."

"Think we should call him, give him a heads-up that he has company?"

"No, he'll freak out. It'll only make things worse," said Lock, waiting for a gap in oncoming traffic before touching the gas pedal, and pulling out wide, overtaking the three vehicles between him and the Mustang in one sudden burst of speed.

"What about the cops?" said Ty.

Lock thought about it for a second. He was studying the road. More importantly, he was studying what was on the other side of it. The lack of pedestrians. The absence of a high curb. And the way it opened up near the interchange with the 405 freeway.

He had something in mind, and he wasn't sure that adding a third party with guns would make it easier. Giving it a second's thought, he knew it wouldn't. It would only complicate matters.

"If we see one, I'm sure we can flag them down."

"You got it," said Ty.

"Oh, and holster that," said Lock.

Ty looked puzzled.

"What we gonna do?" he asked. "Give them a stern talking-to?"

"Something like that," said Lock, his hands moving into position on the wheel. "Call Li and put him on speaker for me."

Ty holstered his gun and made the call to Li Yeng. They could see his blue Lexus up ahead, the Mustang closing in on it. As the phone rang, Ty tapped the speaker icon, and put the phone into a holder on the dash.

"Li," said Lock, when he picked up.

"Mr. Lock, good to hear from you. Have you reconsidered what we discussed?"

"In a way, yes. There's no reason for alarm, but you have some unwanted company so I need you to do exactly what I tell you when I tell you to do it. And that starts with keeping your current speed and direction exactly the same."

"Okay," said Li, a nervous hitch in his voice. Lock could imagine him checking his rearview right about now.

"Keep your eyes on the road ahead, unless I tell you otherwise," Lock added.

"Understood," said Li.

"Okay, I'm going to stay on the line here. Disregard anything you hear in the next minute, apart from my instructions. Things might get a little loud, but just stay focused on getting to the freeway on the ramp. You know where it is, right?"

"The 405, yes—it's just up here."

Lock looked ahead. Traffic was light. That was good. He didn't want to involve anyone else in this. On the next block there was a turn lane that led into a long-term parking lot for the nearby airport. It was shorter than he would have liked, but it would have to do. If he was going to pull this off, it was way safer on a surface street. Do it on the freeway and it would be mayhem.

The Mustang was still tucked in behind Li's Lexus. Lock moved up on it, closing the gap between his Audi and the Mustang, but not so much that the teen gang members would get spooked.

"Okay, Li, you there?"

"I'm here."

"Good, okay. You see that turn lane up ahead?"

There was the slightest pause.

"Uh, yeah, I see it."

"Okay, I want you to put on your blinker, and move into it when you get up there. I also want you to hit the gas just before you move into it."

"Thought I was heading for the freeway."

"You are," said Lock. "Soon as you hear a collision behind you, you move back out of the lane, and head to the freeway."

"Okay, I don't get this."

"That's fine. You don't have to," Lock reassured him. "You understand all that?"

"I think so."

"Good. Then repeat it back to me."

"Signal. Speed up as I move into the turn lane. Wait for a crash behind me then get back out."

"Perfect," said Lock.

He watched as the Lexus's turn signal began to blink.

He assumed that inside the Mustang the two gang members must be thinking that all their Christmases had arrived at once. Way easier to kill someone in a parking lot than shoot at them from the freeway.

The Mustang's blinker didn't light up, but it did inch across the road and slow a little, anticipating Li's next move.

Lock studied the road ahead. There was no traffic coming in the opposite direction.

"Okay, Li, hit the gas—now!"

Lock already had his foot poised over the Audi's gas pedal.

The Lexus shot forward. A fraction of a second later so did the Mustang.

After that, everything happened at lightning speed as, first, the Lexus, then the Mustang made their move, one matching the other.

As they began to move into the turn lane, Lock kept the Audi on a straight line. He moved up on the inside of the Mustang at speed, his hands set on the wheel, his focus intense. Next to him, Ty braced for the impact.

When the front wheel of his Audi was exactly level with the rear wheel arch of the Mustang, Lock pulled down hard on the wheel.

Both cars travelling at speed, the Mustang spun out as the front of the Audi made contact with its rear.

"Keep going, Li," shouted Lock, as metal grated against metal.

Lock watched as, with the cars behind him braking to avoid the accident, the Lexus darted back out, heading for the freeway on-ramp.

The Mustang was now pointed in the opposite direction. The driver started to turn but a truck had moved up behind him. Vehicles on both sides had him hemmed in.

Lock rolled to a stop. Ty was already out of the vehicle, headed for the Mustang, as the gang members bailed, their mission aborted.

From experience, Lock knew they would have stolen the vehicle. Even they weren't dumb enough to use their own car to hunt down and kill someone.

Lock watched as Ty picked the slowest of the two, and chased him down. His opponent had youth on his side, but Ty had long legs and natural athleticism. As the gang member turned to face his pursuer, Ty tackled him to the ground.

The kid was reaching for something tucked into the back of his waistband, but Ty cinched his wrist with a massive hand, peeling back his fingers past breaking point. Even with the honk of horns as traffic built up, Lock could make out the screams of pain.

Ty hauled the kid to his feet and marched him back toward the Audi. Lock turned the Audi around, and met Ty halfway. Ty opened the rear passenger door, threw the kid inside and climbed in after him. Lock hit the central locking. The doors clunked shut.

"You can't do this, you assholes," the gang member protested.

"I think you'll find we just did," Ty told him, his game-face expression quieting the kid somewhat.

"Hey, you ain't cops," said the kid.

Lock pulled out, and hit the gas, heading away from the now abandoned Mustang, and setting the navigation for Orzana's auto shop in East Los Angeles. Not that the kid was to know that was where they were headed.

Lock studied him coolly in his mirror. "That's right," he told him. "We're not cops. We're way worse."

60

With the front fender smashed and a major dent in its bodywork, Lock's Audi limped down the ramp and into the parking garage of his new apartment building on Wilshire Boulevard. He and Ty had deposited the teenage gang member with Orzana, along with a warning that if this wasn't over it soon would be.

Lock had the leverage of Orzana's involvement in the kidnapping and Orzana knew it. His final piece of advice to the auto-shop boss was "Take your money and enjoy it while you still can."

Orzana had bluffed and blustered and claimed no knowledge of the attempted attack on Li Yeng. Lock knew he was lying. So did Ty. But they let it go with an assurance that Orzana would ensure there was no repeat.

Lock pulled into one of the apartment's two designated spaces. He and Ty got out. Lock stopped for a moment to assess the damage.

"You know cars are never quite the same after a crash," said Ty.

"I was thinking of trading it anyway," said Lock. "I'll speak to the insurance company in the morning."

"What you gonna tell them?" said Ty.

Lock mulled it over. There were some laws he didn't mind breaking, as long as there was a compelling reason. Insurance fraud didn't really fall into that category, and he wasn't sure his policy covered fishtailing another vehicle off the road. "Maybe I'll just get it repaired on my own dime."

Ty grinned. "It's not like you don't have the money. I mean, look at you, cold chillin' in a condo on Wilshire."

A car horn sounded behind them. They turned to see Carl Galante leaning out of a brand new black Mercedes.

"I guess working for a billionaire does have its advantages," Lock conceded, as he directed Galante towards the visitor parking.

They waited for him to turn off his engine and get out. He paused to check out Lock's damaged Audi as he walked over to join them.

"Let me guess, you let Ty here drive?" said Galante.

"No, that one was on me," said Lock.

"Everything good?" Galante asked him.

"Yeah. Just had to tie up some loose ends. Emily and Charlie are on their way home. What are the LAPD saying?" said Lock.

"I'd keep a low profile for a while, if I were you," said Galante.

"We plan on it. Isn't that correct, Tyrone?"

"Yeah, sure. Hey, I don't go looking for trouble, it just has a habit of finding me."

The three men walked toward the elevator. The doors opened, and they got in. Lock hit the button to take them up to the lobby. They'd catch the next elevator in the lobby that would take them up to the sixteenth floor and the new apartment Lock was going to share with Carmen.

When they hadn't been able to agree on whether she should move in with him or vice versa, a new place had seemed like the obvious compromise. Lock hadn't lived with anyone since his fiancée back in New York, but this seemed like a natural next step. Life went on, and he loved Carmen. The housewarming party had been her idea, and he'd been happy to go along with it.

"One other thing," said Galante, as they stepped out into the plush lobby.

"What's that?"

"They got the autopsy back on the kid's biological father, Tang Bojun."

"Why'd they have an autopsy? Dude must have been shot like seven or eight times," said Ty, his comment drawing an alarmed look from the building's concierge.

Lock directed an apologetic "What are you gonna do?" look in the direction of the concierge. "Go on, Carl."

"Guy had a tumor the size of a melon in his liver, plus some others scattered around his major organs. All of them malignant. If he hadn't been shot, he maybe had only a few months left. If that. Could have been weeks. He must have been taking steroids or something to function like he was."

"That's why he didn't want to wait when he got the news," said Lock.

"Looks like it," said Galante.

They got into the elevator.

"Sorry," said Galante. "Here's me talking about this stuff when you and Carmen are all set to start your new life together. I don't mean to be a downer."

"It's okay," said Lock. "I feel better knowing."

They settled back into the silence that for some reason was customary in an elevator. Lock took the time to say a silent prayer for the man who'd laid down his life for a daughter he'd never been able to know. He wasn't sure what lessons could be drawn from it. Maybe there weren't any, except that it was no bad thing to count your own blessings.

61

L ock stood by the window, a glass of single malt whisky in his hand, and looked out over the lights of Los Angeles. Behind him, the party was in full swing. People were talking, laughing and sharing stories. Over by the large open-plan kitchen area, Ty was in his element, surrounded by several attractive female friends of Carmen's. It seemed like a million miles away from the events of the past week.

In the night sky, a jet's tail light flashed red as it came in to land at LAX. Lock tracked it, thinking again of Emily, out somewhere over the Pacific, cocooned again in a life of luxury and privilege. He took a sip of his Scotch, enjoying the biting but warm sensation of the spirit.

"Great place."

Lock turned toward a male attorney around his age whom Carmen had introduced to him as Jake. She had dated him very briefly before she'd met Lock. He could tell that Jake still had feelings for her. Lock didn't blame him. She was a rare blend. "Yeah, it's pretty nice, isn't it?" he said. Small-talk at parties wasn't his forte.

He could see Carmen in the living area chatting with an older couple. She caught his eye and smiled, but her expression said, "Play nice." He raised his glass in her direction. She winked.

He turned back to Jake but didn't say anything.

Jake cleared his throat. "Carmen tells me you're in private security."

Here we go, thought Lock. He tended not to discuss his work in polite company. Like politics and religion, he'd found it was a subject best avoided. "Yes," he said, hoping they'd move on to sport, not that he had much to say about that either.

"But she said it was like high-end stuff," said Jake.

Lock nodded, hoping the guy would take the hint.

"Must be why you can afford a place like this," said Jake, taking in the new apartment high above the city with a sweep of his beer-bottle-clutching hand.

"We've had a good month."

Jake took a sip of his drink. "Doesn't it get kind of boring, though? Y'know, babysitting rich people."

Lock smiled to himself. There were many words that could have been applied to the past few days, but boring wasn't one of them. He took another sip of single malt, and tried not to look too amused.

"I don't mean to . . ." Jake trailed off. "I mean a lot of the stuff that crosses my desk, it's pretty dry. Trusts, estates, that kind of thing. But, hey, it's easy money." He raised his bottle to clink Lock's glass.

"Here's to it," said Lock. "Easy money."

ALSO BY SEAN BLACK

The Ryan Lock Series in Order

Lockdown (US/Canada)

Lockdown (UK/ Commonwealth)

Deadlock (US/Canada)

Deadlock (UK/Commonwealth)

Lock & Load (Short)

Gridlock (US/Canada)

Gridlock (UK/Commonwealth)

The Devil's Bounty (US/Canada)

The Devil's Bounty (UK/Commonwealth)

The Innocent

Fire Point

Budapest/48 (Short)

The Edge of Alone

Second Chance

The Deep Lonely (Short)

The Red Tiger

Ryan Lock Thrillers: Lockdown; Deadlock; Gridlock (Ryan Lock Series
Boxset Book 1) - (US & Canada only)

3 Ryan Lock Thrillers: The Innocent; Fire Point; Second Chance

The Byron Tibor Series

Post

Blood Country

Winter's Rage

～

Sign up to Sean Black's VIP mailing list for a free e-book and updates about new releases

Your email will be kept confidential. You will not be spammed. You can unsubscribe at any time.

Click the link below to sign up:

http://seanblackauthor.com/subscribe/

ABOUT THE AUTHOR

To research his books, Sean Black has trained as a bodyguard in the UK and Eastern Europe, spent time inside America's most dangerous Supermax prison, Pelican Bay in California, undergone desert survival training in Arizona, and ventured into the tunnels under Las Vegas.

A graduate of Oxford University, England and Columbia University in New York, Sean lives in Dublin, Ireland.

His Ryan Lock and Byron Tibor thrillers have been translated into Dutch, French, German, Italian, Portugese, Russian, Spanish, and Turkish.

CPSIA information can be obtained
at www.ICGtesting.com
Printed in the USA
LVHW010512081222
734805LV00030B/922